LIGHT

SEYMOUR EPSTEIN

LIGHT

HENRY HOLT AND COMPANY
NEW YORK

Published by Henry Holt and Company, Inc.,
115 West 18th Street, New York, New York 10011.
Published in Canada by Fitzhenry & Whiteside Limited,
195 Allstate Parkway, Markham, Ontario L3R 4T8.

Library of Congress Cataloging-in-Publication Data
Epstein, Seymour, 1917–
Light / by Seymour Epstein.—1st ed.
    p.   cm.
ISBN 0-8050-1067-X
I. Title.
PS3555.P66L55   1989
813'.54—dc20   89-2201
                                              CIP

Henry Holt books are available at special discounts
for bulk purchases for sales promotions, premiums,
fund-raising, or educational use. Special editions
or book excerpts can also be created to specification.

   For details contact:
   Special Sales Director
   Henry Holt and Company, Inc.
   115 West 18th Street
   New York, New York 10011

First Edition
Printed in the United States of America
10   9   8   7   6   5   4   3   2   1

FOR CANDIDA—
with much gratitude

PART I

1 Yesterday the overcast flowed over the front range like an aerial ocean. It began snowing by midafternoon and visibility was cut down to yards. I couldn't even see the tennis courts below. The forecast had been, as usual, many hours off. The prediction had been for snow to start yesterday evening, and I had been hoping that they would be right this once. The quicker that front came through, the clearer the airport when Jessica lands in Denver. Clearly, now, she'll be coming in behind the front, but bad weather can trail for hours, even days. Her plane is due three-forty. I'll have to phone-check the flight before starting out for the airport.

Right now I'm sitting in the usual chair, the one I turn to face the sliding glass doors that frame my view of the mountains. Mario, our well-informed doorman, has told me that the empty lot across the street has been bought by a big developer, and that by this time next year my view will be kaput. A twenty-story apartment house is in the works. Mario looks like that long-gone movie actor, Wallace Beery, and he does a decent imitation of Rodney Dangerfield. He bugs his eyes and tips his head and growls, "I don't get no respect around here." It seems to me he's more funny than the original. The success of certain American comedians has always puzzled me.

Naturally, I always included a hopeful invitation to come to Denver before heading back east for the Christmas–New Year's break. There would be the time, apparently. The classes she had taken that semester required term papers rather than exams, and since she had finished those papers she was able to take off earlier than expected. She could spend some days with me and get home in plenty of time before Christmas.

I had taken it for granted that she was going to head straight home for the holidays. She would phone me, of course, wish me a happy this and that, and then speed home to all the seasonal fun awaiting her. I could just picture it—ballet, meeting with friends, eating binges at the South Street Seaport, plays, days of movie-hopping. She had once confessed to me this secret vice. It usually started at noon and finished somewhere around midnight, taking her all over the city to pick up a French film here, an English film there, a German film crosstown, eating candy bars and hot dogs and popcorn all day, a debauch that filled me with vicarious delight.

When she was six, seven, eight, we had a regular routine of going to the Bronx Zoo on sunny Sundays. We would drive there in the late morning, have lunch in the cafeteria, and then begin our tour of the houses—the apes, the snakes, the big cats—the last being her favorites. Sometimes—I'm not sure why, maybe because it was rutting time—the stench of the place was enough to blow you away. "Pee-yoo!" exclaimed Jess, clamping her nose with her fingers. "Shall we skip it?" I would ask. "No," she would say, "I'll walk like this," keeping that tourniquet on her nose. It was a measure of her fascination that she would go thus stoppered rather than miss her lions and leopards and tigers and jaguars. She loved animals. Their *eyes,* their nice eyes. We had a schnauzer, for years.

She wondered why it wouldn't be possible to take a cub, a lion or tiger cub, and rear it at home as you would a dog or cat. Her theory was that if a big animal got used to people early in life, it could be domesticated like any smaller creature. Instead of its natural prey, it would eat inexpensive cuts of meat from the supermarket.

"When they grow up, they eat quite a lot," I tried to point out.

"How much?"

"I think I read somewhere that a full-grown lion or tiger could eat as much as thirty pounds of meat at one time."

"How much is that?"

"How much is that—well, let's see—that would be about two big Thanksgiving turkeys."

"All by himself?"

"Or herself."

That occasioned quiet calculation. "Every day?" she asked.

"Oh, I guess maybe two, three times a week."

"But if he lived in a house instead of the jungle, he wouldn't have to eat so much."

Which was astonishingly shrewd.

"That's probably true," I said, "but where would you take him for a walk?"

"In the park."

There was a park within walking distance of our house in Forest Hills. Clearly that park had taken its place in her secret strategies. But she hadn't counted on that enormous intake of food. It presented a problem in more than just room and expense. She had seen large dogs on the street and in the park, and she had made a proportionate calculation. She said, "Maybe we could go to the beach, where Grandma lives." She meant my mother, who was alive at the time and living out in Sheepshead Bay. Jess must have remembered the off-season, unpeopled stretch of sand, enough acreage to accommodate the "do" of a two-turkey lion. I was reluctant to put an end to her big-cat dreams. I enjoyed the turns of her imagination as it sought to fit a jungle beast into her life.

Once, when Ellen had joined us on one of those zoo trips and Jess began playing her theme, Ellen had said decisively, with a quick glance at me, "You know, dear, there's a law against having lions or tigers for pets. When they grow up, they're dangerous." Which put an end to the fantasy game Jess and I had been playing.

Fate is being nice, for a change. By lunchtime, the overcast had broken and the visibility had much improved. I can see the mountains again. I hope the damn thing doesn't close down before I get Jessica to the apartment. I want her to see this. The peaks of the front range are covered in a white that seems almost phosphorescent in this light. The foothills remain patchy. Here and there blue sky appears through a tear in the clouds, but mainly it's the Japanese mural again. Shades of gray and blue as each range catches its portion of subdued light.

I haven't seen Jess since the early part of this past summer. Early July, it was. I took my vacation in New York. It was her summer break. Look at it this way: Suppose Jess had married some guy who had been sent overseas by the State Department or IBM—she might be gone for years at a time. Or if she decided to do a stint in the Peace Corps. She might go off to Bolivia or Botswana for God knows how long.

What I'm doing is thinking one way in order not to think another. By looking at the foothills and blowing mental bubbles, I prevent myself from thinking about what I should be thinking about. I should be thinking about my daughter not only as daughter but as woman as well. She is very much a part of my experience, my intention. My present intention is to really think about, and no doubt write about, the man-woman thing. I confess to being much perplexed by the man-woman thing. I had always assumed—unconsciously, perhaps; silently, perhaps—that there was an ideal you worked toward, and that through a combination of luck, intelligence, and goodwill, you would one day find yourself at the shining peak of man-woman felicity. Now I'm not at all sure that nature gives a particular fuck as long as men and women do. Beyond that, there are no intrinsic rules. Different societies have different rules. Different times have made different rules. I'm not sure what the rules are now, so I'm having an investigative look.

Which gives a sharper edge to my daughter's impending visit. After all, Jess is a woman—a twenty-year-old woman, which is woman enough, which is woman in the fullness of mind, personality, character, and sex. Perhaps not *total* fullness. There may still be some developing to do, but Jessica, bless her heart and head, always seemed to be tumbling precipitously toward womanhood ever since she lifted her little ass off the floor and tried her first few faltering steps.

She was delightful . . . okay? I mean she was everything you would want a child to be. She was healthy, curious, bright, mouth-wateringly cute. I read stories to her and her soul was like a little vacuum that sucked up details and stored them in that Edenic place where the Bible-writers went to imagine the world's beginning.

Fate and Ellen collaborated in keeping ours a one-child family. Ellen did become pregnant again, but she lost the child, and with one thing and another it was decided we'd be best off with just Jess. It was Ellen who made that judgment, and as things worked out she was right.

As I say—a wonderful child. It seemed as though that childhood would go on forever. Any parent will know what I mean. She was so *small*. How old was she before she could heist herself on the throne? Three? Four? She had such smoky blue eyes. Then, all of a sudden, privacy began. The bathroom became as sequestered a place for her as it was for Ellen or me. Except when she was sick, of course. Then the second "all of a sudden": She was going to school and it was about that time that she began to decide for herself what she looked best in. Dresses, shoes, overcoats. I remember Ellen saying, "She was the one who picked it out. I had two little dresses off the rack, and she went over and picked out a third. 'I like this one, Mommy,' she said. There was no question about it. The one she had picked out was the one that looked nicest on her." Third "all of a sudden": the closing of many doors besides the bathroom door. Interior doors. Which is not to say that Jessica was a brooding, reclusive girl. Not at all. She was open and happy. She shared a good deal of herself with me, and I'm sure she shared even more with Ellen. But now there were many friends and the secrets of friendship. Now the air was thick with rumors of sex, and there must have been much secret contemplation about that. At ten, her dolls became mementos. She kept them out of nostalgia. Then (not so all of a sudden; I had seen it coming) she was her very own person. I place it around her twelfth birthday, maybe thirteenth. This is the canvas I have retained and framed:

We were doing the pre-Christmas thing that had become ritual with this semi-apostate branch of the Light family. A movie, then a walk around Radio City to see the skating rink with its decorated Christmas tree and the promenade with its wire-wound angels. Jess and I were together. Ellen was to join us at the restaurant on Second Avenue that had become part of the seasonal ceremony. A French restaurant that Jess adored for its bread and linen tablecloths and pâté. There was something that Ellen had to do that had kept her apart for a few hours. Visit a relative in a hospital, I think.

Jess and I had gone to a movie that starred Walter Matthau and Glenda Jackson—the laff riot of the year, so the paper said—and I had squirmed more than a bit at Matthau's sexual adventures. I hadn't as yet found a comfortable attitude toward Jess in matters of sex. I had never had a "talk" with her. After all, she had a mother. I assumed that she knew more than I did at a comparable age, but since there hadn't been any ongoing exchange about life's basics I recall being distinctly ill-at-ease seeing that fairly harmless movie with Jess. Particularly the slapstick scene where Matthau and Jackson get into bed, more or less clothed, but going through a series of contortions to test whether sex could be accomplished with each partner keeping one foot on the floor.

"Did you think that was funny?" I asked Jess.

"Wasn't it?" she asked back. "I saw you were laughing."

"Sometimes you laugh because you're expected to laugh," I said.

"Then you didn't find it funny?"

"Well, yes, I did find it funny, but I guess what I'm asking is in just what way it was funny—for you?"

Jessica, I recall, half turned and gave me a curious, smiling look. She knew I was skirting around unexplored territory. She said, "What I found funny was Walter Matthau acting like a big make-out artist. He always reminds me of somebody's uncle. He's like somebody you expect to find in the deli having a corned beef sandwich with a friend."

I laughed. She was going to be good with words, my Jess. But I wasn't about to be detoured. I had let myself be detoured too often in the past.

"And what, may I ask, is a make-out artist?"

She made a face and lifted one shoulder. Who was I kidding? Nevertheless, I wanted to hear it from her. "Tell me," I insisted.

"Oh, Dad."

"Do me this little favor."

"A make-out artist is a guy who's always trying to make a girl go to bed with him."

"I see—yes—that's a workable definition. Are there any make-out artists in your circle of friends?"

She sighed, asked, "Are we going to have a big sex talk?"

"Is it too late for that?"

"Much."

So we strolled with the strollers in the Radio City arcade, listening to the jingly Christmas music that was being piped into the evening air, while I contemplated the fact that instead of informing my daughter, my daughter had informed me. She had informed me that I could begin treating her as a woman whose sex was fully established, not as a sort of genderless doll favored by fairy tales and fathers.

We began to make our way out of the Radio City enclave, past the hot-chestnut sellers, across Fifth Avenue, toward Second Avenue, where Fredo's would serve us that unbelievable pâté and the crunchy bread. I was sure that Jess was thinking all the way of what had passed between us, and she must have concluded that we had arrived at a new place as father and daughter. She began to ask her own probing questions, questions about me that she had never asked before, like: I had been in television, then was out of television, and now was back in television . . . yes?

"Yes."

"And you wrote that book, but that was all, just that one book?"

"Yes."

"And you wrote that show for TV . . . *The Search*?"

"Right."

"Why all those things?" she wanted to know.

"Why all those *different* things or why all those *many* things?"

"Either. Both."

"Why do you ask?"

"Just curious."

"Have you been comparing me to other fathers, the fathers of your friends?"

"Not exactly."

"Inexactly."

"I suppose every kid does that," she said. "Compare her parents to other parents."

"And have I been found wanting? Or just the opposite—excessive?"

"You haven't been found anything," Jess said. "I'm just asking."

It wasn't a story I had found necessary to tell before, so there was some fumbling and hasty stitching in the telling. My daughter had been musing over her father's patchy career, and her father had to improvise an explanation that would respect the truth while leaving his image relatively undamaged.

I told her that doctors study and study and sooner or later they emerge as doctors. Ditto lawyers, architects, and engineers. What is there to do with a specialty but specialize? But there were others, like her father, who didn't specialize, and then it was a question of how well and how quickly you can apply some native ability, talent, or muscle to an unobliging world. Some men and women sell things to other men and women with not much more competence than a ready smile and a way with words. Some men climb on huge rigs and spend their days and nights pounding across the interstates, fueled by diesel oil, loud music, and gallons of coffee. Others get into one field or another by accident or affinity—

"What's 'affinity'?"

"A natural attraction, one to the other."

"Were you naturally attracted to television?"

"At the time."

"Go on."

I went on, telling her that I got into television by accident and by affinity. The accident was a man I had met when I was in the army; the affinity was to the activity that man was engaged in. Then there was the lighting apprenticeship, then the assistant directorship, then the pilot show I wrote . . .

We were walking on a side street in the Fifties, I remember. I also remember I was feeling a growing resentment at being probed by a child who didn't have the experience to judge but who did have the right to ask. One is supposed to be honest with one's child, right? I was trying to be honest with Jess, but I found that being honest with my own daughter demanded a purity of mind and motive that wasn't necessary in the knowing world of adults. Adults understand the blank spaces; children do not.

I offer these vignettes of personal history as possible insights. Odd things stick in the mind, and there may be deeply buried reasons for their doing so.

2 I drove to the airport after confirming with United the arrival time of that flight from Detroit. I walked from the parking area to the terminal. This terminal has been in a continuous state of expansion ever since I arrived here. I guess that says something about the desirability of the region. Well, why not? It's quite beautiful, a hell of a lot less expensive than New York, and the living is easy.

I haven't seen Jessica since last summer. Six months. A mountain range or an ocean's width in the life of a twenty-year-old. All possibilities are still ripening on the vine. Ambition, career, love, marriage, family. Or none of these things. Perhaps Jess has taken up some exotic religion, dresses in silky robes, has implanted a precious stone in her left nostril, a bloodred emblem between her eyes. What do I know? Perhaps she's married. Not at all impossible. Or pregnant.

Or has given herself over to some fierce cause, ready to sacrifice all for universal sisterhood.

Naturally, I don't expect that the cheery, slightly smug "on time" actually means on time. Planes are *always* late. So I'm prepared to sit down, open the paperback book I slipped into my overcoat pocket on my way out of the apartment, and continue reading the book that was recommended to me by the helpful girl in the bookstore. I had asked for a book that would take the woman's point of view with regard to men.

The girl, who was rather pretty in a Botticellian way, gave me a quick look and a pale smile. "Fiction or nonfiction?" she asked. "Nonfiction," I said. "Fiction tends to obscure the matter. Don't you think so?" She only smiled and then directed me to the right section and made several recommendations. I wound up with a strange book. It's nonfiction, all right. It's the woman's point of view with regard to men, all right. But so far (I'm into it about fifty pages), it strikes me as an intentionally nasty piece of work. What I don't like about it is simply discovered and simply stated. The author takes the view that all of past history shall be judged for its cruelties and crimes against women by today's standards. The hairy ancients who wrote the Old and New Testaments were just as culpable as any contemporary wife-beater. The Hebrew proscription against menstruating women and the Chinese custom of binding a girl-child's feet are widely separated symptoms of the same male sickness. The guilt passeth unto the latest generation.

Is that fair?

The people in the waiting area were there to board the same plane that would be bringing Jess to Denver. They would be going on to Salt Lake City and San Francisco. The young woman in the fuzzy blue coat standing by the railing was also waiting for Flight 702, and her persistent stare (at me) and that half smile I took to be a case of mistaken identity . . . or possibly the look a daughter might give a father while waiting for the preoccupied old fool to recognize what was right there before his failing eyes.

I try to gather my dignity and my sense of humor as I start toward Jess, as she starts toward me. By God, she is a stunner! That coat she's wearing is the color of her eyes. I'm certain I've never seen that coat before. No hat. Her gorgeous hair is—I don't know what it is—it's profusely *there.* Drawing close, I can make out the familiar angularity of her smile. I take hold of the arm she's about to wrap around me.

"And would you mind telling me how long you would have let me go on staring like a blind idiot?" I demand.

"I couldn't believe it," she said. "You were looking right at me. Have I changed that much?"

"No, you haven't changed that much. I wasn't expecting to see you, so naturally you couldn't be here. Your plane must have landed early."

"Fifteen minutes."

"What's this you're wearing? I don't recognize it."

"It's a sweater coat. I bought it in Ann Arbor."

"Looks good on you."

"Hello," she said.

I gave her a hug and a kiss. I smelled perfume. Then I held her out at arm's length again. "On reconsideration," I said, "you have changed."

"How?"

"I don't know how. Give me time. Is this your only bag?"

"Are you kidding? I have a big suitcase coming through baggage. I'm going to be here three, four days, I thought. I'm going to be all over the slopes and all over town. Did you warn Denver that I was coming?"

"I thought it was a week," I said. "I have plans for a week. You said at least a week when we spoke."

"You're making that up."

"How was the flight?"

"Awful. There was the guy next to me who wouldn't shut up for a second. He was incredibly handsome, but a horrendous *nudnick*. Yak, yak, yak. About nothing at all. But in the minutest detail. His skiing, his car, his job, his boyfriends, his girlfriends, the great restaurants that have through blind luck had the honor of his patronage . . . like that."

I smiled. I was already in seventh heaven. I loved that "honor of his patronage." Jess is into her senior year, and I think it's already possible to see the kind of mind and personality that's been fashioned. We were walking toward the baggage area. I was carrying her nylon knapsack. I said I certainly knew what she meant about gabby *nudnicks*. I was familiar with the type who thought garrulousness was next to godliness. Still, we mustn't judge harshly. Some people were brought up in the tradition of neighborliness. Not like us New Yorkers who sally forth each day tightly zipped against all human encounters except those marked on our calendars . . .

"Listen," I said. "I took the liberty of reserving a room for you at a very nice hotel not far from my apartment. You could have stayed at my place but it would have been kind of crowded. This way you can watch the late shows, sleep till all hours, have a leisurely breakfast, and whenever you're ready you give me a jingle and I'm over in two minutes."

Jess gave me a quick look. "Okay," she said. "Whatever is comfortable."

The clerk at the hotel or motel—they call it a "Manor"—naturally had no reservation for Jessica Light because none had been made, but I put on a gentlemanly act of annoyance, complaining that the reservation had been made days ago . . . etc. Talk about luck! Another clerk sidled over to say that there had just been a cancellation. A single, fortunately.

The lobby was positively atwinkle with Christmas. Garlands and silver tinsel and a Christmas tree hung with the usual decoration. Noel! Very nice! With Jess here, I was very much in the spirit of the thing. I went up with Jess to inspect the room, saw that it was as trim and hygienic as such rooms are supposed to be.

"This do?" I asked.

"You should see my room at Ann Arbor," she said.

"I have," I reminded her.

"I mean since I've moved."

"I didn't know you'd moved."

"I have . . . anyway, this is great."

"Good. I'm going to leave you alone now. Have yourself a shower, a bath, a lie-down, whatever. An hour? Two? I'll get back around dinnertime."

"I don't know what's the big rush to be off," she said. "Why leave? I just got here."

"I thought you might want to—you know—unpack, arrange, relax."

Jess looked at me wryly. "Are you going to fuss?" she asked.

"Scout's honor."

"Okay," she said. "Maybe I will take a hot bath. I haven't had a hot bath in months. Showers only."

"Good. I'll be back around five. We'll have a drink, if your father allows you to drink, and then we'll go to dinner. What's your preference these days—meat, fish, Chinese?"

"Love Chinese. You know that."

"Knew that. Things change. But Chinese it is. I know a place that has the last great chef of the Ch'ing dynasty."

"How old is he?"

"Hundred and thirty-six."

"See you later, Dad."

It wasn't cheap. Sixty bucks a night for a single. But think of what comparable accommodation in the Big Apple would cost. Nevertheless, the question remains—why? The truth is that it hadn't occurred to me to have Jess stay anywhere but in my apartment, but when I recognized my own daughter standing there in Stapleton Airport in her royal-blue sweater coat with that amused look on her thoroughly beautiful, thoroughly mature face, I knew that having her stay in my apartment was out. She would have to stay elsewhere. Let me say it quickly, just to get it out of the way: I harbor no incestuous feelings toward my daughter. Yes, yes, I know, merely to have mentioned it, and so forth. I suppose the ancient taboo occupied a small irregular corner of the large complex consciousness that forced me to that quick decision.

Certainly it wasn't a question of space. She probably lives in a quarter of that space in Ann Arbor. The real question was one of *time.* I mean time for *adjustment.* I hadn't seen her in six months. We hadn't lived under the same roof for two years. Suddenly I'm confronted with a woman whose womanly ways, thoughts, feelings, and—yes—involvements I know very little about. The continuity from child to adult has been broken, and I knew instinctively that I couldn't put it together quickly enough, or confidently enough, to make for a comfortable few days. Traipsing in and out of the bathroom . . . *Good morning, Jess. Sleep well? Would you like your eggs scrambled or once over lightly, like you used to have them? . . .* I know women are better about these things than men, even in a father-daughter situation, so it wasn't Jess I was concerned about. It was me.

You see, I've been "Papa" or "Dad" or, sometimes,

"George," ever since she's been old enough to make out any consistent presence. She, on the other hand, has been a child for eons, a teenager for centuries, and a woman only recently. Now she brings that overwhelming womanhood to Denver, where her father is hanging out for the present, and her father is at a loss. I need time. I don't have the posture, the attitude, the ease. Yes, there *is* sexual embarrassment! God knows I know she's no virgin, but I don't quite know how to handle it . . . *Been laid much, Jess? One guy, or are you sort of playing the field?* . . . But that's the least of it. We could handle that by avoiding it. It's the time abyss that has brought me to an abrupt halt, made a quick adjustment of plans necessary. I could deal with Jessica the child, but I couldn't face the awkwardness there would be for me and the child of my mind in the prospect of a grown woman parading around my small apartment.

I swung off before the Eisenhower Tunnel and drove over Loveland Pass. I wanted Jess to see that majestic view and breathe that thin air. Snow had been walled up alongside the road like a geological slice of white rock. I stopped at one of the lookouts and we got out of the car. It was sunny and arctic. Jess was wearing a goosedown jacket and a long, white, woolen scarf—bought that morning at the Aspen Leaf. She was wearing the heavy slacks she had brought with her. I had urged her to buy some insulated ski pants as well, telling her that this was her Christmas-Chanukah present, so she might as well make the most of it, but she declined the ski pants, saying that a ski jacket could be used anywhere, for many different occasions, but God knows when she'd have a chance to use those stuffed trousers again. I said okay but warned her she might freeze her fanny.

Incidentally, she had brought with her her present for

me—hers and Ellen's. Two tattersall shirts bearing the label of a fancy Ann Arbor men's store. I remembered the name of the place from my last visit there. One shirt from Jessica; one from Ellen. I smiled inwardly at that, feeling a touch of time-sickness. I like tattersall shirts. Ellen knew that. Ellen also knew my size. Ellen knows a lot about me, naturally. The odd thing, however, was that she had Jess buy and bring her gift for me rather than mailing it. I was having mine mailed to her directly from the store: a new, illustrated biography of Verdi. What was wrong with having Jess bring her present? Nothing. Very sensible. And yet . . .

Jess must have guessed the profligate mood singing in my blood like a shot of 100-proof vodka. It was so good to have her with me! I wanted to buy her things! For my sake more than hers. Because I'd been putting money in the bank for months, because the holidays were closing in and I had made no plans to go east, because Jess had, quite on her own, made the decision to spend some time with me before going home. That she had done that, that she was here, mounted up with each passing hour. I had been feeling so alone, so (let's face it) *sorry* for myself, that any relief was bound to be explosive. Now I wasn't feeling sorry for myself. These purchases were expressions of my gratitude.

"You can see timberline there," I pointed out.

"What's timberline?"

"Timberline is the place above which trees won't grow."

Jess gazed out toward the indicated place on the mountain's slope, her face swathed in white wool. She spoke through the wool. "Too cold?" she asked. "Is that the reason?"

"Too cold. Not enough sun, if it's on the wrong side of the mountain. Timberline is generally at the location of the fifty-degree isotherm during the warmest month of the year."

Jess smiled at me with her eyes. Lapis lazuli in crystal air. Some freckles were showing. "You're showing off," she said. "You looked that up."

"I'm not denying," I said. "How do you find out things?"

We drove on, past Arapahoe Basin, on to Keystone. Jess had assured me that she had taken ski lessons, had gone skiing several times in northern Michigan with friends. And didn't I remember the time about five years ago when she had gone skiing with a group of girls at the Snow Bowl in Vermont? No, I didn't remember that. Well, I must not have been paying attention. *That* had happened frequently enough in the past, my not paying attention. Anyway, Mrs. Davis and Mrs. Jessup, mothers of two of the girls, had chaperoned the expedition. They drove up in two cars and stayed at a wonderful chalet. She'd been gone for three days. . . .

We spent some time fitting Jess out in boots, skis, and poles, and then we made our way over to one of the ski lifts. "Now, you have been on one of these things before, haven't you?" I asked again, and she replied, "How else would I get to ski down?" What worried me was not the getting on but the getting off. Tumbling down that little hill at the top wasn't dangerous but it was discouraging. I thought I detected some nervousness on her part, so I said, "Hold your pole in your left hand and hang on to me with your right." Jess turned and looked at me with an open mouth and crossed eyes, a pantomime of terror.

The evergreens to the right were cradling pillows of snow from a recent downfall. To the left was a steep slope on which the better skiers bounced over moguls. "Warm enough?" I asked. "Toast," she said. I searched for a concise way to express what I was feeling, but it was all too complex for economy. I would have had to incorporate what we had discussed last night over the Hunan beef and sweet-and-sour shrimp. It would have had to touch on the two of us riding a ski lift up the Rockies, the past ten years, the next ten years, the state of Jessica Light's heart and mind, the state of our disastrous world, mortality, immortality, and so on. What few, select words would encompass all that?

"Ain't this somethin'?" I settled for.

"Fabulous!" she agreed.

Gloves, too, I had bought. And ski goggles. The gloves she had brought with her would never do for skiing. The ones I bought were insulated with the latest scientific materials, gathered at the wrist to keep the warmth in. It's not that I want to come on like the munificent daddy, but I am trying to give some measure to the pleasure it gave to me to be in Jess's company once more. It's crass, I know, but that little shopping spree was a terrific emotional fix for me. Redress for missed occasions.

"Now!" I yelled.

Jess took my arm and we got up a little too slowly. The turning ski chair gave us a boot in the rear and we slid down the hill, separating to use our skis for braking. Near the bottom, Jess windmilled and flopped. "Okay?" I asked. "Damn it!" she said. She got up and looked at me crossly, indicating that all this fatherly solicitude was getting to be a pain in the ass. Was it? Could be. But, damn it, I didn't want her hurt. I didn't want her going back to her mother with a broken leg.

"Ready?" I asked.

"Let's go," she said.

"Start slowly," I foolishly cautioned.

"Yes, Daddy."

Yes, Daddy!

I let her go first. She snowplowed down, straightened out, gathered speed, snowplowed again, brought her skis together, did a slow but nice traverse, then another, and I allowed that she'd be all right. I started down myself, determined to stay behind her. I do a cautious stem christie, not very graceful, but then I don't fancy a fifty-year-old fall with the attendant casts and boring immobility. I don't have an entourage of buddies to inscribe graffiti on my plaster of Paris. It wouldn't be any fun at all.

There was quite a bit of crosswind. It picked up the snow and unfurled sprays of gold. I recalled Jess's career announcement, and I wondered why I felt so completely unsurprised. She had told me last night that she was definitely going in for graduate work. She had applied to the Columbia School of Journalism and had been accepted. She told me she had been studying Russian this past year. Did I have any idea how hard it was just to learn the Russian *alphabet*? I confessed I had no idea, never having tried. And why, I asked, had she decided to study Russian? Because, she said, what was wanted in journalism these days was *specialty*. So she had decided to concentrate on languages and history. She had French reasonably well, and now she was concentrating on Russian.

Ridiculous, I know, but I felt more than a little put out that all these career maneuvers had taken place without my knowledge.

We made it to the bottom without disaster, and then immediately took the chair lift up again. Jess seesawed her skis in jubilation. "I love it!" she crowed. "Can we come here again before I go home?" My heart contracted in joy-pain. How often in the past, whenever she was enjoying something, had she demanded some guarantee that this happiness would be repeated. "Why not?" I said. "As long as the weather holds."

We ate chili dogs in one of the many eating places scattered around the area. Jess had already taken on the owlish look of the sunlight skier, her goggles having left a pair of whitish rings around her eyes while the rest of her face glowed ruddily. I asked if she had let her mother know of her intention of coming to Denver for a visit, and she treated the question with the wry impatience it deserved. Of course she had let her mother know. Why on earth would she have kept it a secret? No reason, no reason, just asking. It was like talking in the middle of a dry thunderstorm. There was a continuous roll from the ski boots pounding the wooden floor. I apologized more than once for not catching the opening or close of some of Jess's remarks. She raised her voice and asked, "So are you going to stay here?"

"Permanently, do you mean? I don't think so. I'll be coming back east."

"When?"

"I haven't set a date."

Jess nodded reflectively, hesitated a second, then asked, "Are you and Mother going to get a divorce?"

I was sitting so that I could see through an open door onto the last descent of one of the steepest slopes. Two expert skiers, arms held like ballet dancers, slalomed down in quick, sharp turns. I felt a stab of deficiency as I thought of all the things I had left undone, all the things there was no longer the time to learn to do. Like ski with such grace. Like learn Russian. The loss I was feeling attached itself to Jess's last question. I wondered if Ellen had something to do with Jess making this stopover before going east. That didn't seem like Ellen's style. But how could I be sure of Ellen's style after a two-year separation? People change. Do they? I don't know. Maybe yes, maybe no, but in any event circumstances change, and the same people begin to adjust or reject, and that can look like change from the outside.

"Do you think your mother wants a divorce?" I asked.

"I really haven't discussed it with her . . . I *should* say, she hasn't discussed it with me."

"I see . . . well . . . did you want to discuss it with me first?" I asked her.

"I wasn't aware of any particular order."

"My answer is no, I'm not looking for a divorce at all. There's no reason for it, from my point of view. Do you think your mother is looking to be legally free?"

"If you mean did she *say* she wants to be free, the answer is no, she didn't say that. But I should think that by this time . . ."

"What?"

"One might ask by this time what's the point of it all," Jess said. "I *mean*—"

"You mean what?"

"You here. Her there."

"Did you say something of this sort to your mother?"

"Dad, please don't do that."

"Do what?"

"Fence that way. Turn everything around. I'm talking to *you*."

She was right. I was fencing. On the other hand, why shouldn't I try to find out things? Jess was regularly in touch with her mother. I knew that. Certainly more in touch with Ellen than she was with me. As she should be. She was still living at home—that is, with Ellen—when she wasn't at school.

"Okay," I said. "No fencing. The truth. Do you want the truth?"

"Haven't I been getting it?"

"You have. Here's more. The truth is that I'm trying to get my act together. Specifically my man-woman act."

"What does that mean?"

"That means that I seem to have lost some instinct. Or maybe I only thought I had it. It seemed to me at one time in my life that there was an ideal out there that one must try to realize. An infinitely adjustable thing, depending on the particular man and woman, but attainable. Now I'm not sure. Now I'm investigating. Will you help me in my investigation?"

"How?"

"Tell me about your man-woman thing. I'd give heavy odds on there having been one recently. Am I right?"

Jess shook her head, shrugged, nodded her head. She said, "Not now. I want more skiing."

"And you shall have more skiing," I said.

It began in the car, on our way back from Keystone, and it continued over dinner, which we had at the Plumtree Room of the Manor. I left Jess in her room to wash up and change her clothes, while I went back to my apartment to do the same. On the drive back, I noticed the first flakes of the new weather system. The forecast had glumly told of "heavy accumulations." Ordinarily, I don't mind meteorological biggies. I'm not sure why. Maybe because they preempt the stage, slow down the whole damn process. This time, I did mind. I've seen these Denver blizzards. Jess could be marooned in her "Manor," I in my apartment.

Jess retained her owlish look in the red-and-gold restaurant. Nothing like snow-reflected sunlight to give you a handsome burn. I had noticed in my bathroom mirror that I had my own slope tan. "So," I said, "his name is Bryan Daniels, and he has green eyes and sorta light hair, blondish, straw-blond. What else?"

"He's in Biz Ad," Jess said.

"Which is—Business Administration?"

"Yes."

"Continue."

She continued. What was Bryan Daniels like? Well, he was like this: He never raised his voice; even when they had arguments, he never raised his voice. Did I think that was a matter of home environment? Very likely. I had been known to raise my voice. Not frequently but on occasion. Anyway, Bryan could play the guitar. He could play it well enough to appear in a fraternity combo. Bryan had made the dean's list this past year. He was a senior, like her . . . and what else?

"And you are—or were—in love with him?"

"I guess so."

"And?"

And nothing, really. They had talked about going somewhere together over the holiday break, but they had gone nowhere. Bryan thought maybe he ought to touch home base—which was Seattle. And she thought maybe she would visit her father in Denver before heading east. Bryan had asked if her parents were divorced, and she had said no, they weren't, that her father was doing some work in television in Denver. That's as far as she took it. Just the bare bones. Anyway, there was nothing definitely understood or misunderstood. They would probably see each other again in January, but the chances were they wouldn't be seeing each other exclusively . . .

"And is the end of that exclusiveness something you're going to be dragging around with you throughout the holidays?" I asked.

"Probably," she said.

The waiter had come and gone. Jess had ordered Perrier and I had ordered a Jack Daniels on the rocks. Now the waiter was back with our drinks. Were we ready to order? We were. Jess ordered the trout amandine, and I ordered the prime rib. "Are you still a big red-meat man?" she asked me. "I wouldn't say so," I said. "Couple of times a week. Not every night like I used to. My doctor here says he wishes he had my cholesterol count. Condition? Is it a condition or a count?"

Just on the other side of this banter was an entirely different set of images and conjectures. When Jess spoke of "going somewhere together" with her guitar-playing Bryan, I immediately gathered that such togetherness would be a continuation of an ongoing togetherness. What I noticed was the difference in our attitudes and assumptions. This was the first time in our mutually important father-daughter relationship that Jess's sexual activity was taken as an established fact. Of course, I knew it. For Christ sake, I *read.* I have, I've always assumed, a contemporary nose. But what a man knows and what affects him intimately are in different parts of the forest. Jess wasn't trying to shock me or educate me. She was merely informing me on the state of her life. I had asked, hadn't I? Yes, indeed. And, believe me, I sat there with a mature, unruffled look on my face as the primal scene stamped itself like a branding iron on a train of tender memories. And why should not my daughter, my Jess, take her place in the man-woman world? She should, she should, and in a corner of my consciousness I solemnized her womanhood, but the much larger part of my consciousness was busy with tracking its immediate state of unhappiness.

"I know these things happen," I said. "God knows I know. But there's usually a reason. I won't insist, but I do wish you'd tell me. I know I can't help, but the telling itself might help."

Jess turned her attention to a corner of the tablecloth and arranged some crumbs with the tines of her fork. She was tired, all right, but within those droopy eyes was serious sorrow. She was measuring her loss and it was a big one. I wondered what kind of a fool this young Bryan Daniels was that he could chuck in such a winning hand. All right, George Light was the girl's father, too fond, no doubt, but even fond fathers retain some objectivity. This was not just another pretty girl.

"It'll sound stupid . . ." she began.

"Not to me."

Jess hesitated, still keeping her gaze on the tablecloth. Without looking directly at me, she said, "You once said that most decisions were a form of surrender . . ."

"Did I say that? I don't remember saying it, but I'm ready to agree with myself."

"I remember a lot of what you said," Jess said.

"I'm pleased," I said, "but a little apprehensive."

Now she looked up and locked on to my eyes. She told me that Bryan was planning to become a rich man. He planned it coolly and consistently, and he didn't see what was wrong with such a plan. It wasn't a matter of greed or ego with him, but a natural goal for his particular skills. Just as, say, the polio vaccine was the natural end of Dr. Salk's research. Bryan knew that he had a feel for the nature of money. Money in large quantities behaved in a certain way, and Bryan had discovered that he had an instinct for that behavior. It wasn't all of life, he understood that, but he also understood it was one of the things in this world he understood best. There was nothing he could do about that, was there? It was a case of early recognition. He would probably get a job in an investment house. They were looking for people like him. He didn't care which city. They could go to New York, if that's what she would like. . . .

"I think I see," I said.

"What do you see?"

"Do you happen to have a snapshot of Bryan?" I asked.

She nodded. She reached for her bag, took out her wallet,

flipped through the plastic holders (I thought I caught a glimpse of my own picture there), and finally extricated a photograph. She passed it over to me. I could see what she saw. I could sense the weight of what she was giving up. Bryan had a smile that would light up a fifty-foot radius. A fine-looking sonofabitch, this *shagitz,* Bryan Daniels. But I still wasn't sure of her reasoning . . . or reasons.

"So . . . why?" I asked.

"You said before that you thought you saw," she said. "What did you think you saw?"

"What I saw . . . I saw that his center might be your margin, your center his margin. Love might soften it, disguise it, but it would never change it."

She held out her hand and I passed back the photograph. She had some trouble finding the plastic slot. Finally, she stuck the photograph anywhere and returned the wallet to her bag. There were tears in her eyes—or the containment of tears.

"I guess I'm pretty tired," she said.

"I can imagine," I said.

"Do me a favor, will you, Dad? You order dessert for yourself. Please? You sit here and enjoy your coffee and dessert, and I'll go to my room. What I'd like to do is take another hot bath and get into bed. Would you let me do that? Right now?"

I held up both hands in total assent.

3 The next morning—eight, my time; ten, Ellen's—I telephoned. It was Saturday. Ellen was sure to be at home, wanting to know if Jess had arrived safely, if everything was going well, when she could expect Jess to be coming home . . . etc. Of course, Jess may have telephoned and spoken to her mother by this time, but even so I thought that Ellen would appreciate a report from me.

"We've got a blizzard going here," I told her.

"So I gathered from the morning news," Ellen said.

"But Jess is safe and sound. Has she been in touch with you?"

"Not yet."

"We had a wonderful day yesterday. We skied."

"Skied! But she didn't have the clothing for that. . . ."

"One buys and rents," I said.

"Those are awfully steep mountains, aren't they?"

"Oh, there are all kinds of slopes. Slopes for beginners and for hot dogs. Slopes for Christians and Jews."

"What?"

"Kidding."

"Is Jess staying with you?" Ellen asked.

I told her about the room at the Manor. I gave her the telephone number of the place, in case she wanted to speak to Jess directly. I was fairly certain that Jess hadn't told Ellen about the bust-up with Bryan Daniels. After all, Jess hadn't volunteered the information, I had extracted it. It was a loose tooth, didn't need much pulling, but even so I suspected I was the first to know. Normally, Ellen would be, but Jess wasn't with Ellen, she was here, with me. It was the kind of hurt a girl like Jess would want to digest before sharing. There's always some humiliation in failure. I doubt she would have told me anything if I hadn't pried and probed. She may have been playing out in her mind a variety of confessional scenes with her mother, but fate offered her father instead. That's life.

"When I spoke to her last, she said she was going to be staying with you," Ellen said.

"That was my original thought, too, but when I saw her standing in the airport I decided against it."

"Really? Why?"

I thought I caught a slight hitch of amusement in Ellen's voice. It occurred to me that she may have pictured Jess in my bachelor digs a little more promptly and realistically than I did.

"Why?" I stalled. "Well, because fitting her mentally into my small apartment was one thing. In the flesh, it was quite another, if you see what I mean. When I saw her in her blue sweater-coat, and her boots, and her grown-up grown-upness . . ."

"Yes?"

"I couldn't see it," I said. "Does this make any sense to you?"

"Sort of."

"I suppose you know about Bryan Daniels," I said.

"I know there is somebody by that name," she said. "I've never met him. Why do you ask?"

"How long has it been going on with this guy?"

"I'm not sure. About a year, I would guess."

"A year. That's almost twelve months, isn't it? What I'm wondering—I'm wondering why she hasn't said a word to me about it in all this time. I wonder why she didn't let me know until it was all over."

"*Is* it all over?" Ellen asked.

"Apparently. She wrapped the whole thing up for me yesterday. The beginning and the end, leaving out, I might add, much of the middle. From what she tells me, Bryan is a young man on the make. Looking for the big buck. Nothing wrong with that—unless something is wrong with it. Evidently Jess saw something wrong with it. She didn't want to dedicate her life to big bucks. Why do you think she didn't tell me anything about this before?"

"Maybe because she was afraid this would happen."

"But she told you, didn't she?"

"Yes, she did. But there is a difference, wouldn't you say?"

"Ah, yes, well . . . I grant you a difference. I understand she's in touch with you more, the gender bond, all those good things. But this was no small item. This was important. Here's a guy she might have married, seriously in love, slept with him, I assume. . . . Do you know if she slept with him?"

"George."

"Simple question."

"Ask her."

"I'm asking you."

"Don't take that tone," Ellen said, quietly and firmly.

"Sorry."

It wasn't the first time I'd had to step back from former

assumptions. In the past two years Ellen had had several opportunities to remind me that she wasn't my East Coast agent, providing information on request. She wasn't obliged to answer all my questions. I was the one who had thought a break would be best, had removed myself from the scene. I was the one who had the affair. Actions have their consequences. Ellen didn't spell it out, but the intimation was strong and clear. She wasn't going to be vindictive—it wasn't in her nature to be vindictive—but neither was she going to be, do, or say any more than she thought necessary. Yes, she was taking into account that Jess was my daughter, that I loved her, that, equally important, perhaps most important, Jess loved me. She would do nothing to prejudice that fact. She understood the importance of that fact, for everybody, but she would not be intimidated by that fact. That's the way things stood.

"I assumed you knew that your daughter is no longer a virgin," Ellen said.

"Rumors have reached me," I said. "No, Ellen, it's this— she doesn't have to fill me in on details, but I am a little surprised that I heard no mention of the Bryan Daniels affair until it was all over. You say it's been going on for almost a year. God knows how many times I've telephoned Jess in this past year. No mention of beautiful Bryan. No mention of the fact that she had applied to the Columbia graduate program. She used to tell me things, Ellen. You know that. What I'm asking is why I'm on the outside looking in? All right, things have happened, I'm in Denver, you're in New York, but I never before had this feeling of being locked out. Jess told me things. We were friends. I just wondered if you had any idea why I'm being left out."

"Is that supposed to be a serious question?" Ellen asked, her voice going flat, cold.

"Of course it's a serious question."

"Then there must be something the matter with you. I don't believe what I'm hearing. Where is she now? Is she with me or with you? Whom did she tell first about breaking up with Bryan Daniels, me or you? She could have come right home, you know. She *chose* to be in Denver. She wanted to see *you*. She hadn't told me about the breakup with Bryan, but she has told you. If I kept your kind of scorecard, I could say *I* was being left out."

True! How the hell was I ever going to break through to a new understanding of the man-woman thing if I fell into the old *shtick* so easily? Ellen was always good at adjusting perspectives. Even when she did it with a good deal more tenderness, she was good at it.

"How," I asked, "do you manage to keep separate your relationship with me and your relationship with Jess?"

"I don't understand what you mean."

"I mean that you don't let what happens between us wash off on Jess. You never did. You've always managed to keep it steady and whole that I'm her father."

"Don't you do likewise?"

"Yes, I do. I swear I do. It's no problem for me. I can see how it might be a problem for you. That's why I'm asking."

Ellen replied that it was very simple. All she had to do was keep our different histories in mind. Jess's history and mine. She had no trouble keeping all our separate and commingled histories in place. And while she was telling me this, I wondered whether this was a universal feminine trait or pure Ellen. My quick decision was that it was the latter. It was not a universal. Women were quite capable of kicking, gouging, biting, stabbing, poisoning. Look at Lady Macbeth. Look at Becky Sharp, Jezebel, Lucrezia Borgia, Medea, etc.

I asked, "Did Jess think I was going to be the sit-com, dunder-headed papa about Bryan? Nobody good enough for his darling?"

"She knows you're not like that," Ellen said.

I took quick advantage of the softer note in Ellen's voice. "Give me an informed guess on why Jess kept the whole business from me."

"It would only be a guess."

"I'd be grateful."

"It's possible Jess thought that if she told you about Bryan—maybe even about graduate school—that you would think she was—well—sort of fashioning her life in an opposite way."

"Opposite. Opposite of what? Of whom?"

"Of you."

"You've lost me. How would Bryan be opposite? In what way?"

"Oh, George."

"Please, Ellen, I'm not trying to be deliberately obtuse. I really don't understand."

Ellen explained. She said that Jess's choice of a boy like Bryan Daniels might be seen as a living rebuke to her father's fugitive career. (It wasn't entirely true that I had no idea what Ellen was hinting at. Something of the sort had scurried through my mind like a mouse.)

"Ellen!" I protested. "That's way out in left field! She needn't have told me about Bryan's hotshot ambitions. Anyway, what difference would that make to a girl like Jess if she really loved the guy?"

"It wasn't only a question of how you would see the boy, but how *she* was seeing him," Ellen said. "She is your daughter. It's possible she found something in your life she prefers to being a rich man's wife."

I could see it. I could see that Jess might have had a quixotic something implanted in her that would make young Mr. Daniels's set and solid ambitions less than thrilling.

"Got any holiday plans?" I asked Ellen.

"Changing the subject?" she asked.

"You might say."

"What did I ever do over the holidays?" she asked.

"Oh, I don't know," I said. "I seem to recall some pleasant times. Does that mean you're not going anywhere?"

"George, it's none of your business."

"True."

Ellen followed that up by telling me that she was going upstate to a resort, something like Grossinger's but not Grossinger's. "With a friend?" I asked, trying to make it sound like friendly curiosity, the merest courtesy, prepared for her to tell me that it was again none of my business. But she surprised me. She said, "Yes, I'm going with a friend."

"Good," I said. "Then you won't be alone. Well, I'm sure we'll be talking before that."

"Yes," she said. "I'm sure we'll be talking."

"Take care."

"You, too."

I hung up quickly, quickly, before I had a chance to say something gravid with future regret. Like: *Male or female?* If I had asked and she had said, "Female," I would have had to carry my crippled self-respect on my back for weeks, even months. But even while carrying, I would have wondered if she had told me the truth. And even if I were sure she had told me the truth, I would have had to live with the contemptible rat who had to—*had* to!—ask.

Rationally, I concede Ellen's absolute freedom. Mine the instability. Mine the infidelity. Yet if Ellen were to tell me—as she had every right to—that she was going to the Grossinger-like place with this attractive, straight-arrow of a man, recently widowed, partner in a management consulting firm, with two grown children, a head of remarkably full, iron-gray hair (my own having thinned considerably), enviably full of sound investments and maturity, I would have slipped slowly and agonizingly into a vat of smoking acid. For even if it was fair play, there would still be the inexpungable image of my Ellen holding out her arms to Mr. Iron-Gray, welcoming his eager manhood.

So, frankly, I'd rather not know. I'd rather have the liberty to smudge the erotic line drawings my mind so readily sketches for me. Allow myself the old assumption that Ellen is too upset, too busy, too monogamous, too *something,* to fuck around.

What I'd rather think about are those previous speculations about Jess. About what Ellen thought might be behind Jess's decision not to attach herself to the sun-bright god of *gelt.* Did that mean that Jess would become one of those highly principled young women from whom I could expect to hear once or twice a year out of some place in Asia or Africa where she was covering the latest horror for the Syndicated Syndicate? . . . *"We have a report now from Jessica Light, who is standing by in Umbulu. Come in, Jessica . . ."* It sounded right. Sometimes names lend themselves to particular destinies. Jessica Light sounded right.

Would I want that? Not that what *I* want is of any particular significance. Jess will pursue the life *she* wants, whatever that happens to be. It didn't happen to be a lifetime attachment to ambitious Bryan Daniels, and Ellen speculates that that decision may have had something to do with my influence.

I don't know if I believe it or not. I do see now that my influence may have extended in directions I hadn't imagined. Perhaps there were ingredients in that influence I hadn't suspected. Pity? Am I an old nut howling on the heath, damning all? Is she a Cordelia, heart wrenched at the spectacle of her dingbat father?

I choose to think that there is a stubborn, freedom-loving gene in the Light line.

4 I waited until eleven o'clock before calling Jess, and even then I
woke her up. She had been up at eight, she said, had turned
on the tube, learned that the city was paralyzed, and like a
practical cat had gone back to sleep.

"Smart idea," I said. "There'll be nothing better to do
than that. I'm afraid it's even worse in the mountains. Not
a chance of making it to the slopes."

"I gave up on that idea last night," she said.

"Well, look, why don't you brunch or lunch at the hotel,
and I will try to venture out by midafternoon. I figure that
by that time the snowplows will have been through the main
avenues. I'll do some phoning around and find out if some
of the restaurants will be open for dinner."

"Why risk it? You get stuck somewhere and we'll both
be miserable. I got a couple of books to read, or I can look

at the tube, or I can go down to the lobby and flirt with the help."

"Do you do that?"

"What? Flirt? Do you know a woman who doesn't?"

"Your mother doesn't."

"How would you know?"

"How indeed? Does she?"

"Give me a ring before you sally forth," Jess said. "If you're not here in a reasonable amount of time, I'll have the huskies sent out."

"Will do."

That she got from her mother, that little segue around unwanted questions. Pick up the conversation at the point of choice. Pretend that the superfluous or provoking hadn't happened.

I have cable TV, naturally. I'm in the business. I leave on the news channel as I go to shave. The Iran thing is going full blast. The second Iran thing. Sales of arms to Iran, the proceeds allegedly going to the Contras. Nich-ah-ra-gwa. Either there's something I'm not understanding or the enormity of what's happened escapes understanding. Sold arms to *Iran*? The country that spread-eagled the eagle and plucked its feathers out, one a day, for 444 days? . . .

Brushed and combed, shaved and ruddy, I'm fairly presentable. Aquiline nose, brown eyes with a slightly downward cast at the outer corners. It's possible that in one of those eastern invasions around the Fertile Crescent, a soldier of the Khan had his way with a Light ancestress. . . . I know, this is ridiculous, verbalizing my appearance in this way, but I think it has some relevance. I'm not just a voice. I have other features. Mouth, for example. One of my peculiarities. There's a slight skewing when I talk. I'm not really sure why that's so. It might have something to do with my early efforts to avoid the Brooklyn inflections I grew up with. Rather early in life, I began to fashion an idiom I preferred rather than the one I inherited. The process was long and deliberate. I have a good ear. I can repeat what I hear with fair accuracy. It's always been a question of duplicating accents of choice.

Like the time I was going to Paris and had a chance to use my college French on a lady in the train taking me from Germany to France. I was wearing the uniform of the U.S. Army. We exchanged a few amenities in French: *"Vous êtes Américain, non?"* ... *"Oui."* ... *"Mais vous parlez comme un Parisien!"* ... She was being gracious, but it's true that I can pick up verbal nuances.

That Paris trip, incidentally, was the result of accumulated leave time. I had no desire to wander around in Germany, so I had planned ahead to visit those places Fitzgerald and Hemingway wrote about. I found a nice hotel on the Left Bank. The room had one window with authentic metal shutters that, when folded open, revealed a street with a church at one end and a café at the other. I couldn't believe I was actually there.

My mere two weeks would be a teaspoon rather than the ladle of time I thought I needed. Just the museums! And Notre Dame! And the walks, the bistros, Versailles, the Bois ... but on the fourth or fifth day I found myself fatigued with history and art, wanting company ... and I found company, at that café on the corner.

Outdoor tables, aproned waiters, the traffic on the boulevard St. Germain sputtering by. I sat at one of the outdoor tables. It was one month beyond the fabled April, but there was a mellowness you could scoop out of the air and rest your head on. . . .

"Hello," she said. "Are you waiting for someone? May I have this chair?"

On my feet like a corporal and a gentleman. "Please!"

"All the tables seem to be taken," she said.

"Lucky for me," I said.

"I'm waiting for a friend," she said.

"Oh."

Marie was as gamine as any half-baked American could have wished. At least she appeared that way. Two things occurred to me: one, that I had lucked into dreamy chance that would carry me along to some fine conclusion; and, two, the army's standard films and lectures on the ghastly results of VD. Neither thought overstayed its welcome. I was too quickly engaged with Marie. Marie what? I was told but I'm not sure I've retained it correctly . . . Angeli or Angelini . . . definitely something Italian along those lines. Let's make it Angelini.

Within five minutes, I made out that Marie wasn't as young as she first appeared. She had black eyes and black hair that was fashioned in the Louise Brooks style but lacking the Louise Brooks gloss. Nor was it jet black; rather, the color of an old penny. And the bangs lacked precision. I don't remember what she was wearing, except for an oblong pin at the neck of her dress. Onyx with a tiny gold design at the center. Initials, I was told. Her initials? No, her grandmother's. The pin was an heirloom from Italy.

I learned that her mother was from Fiesole and that she had married Marie's father, an Englishman from Swindon. She, Marie, was actually born in the fabulous city of Florence, where the family had lived for several years. Her father was an artist, a painter, and he had come to Florence because he wished to live for a while in the very heart of art. Eventually they were forced to return to Swindon, where her father worked as a draftsman. He was killed in a railway accident. She was only ten at the time. Her mother went to work for a baker. Her mother knew how to make all kinds of pastries. During the war, Marie had lived just outside London.

Of course, it wasn't retailed like that. It came out piece-meal, between glasses of wine or vermouth or cognac. I wove in some of the roots of my own family garden during that soft, biographical evening, making a marginal note of the fact that those friends of Marie's had never shown up. Marie told me that she had left London for Paris after the war. She took her mother's name. Her surname had been something solidly English to that point. Frankly, she had never liked England. The English could be very unfriendly. In Paris, she got a job in an export firm, being fluent in three languages. . . .

What I reconstruct I reconstruct out of the early-evening haze of alcohol and euphoria. I couldn't begin to guess how much of it was true, how much the inspiration of the moment. My guess is that it was largely an improvisation that floated somewhere between mean facts and impromptu fantasy. The exact proportions don't matter. I thought I was being awfully lucky, and my own improvisations were designed to keep that luck going.

I suggested we go to my room, which was just down the block. Marie shook her head and said that perhaps it would be better if we went to her room, which was some distance away, which was, I found out the next morning, in sight of Sacré Coeur. We found a cab and the trip cost me lots of francs. I should mention that part of Marie's attraction was an accent so richly composite that I felt half hypnotized by its strange melodies. She spoke English with a faint cockney that confirmed that part of her story. The Italian part was also confirmed by occasional vowel sounds that broke the surface of her speech like quick, small fish. She mixed all the languages when we made love, indicating to me that her friends, or clients, or whatever, were an international lot and that she or her unconscious had assembled this erotic babble for the high moments.

Her room was just that, a room. Her kitchen was a few appliances set against one of the walls. The rest was a bed, a table, some chairs, a telephone. There was a bathroom of sorts through a curtain. It had a bidet. There was a pull-chain light on the toilet side of the curtain that remained on throughout. Marie took off all her clothes in the semilight, but oddly she didn't invite me to do the same, even though my primed condition was evident. She put on a dressing gown with a silver brocade running vertically on either side. Then she produced a bottle of wine and two wineglasses, setting the wineglasses on the table. She poured the wine and handed me one of the glasses, raising hers in a silent toast, to what, I wasn't sure—until, with her free hand, she cupped the impatient ache in my GI tans. So? What? A toast to Priapus? Fine. I'd drink to that. But it was an odd cere-mony. Well, I was in a foreign country, and the woman I was with was even more exotic than the country, with her mixed accent, her vagrant history, and her worried eyes. What I remember about her eyes was that they reflected an offstage concern, like a woman waiting for someone who is hours overdue. A dark brown sadness (they were dark brown rather than the black I had originally thought).

"What is the date?" she asked.

"The date?" I gave her the date.

"I must pay the rent," she said.

"Yes?"

"Yes."

Then I understood. She wanted a contribution toward the rent. Or all of it. I asked her how much the rent was and she told me. I don't remember the exact figure, but it wasn't much at the then rate of exchange. So—that's what the odd ceremony was all about. We had toasted the next month's rent. Well, what the hell! How did I feel about that? I felt three-quarters foolish and one-quarter indignant. What did I think this whole evening was all about? Who did I think sat herself beside a stranger in a Paris street café, then takes the stranger to her room a few hours later? Of course I gave her the money for the rent, and the same sum again for her worried eyes, and for the plumpish body I had made out during the dressing-gown passage. I smiled at my own naïveté, but at the same time there remained an undissolved clot of sucker-resentment in the general sexual melt. I didn't think I was entirely to blame. A workaday whore would have had a more pragmatic sense of time, wouldn't have spent the whole evening with a single customer. That's what had thrown me off, the *time* she had spent with me, allowing me to believe that I must be more than just another score to this wistful lady.

This wistful lady . . . who is now rubbed into my memory with a tincture of burnt sienna, either from her cosmetics or some sense displacement. She lost all her melancholy in the act of love. The many implied languages actualized as she strung together a litany of real or pretended passion. A warm, nonstop purling against my ears, my neck, my chest, my groin . . . It was wonderful, it was oh so wonderful, so formidable, so lovely, so *douce,* and please, please, be careful, do be careful, do be considerate, do go slowly, go ever so slowly, there, there, oh there! . . . The script was all hers, and I leave out many Italianisms and Gallicisms. I tried to let myself be cued in to the strange rite or exorcism, but I was young and far from practiced and my chief concern was containment rather than embellishment. Less would have been more for me. I didn't need encouragement. I didn't need stimulation. And when I took over with a blind, heedless finality, Marie gasped and stiffened, as though she were a virgin, as though this brutal invasion hurt, for all its rumored delights.

We made love four times that night.

The next morning Marie informed me in a reflective way that the second connection was by far the best.

We fell into a kind of honeymoon for the remainder of my stay in Paris. Perhaps "marriage" would be more like it. It wasn't a time-out-of-mind romp. We were like a married couple who had been saving for years for this trip abroad and were determined to enjoy it responsibly rather than recklessly. Marie set the tone. I wasn't aware of her doing so until we were well into it. She knew Paris, therefore what more natural thing than for her to make the decisions as to where to go, where to eat, what to eat, how to divide the morning, the afternoon, the evening. What I should have realized (and didn't) was that she had set aside her usual life to spend her time entirely with me. The fact that she would do so gave a deeper shade of ambiguity to her life. If she was a full-time hooker would she have been so lovingly acquainted with so many museums and theaters and bookshops? She seemed to know of a café in every section of the city where the food was good and the prices reasonable. She seemed to know of a church in every section of the city where there was an unusual rose window. (By that time, I gave full credence to that part of her story about an artist father.) I was given the perfect tour of Paris, with just the right mixture of history, art, food, wine, sex, and other penetralia most tourists never get to enjoy.

I paid for everything, of course.

"Where do you get so much money, George?" she asked.

"Army pay."

"The army pays you so much?"

"I had nothing to spend it on. I saved it up."

"But so much? You must have a rich father."

"He's not poor."

"Does he send you money?"

"Occasionally."

Again, I was aware that we had slipped into another mode. Marie wanted to know about my life. What did my father do? What was I planning to do after I left the army? How old was I? Had I left, possibly, a wife in the United States? Oh, yes, she knew that this escapade didn't preclude a wife back home. Soldiers are like that. Not that she blamed them, not at all. Well, if I didn't have a wife, then possibly a girlfriend. No one serious? She, too, was not seriously attached, although she had been married. Yes. For six years she had been married and was now divorced. Her former husband was a Polish emigré who had flown for the RAF during the war. His family had been landowners in Poland. She suspected her former husband was now in the United States. He had always talked of going there. They had had a child, a boy, who was living now in a Catholic boarding school. His name was André.

One morning we took the *métro,* and then a bus, and then we walked for at least a mile before arriving at one of those typically French walls with the plaster broken open here and there and the bare brick showing. The coping on top looked like it had been used for random target practice. Why did everything look so *old* in France? I guess because it *was* old. Nevertheless, something New Yorkerish in me rebelled against this decrepitude. Didn't these Parisians ever want to see a spanking new building in their midst, one whose architecture defied age, like the Empire State or the Chrysler?

The ancient wall we walked along ended in an ancient gate that led into an ancient courtyard. Above the ancient door was a bulging escutcheon with a faded gold cross radiating in all directions. We went into a tiled vestibule and Marie addressed a nun. Their murmurs set up soft-footed echoes that ran along the walls and halfway up the staircase at the end of the dim hall. I noticed that the nun had cast a quick glance at me, taking in my uniform, my—what?—Jewishness? Finally the nun walked away, a whisper and a billow of white. Marie and I waited. This is where André lived, I'd been told, where he went to school. I could only try to imagine what kind of arrangement Marie had worked out with her ex-husband, fate, the authorities. While waiting, Marie opened her pocketbook and took out a little mirror, in which she examined her face. I watched as she closed her eyes and expelled a soft breath. She kept her eyes shut for several seconds, as one might do who was very tired or very troubled.

"Here," she whispered to me, "they hid children during the occupation. A priest and three sisters were shot by the Germans."

Everything was transformed. It was as if a tank's cannon had broken through the wall—penile, cruel, immediate—letting in dust and light. Marie, too, appeared different. She couldn't have been one of those hidden children, she was too old for that, but perhaps somewhere in the crazy-quilt of history she had given me was a patch bearing the Star of David.

Feeling that I must position myself in this sudden rearrangement, I said, "I'm Jewish."

"Ah, *oui.*"

I wasn't sure whether that meant *"oui,* I know," or *"oui,* is that so?" I was on the point of asking if she was by any chance—but it occurred to me just in time that to do so would be a rude challenge to everything she had told me. Of course she wasn't Jewish. She was Catholic. She was indicating she knew *I* was Jewish. How did she know? Neither "George" nor "Light" is a particularly Jewish name. Circumcision? That was no longer a sure sign of anything. But perhaps she didn't know that. Maybe I had indicated something to her I wasn't aware of. Quite possible. In talking about my family . . . The long, hollow silence was pocked by distant footsteps, and then I saw the nun returning with a boy at her side.

More French murmurings. Marie kissed the boy and must have said something concerning me, for the boy gave me a quick, scrutinizing look. He must have been about eight or nine. He wore short pants and a navy-blue jacket. His hair was plastered down. He had large, dark eyes, like his mother. It was comical how much like Marie he looked. Even to the shade of his skin—that burnt sienna tone.

What I had not been told about was Marie's plan to spend the whole day with André. We took buses and *métros* and arrived at a children's amusement park. We ate and walked and talked—that is, Marie and André talked French to each other with a telescoped swiftness, while André and I communicated silently with our eyes. Naturally, the boy wanted to know who the hell I was and what I was doing with his mother. I tried to convey that I was no one in particular, an American serviceman, and that I meant his mother no harm. I had no way of knowing how much he understood. His glances made me feel that I was in a large dark room awaiting questioning. All of Europe was in his eyes. All of the twentieth century was in his eyes.

"When must you return to Frankfurt?" Marie asked, when we were returning to her room.

"My leave ends day after tomorrow," I told her.

"Ah, *oui.*" After some moments of hesitation, she said, "So what shall I think?"

Those words made everything fall into place. I understood. I understood why Marie had put everything else aside. I understood why she had taken me to the place where André lived. I understood why I had been allowed to move into her apartment for the length of my leave. She had invested hopes in me. I don't know how many times over the years I have writhed at the memory of my blithe blindness. I had accepted the situation as though I were the Crown Prince of Sheepshead Bay, for whom obstacles were removed and pleasures arranged as a matter of course. Why should this strange woman who had clearly been through the European mill (whatever mixture of fact and fancy she had concocted for herself) undertake a relatively profitless two weeks with George Light, Cpl., U.S. Army, except that she was hoping for some larger, better outcome? *Could she really have hoped for that?* What was she? She was a whore, a *poule,* a hooker, a courtesan. There are so many words for it because there are so many shades of meaning. I couldn't think of her as a street hustler, but where had she picked me up but on the street? Yes, but it hadn't been a quickie in a nearby room. There had been talk and an exchange of intimacies. Yes, but how could I know that in many other instances there hadn't been quickies in nearby rooms? And what if I did know that? Would that make a difference? Whatever word would finally fit, it would still be a matter of bought love. So what? If I brought her back to the States, to Brooklyn, who but I, and she, would know? And even if everyone knew, even if I proudly announced her past, would that have mattered to noble me?

Damn right it would!

Not that I seriously entertained the idea. I merely let it run through my head with other fleeting fantasies. There was no way I was going to bring home Marie Angelini and her little André. Why was she putting me in this absurd position? And she did that, all right. Weeping in her room when we were alone there, saying that she was sure I liked her (I did), that we seemed to get along so well (we did), that she had been through so much (no doubt of it), that there *were* Jews on her mother's side in the distant past, that she had taken good care of herself, had certificates to that effect, had medical assurance that she could still bear children (!), and that we loved each other, didn't we?

We didn't. She didn't "love" me, and I was certain I didn't love her. Not *love*. Not the kind of love I had been taught to expect from Humphrey Bogart and Ingrid Bergman, from all the great poets and the soppy crooners. She wanted a safe haven for herself and her boy. (And how often that knowledge had come back to me, like Marley's ghost!) I was young, healthy, seemingly kind, and, above all, *American*. I would be going back to that munificent fountainhead, that fairyland that could pay its corporals enough money to buy lavish leaves in Paris. Perhaps she could live in a house with her son. Perhaps she could find a place where she wouldn't have to close her eyes, as I had seen her do, and sigh with such bottomless fatigue.

It was this clear hope of a different life that opened for me the reality of the one she lived. I saw it finally in its day-to-day preparation and execution. Imagine having to get yourself primped and primed for a day of cruising, not knowing who or what you might pick up, thinking of André, disguising daily a horde of secrets, hoping that out of one day's mix of chance and arrangement would come a measure of permanence and respite. What I finally saw was the patient, cosmeticked, murderous *exhaustion* of her life. It left me limp.

I wanted to escape—I did escape—and I've been escaping ever since. I spent the rest of my money in a conscience-flurry of gifts for Marie and André. I wish I could say I had bought something sensible—a good woolen coat for Marie, for André—but the mood of escape led me to further foolishness. I bought expensive perfume for Marie and (because I had seen them sailing in the basin in the Tuilleries) a toy sailboat for André, a rather grand one, with rigging and brass fittings.

And I escaped, leaving behind a string of false promises. I would phone. I would write. I would return. I didn't, of course. What good would it have done? But when I recall it now, what I feel is not guilt or regret—it would be too hypocritical to pretend that it was somehow my fault—but a charred, burning-glass hole of reality.

That little mirror she took out while waiting for André to appear. That fugitive glance in the mirror to see what her little boy would see. That faint exhalation. Her eyes closing in fatigue. That instant epitomizes all the rest, and when I bring that episode to mind, as I've just done, I'm left with a frightened feeling I've never really tried to define. I do so now because Jess is here, because Ellen is in New York, and because I've become curious about the man-woman thing.

I love Jess. I love Ellen. I did not love Marie, not in the least, but I experienced with that sad Parisian woman a moment of greater intimacy than I've ever known with my own wife or daughter. I felt the dry despair of her life as though she had injected it into my veins—and I wonder why I haven't experienced a similar insight with those I love.

5 Getting from my place to Jessica's hotel was a slow business. It hadn't been a record-breaking blizzard, but it had been substantial enough to close off side streets and leave head-high drifts. Living in a fairly big apartment house, I had the advantage of equipment that had plowed a path from the building's underground garage to the street. I ventured out at about four in the afternoon, made it over to Colorado Boulevard, which had already been plowed, and then on into the parking area of Jess's "Manor." I found her in her room, in a semidazed condition. She had been watching TV and eating candy bars the whole, long, comatose day. Candy bars and soda pop. I saw the cans of three different kinds of pop scattered around the room.

"Shame on you," I said.

"Oh, God," she moaned. "Things aren't bad enough."

"But all this crap!"

"Emergency rations."

"Like hell," I said. "They've got three different kinds of restaurants downstairs."

"Who has the energy?"

"All right, come on now, let's clean up here, and then we'll go downstairs and have something decent to eat. Then we'll walk outside and breathe in the nice, fresh, white air."

"And then what?"

"Then nothing," I said, getting a little annoyed. "Look, princess, the weather is the weather. You can very quickly be reduced to survival conditions in this part of the world."

" 'In this part of the world . . .' " she repeated sardonically.

I suppose it did sound a little pompous, or fake boots-and-saddles, but picking up on it in that way was a sign of something or other. What? Hostility? Was she pissed off, my Jess, propped up in bed, wearing a floppy turtleneck and a pair of jeans? Had she reconsidered all she had told me and was now suffering a backlash of regret? Was she blaming me for setting her a male role model of capriciousness? Or was she just bored, sorry she had made this trip to Denver? Okay, she was bored, but who was not bored in this situation? Others, however, were out there trying to get the roads cleared, service restored, wires connected, and so forth. Wasn't it rather typical New York to lie disgruntled in a warm, dry, nicely appointed hotel room and bitch about the inconvenience? And was I becoming typical anti-Big Apple after a big two years in the Rockies?

"Unfortunately, the airport is closed," I said.

"What's that mean?"

"Well, we could try for a quick flight out. I think I could manage to get you over there, but I doubt there'd be many planes taking off. It might be more fun, though, hanging around in the airport."

"Oh, please," she said.

"Trying to accommodate."

Jess swung her legs off the bed, sat for a hesitant moment, then went into the bathroom. The first thing to astonish me was the careless way she closed the door behind her. It *wasn't* exactly closed. Not latch-fast. It was just an indifferent meeting between the edge of the door and the jamb. And the reason for her going was made liquidly clear in another instant. I mean, there wasn't the slightest attempt to mask it in any way. When I thought of those years of acoustical camouflage, the countersound of tap water that would invariably accompany her visits! Lord, what a distance she had traveled! What a distance between her world and mine!

The toilet flushed, and Jess reappeared as the bowl was in its last convulsions. She sat in a chair that faced the big mirror over the dresser. She looked at herself critically. I realized that there is no one from whom we accept the human condition as readily and unqualifiedly as we do from our children. It explains a lot. It explains, at any rate, that kind of love.

"I'm sorry," she said. She turned her face this way and that, decided what was needed, and then began to fish in her pocketbook for the necessary implements. She took out little plastic things with colors that reminded me of candied almonds. She began to apply a tiny brush to her eyes. "I'm not ordinarily such a *kvetch*," she said, "but everything seems to be conspiring against me these days."

"What else is conspiring against you—I mean besides Bryan Daniels?"

"Oh . . ." A shrug.

"Tell me," I said. "We've got nothing else to do. Winter blizzards are great for confessions."

"I was hoping to do a year of study abroad," she said.

"So?"

"I was hoping for a scholarship. I didn't get it. That means that someone would have to pay for that year abroad. On the other hand, if I went directly to graduate school, I think I could get some kind of assistance."

"I don't get this," I said. "Has anyone been crying poverty in this family?"

"No."

"Well, then . . ."

Finished with her face, Jess got up and went to the clothes rack. She selected a skirt and held it up for inspection, decided it would do, zipped open her jeans and stripped them off. She stepped quickly into the skirt, but not so quickly that I didn't catch a glimpse of the white bikini-strip that covered her. That, too, shocked me. I'm sure she didn't mean to, or was even conscious of her action, but it did shock me.

I know things are different now, but my generation of males had passed through its adolescence with a crudely calibrated set of responses. Girls who showed more did more. You could see the same amount—or, rather, lack of amount—on a beach, but a beach was the proper place, and that made all the difference. I know these prurient distinctions no longer exist, but it seemed to me that Jess should have been more aware of these generational differences. In any event, Jess switching from jeans to skirt was done without the faintest blush of self-consciousness. This is the way things were, whatever my private scruples.

Going down in the elevator, I argued for Europe, if that's what she really wanted. The money was there. She was not to think about that. But she did think about it. She'd been freeloading her whole life and now. . . . Now what? . . . Well, now in effect there would be three separate households. Things *cost*. Especially in New York. I told her—and not for the first time—about past windfalls, about money I had salted away when her Uncle Henry had bought me out of the family trucking business. Why had I buried that money so incrementally all these years if not for something like this?

"And . . ." she said.

"And what?"

She shrugged, turned mouth and eyes awry, asked if it was worthwhile investing in anything or anyone to that extent.

"Hadn't you better tell me?" I asked.

She shrugged again. I wondered whether she wanted more coaxing, or whether she was truly struggling with the ineffable. We went into the dining room.

A limited menu. Many deliveries unmade. The pork roast was good. Okay, we'd have that. Jess slouched in her chair, a concavity of *weltschmerz,* fingers interlaced, eyes roaming around the uninteresting dining room. Had we reached an impasse? And if we had, whose fault?

"So what do you think about the world?" Jess asked.

"I think there's a serious shortage of natural affinities," I said.

"Meaning?" she asked.

"Meaning that after all the centuries of sex and science, love and art, customs and ceremonies, men and women still stare at each other across an abyss. That goes for fathers and daughters, as well as all other combinations."

Jess looked at me in surprise. She opened her mouth as if to speak, didn't speak, smiled instead. "Well!" she said finally.

"Well what?"

"I'm amazed."

"At what?"

"Your thoughts."

"What did you think I thought about?" I asked.

"Oh, I don't know. I guess I thought you thought about what to do next. Whether to stay here or come home."

"Would you like to know what I've really been thinking about?" I asked her.

"Very much."

"Okay, I'll tell you, but only on one condition . . ."

"What?"

"That you tell me what you're really thinking about."

Jess hesitated, made a face, as if to say: What have I *been* telling you about?—but then I could see a deeper consideration float in her eye. "It's a deal," she agreed.

"Right," I said. "What I've been thinking about is writing about the thing I've been thinking about."

"Which is?"

"The abyss."

"What abyss?"

"The one between men and women."

"Really? That?"

"Is it your feeling that I have very poor qualifications to tackle the subject?"

Jess came upright in her chair. She had an interested look on her pale face. She was in one of her sallow conditions, where her natural prettiness took on the drained look of convalescence. Fatigue. Too much lassitude and brooding in an airless hotel room. Too much candy and soda. That look always brought out the father hen in me.

"You don't have to be an expert to write about something," she said. "You might want to write about it just to inform yourself about it."

"A very astute observation."

"*Are* you going to do it?" she asked.

"I think I may have already begun."

"How?"

"By taking notes. Jotting down gems as they sparkle in my brain."

"Sample me one of your gems."

"After you keep your part of the bargain."

"No, please," she pleaded. "I promise I'll keep my part of the bargain, but first gem me."

Pleased that she was that much interested, I said, "One of my ideas is that the abyss between men and women is the same as that between men and men, or women and women. The problem of separate heads. The general human abyss. I can't know what you're thinking unless you tell me, and often you can't tell me because thoughts fly by like bats—a flap, a squeak, and they're gone. If I were to insist and you were inclined to oblige, you'd almost have to fabricate something. And even when you're perfectly willing to tell, have got what you want to say well in mind, there's the process of transfer to worry about. From your head to your tongue. From my ear to my head. Guaranteed distortion. Guaranteed muddying."

"So it's not exclusively a man-woman problem," Jess rightly observed.

"Not exclusively, although with the man-woman situation another factor enters."

"What?"

"Love. Or what passes for love. Or what one hopes will flower into love."

"How does that make a difference?"

"By making what goes on in the other's head ten, a hundred, a thousand times more important."

Jess nodded slowly, reflectively. Nothing new in my idea, but it always comes as a surprise that others, even fathers, have given some thought to the very things that have occupied you. Ordinary perplexities, but secretly we wonder if others do share them. We usually keep such things to our-selves because we don't want others to think our supposedly grown-up minds are still stuffed with such childish dilemmas. We credit others with more maturity. We imagine that others have the good sense to leave unanswerable things alone, even though we ourselves finger them in the dark like prayer beads.

"Tell me a man-woman thing," she said. "I mean something that's exclusively man-woman, not an everybody thing."

"Survival," I said. "I think women have a much stronger sense of it."

"In what way?"

"No dice. Now it's your turn."

"Funny you should stop there," she said.

"Why funny?"

"Because I'm a woman, and I don't think I've got such a strong sense of survival."

"Tell me."

She made a face. Where to begin? The fact was—well, the fact was that she had pretty much given up on the human race. She knew only too well how pathetically juvenile something like this sounded, that these dramatic statements were usually cover-ups for nothing more earthshaking than a busted-up love affair or a failing grade, but really and truly she didn't think it was true in her case. This feeling she was talking about was there well before Bryan made known his hotshot ambitions. Pressed, she would say that it was more this other thing than Bryan that accounted for her present state of mind.

"What is this other thing?" I asked.

"The world."

"That's zeroing in on it."

"I can't zero in on it. It isn't one thing, or two, or a hundred."

"I went through the same thing," I told her. "Many times."

"No, you didn't."

"Really? How would you know? No one escapes. No one escapes the thing you're talking about, in one way or another. How about a man whose ambitions have always been greater than his abilities? There's a small but effective hell."

"Is that you?" she asked.

"Some would say so—and I've become more or less inclined to agree with them."

"I wouldn't. You've tried. And you've succeeded."

"And you?" I challenged her. "How have you not succeeded? You haven't even begun to try. What's the big problem?"

A little heave of hopelessness. She thought and thought—and then told me about a Lit class she had taken this past year, about a story they had read in class. It was called "Araby," a story by James Joyce. In it a boy visits a bazaar that's just on the point of closing. Everything is dim, a spooky hollowness in the place, and whatever merchandise is left is cheap and tawdry. She identified with the boy. He wanted to find a gift for a girl, one commensurate with his feeling, but he could find nothing. The world seemed to her a tawdry bazaar. Overpopulation. The Bomb. Dishonesty everywhere—in government, on the tube, between people. It was really as though the lights were going out. Did I understand what she was saying?

"Yes, I understand, Jess. I've been through it."

"But your world survived," she said. "Your world survived and made mine."

"And yours will survive, too."

"Do you believe that?"

"You know it will survive."

"I know no such thing," she said, her voice getting a little cranky. "It annoys me to hear people say 'Oh, it will survive,' as if the human race had a contract with God, the cosmos. So much screwing up and then God blows a whistle, like a referee. We Jews were supposed to have such a contract and you see how much good it did us. What I mean, George, is that there was always the hope that the human race would advance toward *something*. A political system that really worked. A sign from Somewhere that we were part of Something. But it's just not going to happen. That's the awful thing. That's the thing that makes my time worse than yours. You still hoped that something was going to happen. I don't. Television is making oatmeal out of people's brains. Russia and the United States are never going to get rid of the bomb. You know why? Because they're more afraid to live without it than with it. Not God, not man, not the present, not the future. It's as simple and unlovely as that— an absolute vote of no confidence."

I was tracking her expression as she talked, trying to make out how much of it she believed herself. Jess was twenty. She became twenty the beginning of last June. Her birthday present from me was one of those new, portable electronic typewriters, the kind with "memory" and an automatic spelling corrector. Not that there's anything wrong with her spelling that I've ever noticed. That little item cost me over four hundred bucks. So what? So nothing. I'm drumming mental fingers. I'm thinking that she's just broken up with a guy with whom she was clearly in love. I've watched her for enough hours to be fairly sure that every external and internal shift, no matter how small, bangs against that bruise. Even so, I think Jess is serious in her pessimism. She means what she says. As far as she's concerned, the world stinks. And I am faced with the peculiar dilemma of agreeing with her assessment while opposing her state of mind. She's not at her best at the moment, but she's still a lovely thing. Look at those eyes. She has no reason to feel as she does, even if her reasons are inarguable.

So?

So I must do something about it. I say, "During the Black Plague, three-quarters of Europe was wiped out. It must have appeared that God had it in for them. They had good reason to believe that the world was coming to an end. I grant you that things look bad, but rescues at the brink are part of the human myth. You mustn't let yourself get too down. You want to be a journalist. Why be anything if it all adds up to zero?"

"I've thought of that," Jess said. "You know what the alternative is . . . ?"

"What?"

"Suicide."

I gave her a pained look, as if she were now truly indulging in childish prattle . . . but my mind improvised a swift and frightful scene: silent room, empty pill bottle, body on bed. Nonsense! Nonsense? What the hell was behind all those teenage, or any age, suicides if not some real and present hopelessness?

"I hope that's not a serious alternative with you," I said.

"No."

"Glad to hear it. The question remains—why a journalist?"

"I figure if I can't do anything about it, I might as well be on the spot and report its happening."

I could have kissed her. However bleak her outlook, her words were instinct with life. I felt relieved. It was an obvious gambit, but such a good one. If you can't lick 'em, join 'em. At any rate, it would keep Jess occupied and interested long enough to work out her own system of salvation—which I was sure she would do.

Or would she? I looked at her, caught her eye, which gave me a half-hearted salute of assurance before turning away. No, she wasn't the suicidal type, but she definitely was not happy, and her unhappiness, I feared, was a steel pile driven deep into rock. Serious things—love, marriage, children, the whole bloody ongoingness of the race—were at best alleviations. A workable vision of life was nowhere in sight.

"I have a theory," I said.

"Tell me your theory."

"My theory is that things are so dark because we haven't seen the light. My theory is that the new spiritual lights are put in only when the old ones are completely busted. I think we're still trying to screw the old ones in tighter, flicking them with our fingernails to see if they won't make contact. But they're out there, the new ones. Depend on it."

Jess gave me a nod and a flat smile. *Nice try, Dad.* She didn't believe a word of it. I wasn't sure I did either.

Speaking of light, the next day's sun clashed like cymbals on the snow. Bright, bright, bright! Brass-bright! Gold-bright! Could we get to the slopes? Reports said that we could. We went. The plows had been through the highways leading to the ski slopes. I had snow tires. We went to the nearest area. There were notices not to ski anywhere except where indicated. No real danger of avalanche, but please play it safe . . . *New York father and daughter perish at Colorado ski slope* . . . We skied until four and then headed back. At dinner that evening, Jess's snow-burn came out like a photograph in a developing bath.

"That's the way to greet the apocalypse," I kidded. "All aglow. But listen, bubbi, I don't disagree with anything you think, say, or feel, but I insist that you enjoy yourself in the meantime. Do you promise?"

"I'll work at it," she said.

I took her to the airport the next day. She said she was very glad she had come. She'd had a terrific time. She was glad we'd had a chance to talk. When did I think I'd be coming home?

"I've got to work out some things, too," I said.

She nodded.

I drove back to my apartment in streets that would be churned to a filthy porridge in the next few days. Denver is not the world's champion in snow removal. The newspapers were forecasting a warming trend, and I knew that the stuff would melt and melt while the wheels churned and churned. Tomorrow my life would resume its *pro tem* routine. I had told the man I work for, Vince Taylor, that I would be taking some days off when my daughter came to town, and that was all right with him, but now it was all over and I would have to get back to work. Unless, that is, I simply chucked the whole thing a little sooner than later. That was a distinct possibility. I don't really need the money, and the activity itself, while not exactly a bore, has become very much beside the point—the point being that I must get a bearing on the rest of my life.

Like Jess? That gave me a jolt. It was all right for someone my age, with my background, to pause, look around, take account . . . but *Jess*? What business had she with these heavy questions? What she should be doing is making choices between one life-enhancing engagement and another. She should be beguiling the margins of her life with parties, movies, plays, ballets, friends, and lovers. The center should be firmly in place. But clearly that was not the case. An hour after I had said good-bye at the airport, I came to the full realization that my Jess had left the sweet shores of childhood and was embarked on her own voyage.

Maybe that was part of her *tristesse.* Could be. But I found no consolation in it. I couldn't believe that what I had seen and heard was just a lapse into adolescent despair. The world she described was the world she saw. I knew that what Jess had revealed to me would be a permanent part of the baggage she would take with her everywhere. She would meet someone else—she was too pretty to go unattended for long—and she would probably get married, have a couple of kids, but I felt a cold premonition that she wouldn't be doing these things with the heart of a joyous woman.

That thought, naturally, gave rise to another. I thought of Ellen, of my own marriage, and how sure we had been of progress and permanence.

6 My job . . .

I work for a man by the name of Vincent Taylor, who is part owner of a cable TV outfit in the Denver area. I met Vince in Germany back in the late fifties when I was doing my army stint in Munich. This was after the Marie Angelini episode. Vince was already in TV, had come to Europe as part of a crew assigned to do a documentary on the occupation in Germany. I was in an engineering outfit that was needed to supply power to the crew. We got friendly and Vince told me to look him up when we got stateside. I did. He got me my first job in television.

I've hinted at it, but I might as well be specific about the fact that I've had a varied career in TV. In and out, I should say. I started out in lighting, worked with directors, have directed myself. I've also worked as a scriptwriter, left television to write a book *about* television. Not exactly an exposé, but it did offend some important people, as a result of which I was out of television for four years.

During that time, I wrote a pilot show about a private eye who is hired by a mysterious millionaire to find out whether certain people were still alive. Through an intermediary (the PE never sees the mysterious millionaire), he is given a dossier on each of his huntees (if that's the word), and in each case the man in question was a Nazi official of one kind or another. The PE is given a no-limit expense account to go to wherever his clues would take him—São Paulo, Singapore, Cincinnati.

Naturally, women cross the PE's path—dark-haired beauties with heavy accents; sunny blondes with heavy equipment—and every time the PE gets close to his quarry all hell breaks loose, with much shattering of glass, much automatic gunfire, and the death or confession of another Nazi.

I sold the pilot, and I was contracted to write the first ten episodes. A new producer, a new director, more and more sex, breakage, gore. It wasn't really sex, but the teasing, rump-pendulating, eye-slanting charade that passes for sex on TV. It had become a stopwatch enterprise with meticulous instruments brought to bear on mass appetite. "Look," I was told at one point, "fuck consistency, fuck what you call integrity of character. These things don't matter. Haven't you learned that by now? What matters is feeding the beast. We've made careful studies. So many minutes of plot, so many minutes of cock-teasing, so many minutes of slaughter. You'd be amazed—although you shouldn't be—at how precisely the ratings follow the formula."

I pulled out after the tenth episode had been doctored to formula. The thing had become vaudeville. I had made a tidy sum of money.

So I've never really been *out* of television after I got in, but it hasn't been a steady course, the kind that looks good on résumés. Oddly, I've never thought of myself as restless, but from the outside it must seem that way. I did get back in after *The Search* (that was the name of my Nazi-hunting series), in news, doing research and writing for a documentary that my former network had developed. That documentary was being phased out just about the time things blew up in the Light marriage.

Ellen found out about Kim. That had been going on for a year. Kim worked in the news section, too. She was young, of course. Twenty-five, about. A nervous, almost panicked sense of self that at one time would have put me off, but at the time her sudden invasion had a violent attraction.

It was about four years ago. She was working with a field producer on one of the news programs. I knew her by sight alone, assumed for some reason that she was either living with or having an affair with one of the young men in that department. I saw them together frequently. One time, lunching at one of those Italian restaurants on Sixth Avenue, I saw them talking away like people who really have something to say to each other.

Then, at the usual office Christmas party, that once-a-year crisis of expectancy, Kim appeared by my side and said, "Don't you like me?"

"I haven't given it any thought," I said, three or four scotches into the occasion. "Why do you ask?"

"Because I've done everything but shoot flares straight into your face, and you haven't blinked once."

"I don't believe it. You just made that up. I'm a man who notices things."

"What kind of things?" she asked.

"Flares. Signals of all kinds."

"You didn't notice mine."

"Maybe you're not using the right pistol."

"That could be."

"Why were you shooting flares in my direction, anyway?"

"To attract your attention."

"Why?"

"Let's dance."

We danced. I can do the kind of dances the young do. I had watched Jess practicing them at home. I even served as her partner. There wasn't much to it other than swinging your shoulders and bobbing your head in the right way. That kind of dancing is ideal for observing your partner. That is, if you want to observe your partner rather than shut your eyes and invoke the rhythms of your unconscious.

At close range, Kim looked like a young woman whose nerves were strung too tightly. I'm not sure how I knew this, but I took it as a certainty. Something in the corner of her eyes. Something in the too-relaxed way she danced. She had a pale complexion, brown-gray eyes, good but unspectacular features. I'm not a sexual marathoner. Never have been. I think I'm as alert to sexual signals as the next man, but it was entirely possible that years of marital repose had dulled my responses. Still, I would have given odds against Kim's signaling system. But here we were and whatever the efficacy of her sending station or my receiving station, the immediate situation was unmistakable.

"Are you sure you aimed at the right guy?" I asked her.

"I might have been mistaken," she said, "but I had the feeling watching you, hearing you talk, that you'd be good to know."

"That's very flattering," I said. "I don't know what would have given you that idea, but in any event I'm glad to know it. Incidentally, I'm married."

"I figured," she said.

"Good in what way?" I asked.

"Look," she said, "if this is making you uncomfortable, I'll go away."

"No, it's not making me uncomfortable. I thought you were with"—I indicated with my head—"that young fellow."

"That young fellow" was standing about six feet away. He was wearing those balloony trousers and a jacket that also seemed slightly inflated. I understood in that instant what Kim confirmed in the next.

"Chuck?" she said. "Chuck's nice, I can talk to him, but I haven't got the right fixtures." Reverting back to my question, she said, "I write poetry. I write very good poetry. If we become friends, I'll let you read some of my poetry."

"Where are you from originally?" I asked her.

"Why couldn't I be from New York?" she asked, smiling.

"Why, indeed? I don't know. I just don't think you are."

"You're right," she said. "I'm not. I'm from Lincoln, Nebraska . . ." where, she went on to relate, her father was a judge and her mother something of a country-club matron. She had gone to the University of Iowa.

She wanted to know if I was under some kind of curfew. If not, we could go to her apartment, where she kept an adequate supply of wines and liquors.

We went to her apartment. She had wine, I had scotch. She leaned toward me, put one hand on my knee, and said, almost tearfully, "Look, let's have sex, please, and then we can talk. It isn't that I'm that horny, but sex just stands there, like a cranky child, getting in the way, until it's put to bed."

As I already half suspected, Kim was not all that sensational a lover. I don't believe she got much out of it, except a release of nervous tension. She thrashed and moaned and cried "Go! Go!!"—but I knew that beyond this necessary paroxysm a quieter Kim waited.

She talked to me about her poetry. She wanted to say

something about the awfulness of love in a world of menace, disease, and death. She wanted to pin down with perfect precision what she considered the most awful human susceptibility: to be aware of beauty and to be voiceless before it. She wanted to write about the strange malevolence of this arrangement.

Simply put, I was at a dead end. In my marriage and in my work. The best I could expect was a couple of cost-of-living increases or, if I got lucky, to head up my own program. I had hoped to write another book, but I found myself less and less willing to wind myself into a coil of purpose that would once again become the center of everything.

"So you decided instead to have an affair with a girl about half your age," Ellen said.

"You figure in it, somehow," I said.

"Oh, George, please!"

"Nothing in it, huh? A bolt out of the blue? Not even a passing thought that something like this might happen? Perhaps even a *hope* that it might?"

"You're being the little boy in the street yelling the usual stupidities," Ellen said coldly. " *'Jimmy made me do it, Mother.'* "

"Sometimes Jimmy does make our little boy do it," I said. "By coercion, by ostracism, by many of the other subtle ways that people have of exerting pressure, or by removing something that was once there."

"I don't recall having had that much influence on you in other ways," Ellen said. "Why this?"

"Christ, Ellen, you were getting light-years away!"

She shrugged and walked away. I almost followed, almost covered myself with more absurdity by piling on the accusations. But didn't. I would have preferred Ellen to stay and fight with me, because, to tell the truth, I wasn't missing as wildly as she was suggesting. There *had* been a considerable cooling off. I'm not sure who started it—it may well have been me, me with my long discontent over aborted ambitions, premature plateaus—and it may very well have been that Ellen was hitting back, justifiably. But a further truth was that Ellen had expended very little effort in drawing me out, in trying to discover the source of my discontent. How much is enough? I don't know. You can only go by past experience, and in that comparative sense I felt a decided falling off.

The importance of this grows in my mind even as I reconstruct. There had been restlessness on my part—I hadn't tried to hide it—but the discontent hadn't been directed against *Ellen*! I'll take an oath on that! What comes back to me now with proverbial twenty/twenty hindsight is the strangeness of Ellen's responses, the coolness of them. Almost as if she'd been *waiting* for this crisis!

"How did you find out?" I asked her.

"How do people generally find out about things like that?" she said.

"I know what I see in the movies," I said, "but I don't trust what I see in the movies."

"Does it matter?" she asked.

"It matters to me. I'm very curious."

"Somebody told me."

There were several people with whom I was friendly enough at the network to have begun social exchanges. Visits to our house, visits to theirs. Ellen had become friendly with some of the wives. One of the husbands might have told one of the wives, and one of the wives might have told my wife.

The question of what we would do hung in abeyance for days, days into weeks, weeks into months. I began to wonder if Ellen was leaving it for me to decide. If so, why? She was, in a strict sense, the injured party. I didn't want an end to my marriage to Ellen, but I had braced myself for that possibility. It wouldn't have surprised me if Ellen had announced that she wanted an end, given the distance between us before this crisis. But she made no definite move in that direction. The months slid by and we appeared to be accepting an arrangement in which we could carry on the daily business of life courteously and efficiently, observing unstated but understood boundaries. Oddly, those boundaries didn't exclude sex. It wasn't done with the preparation and passion of the past, but occasionally I would fumble for the edge of her bed in the darkness of our bedroom, and after a few seconds of hesitation, I would feel the accommodating movement of her body.

I'm not sure of this now, but I think that at the time I surmised that Ellen might be willing to allow the situation to remain in that form indefinitely. She had her job in the city school system, and a good job it was. She was a sort of music coordinator for all the Queens high schools, and some of the Brooklyn schools as well. In recent years, her activities had taken more and more of her time. Jess had begun her freshman year at Ann Arbor. (I've often wondered if things would have developed as they had if Jess had been living at home.) Ellen was busy. Ellen had friends and colleagues, many of whom were unknown to me. There were people with whom she arranged afternoons and evenings having to do with the grant that had burst like a happy bombshell over the music department of Ellen's school, and particularly over Ellen, since she had applied for the grant. Her idea was to stage operettas and even grand opera in the schools. Not in their entirety, of course, but scenes from Mozart, Verdi, Meyerbeer, Puccini, Offenbach. She had made out a very convincing case that rock music was becoming as pernicious an addiction as drugs, and that getting the kids interested in other kinds of music would be a salutary thing in more ways than just the musical.

I said I didn't want a divorce, and it's true, I didn't. I had been much in love with Ellen when we married. I was still in love with her, despite the strain and the coolness . . . Now wait, do I really mean that? *In* love. All right, not *in* love. We'd been married for close to twenty-five years. The fever state had disappeared long ago, but there was an emotional tie that I wouldn't know what name to give to but love.

The romantic aura of our early days still hung about Ellen. Ellen with that off-center cast in her left eye, the hazy ambience it gave her (I think because of the way she tried to compensate), her hesitant smile, the way she had of closing her lips over that smile, as though she were bringing it indoors for safekeeping. Our meeting in that Ninth Avenue discount record shop, where she had worked in the office. We were dry tinder. We blazed. Everything. Sex, talks, walks, exploring each other, explaining ourselves. We married. Ellen, who had already made application for a job in the school system, was accepted. She played the piano well enough to merit a recital at Town Hall. Ellen took off two years when Jess was born, and then returned to her post as musical coordinator for the city schools. . . .

It wasn't as though there was no desire to help each other in our respective careers, but that there wasn't a hell of a lot that we could do. We were in such different fields. I was proud of Ellen's musical skill, would have preferred it if she had persevered as a concert artist, but I accepted her judgment on the limits of her talent. And she was interested in my work, even when I began bouncing erratically on the tracks. When I turned to scriptwriting, she was encouraging, saying that I ought to try different things, that the field I was in had need of so many different talents that I owed it to myself to discover where I fit best before settling on a single activity. Even when I got out temporarily to write that book about TV, she remained steadfast and supportive. We did have arguments over my show, *The Search*, despite having made a quantum leap in earnings on that monster.

She didn't like it. Secretly, I didn't blame her, because in my own seething heart I didn't like it either. I *pretended* I did. I used up a lifetime's supply of sophistry defending the thing, quoting critics on the "inventiveness and intelligence of the script," pointing out that in all the moral hokiness of TV, *The Search* at least had its good guys and bad guys straight. I even had the indecency to invoke the Holocaust, arguing that one owed it to the victims to keep before the conscience of mankind the blah, blah, blah. I guess I tried so hard to make Ellen change her mind about the show because I knew that at the bottom it was just another TV cops-and-robbers piece of cheese, and I didn't want it to be that, I wanted it to be better. I wanted Ellen to rescue me from the truth with a kindly, alchemizing wave of her wand. She wouldn't. She clammed up. She wouldn't watch the program.

But despite our arguments—*mine*, really—it wasn't with, or because of, *The Search* that the serious change set in. It was after, much after. In fact, things were fairly peaceful when I became aware of how far things had gone. I was back in TV, in news, and Ellen was more than ever engaged in her musical programs. I began pulling at her for more attention, but when she gave that attention all I would have to offer was the dissatisfaction I felt over the leveling off of my life. I told her I thought I would like to write another book, this one about the effect of TV on politics, and she said that was a wonderful idea, why not do it? Begin my research while still working, and whenever I felt I couldn't handle both activities quit the job. We certainly had enough money. And even if the book wasn't a big success, the subject would do me no harm when I tried to get another job.

I never did get started on the research. I was afraid of jeopardizing my job again. And Ellen turned away from my fidgeting and back to her own satisfactions. No, it was more than that. What I sensed was not conflict but divergence. . . .

It's about here that I feel I'm playing pin-the-tail-on-the-donkey. I'm blindfolded. I jab at careers, age, attrition, early illusion, late realizations, but when I remove the blindfold I find I'm a foot away from the creature's ass. Our past history, yes, but that was no greater storm and stress than I'd heard about in other marriages. Our different careers? Hell, that's supposed to enliven and fortify, not deaden. And no matter what might pry us apart, there was always Jess, whom we both loved, who was (I thought) the third point of our triangle.

She was—but that didn't prevent me from letting myself be drawn into that affair with Kim. Nor prevent our marriage from continuing in that state of cool crisis, until I met Vince Taylor at that media convention, where he offered me the Denver job.

7 "Why me?" I asked, because I'd never done the kind of work Vince was proposing I do for him. Sales manager, for Christ sake! I'd never been a sales manager. No track record. Mind you, I trusted Vince, saw no reason why he should try to sucker me into something. It had been my experience that no matter how idiosyncratic businessmen were, their money decisions were made for sound reasons. So I naturally asked, "Why me?"

Vince smiled. He had his own cachet, Vince Taylor. A slow manner and a quick mind. "Partly your voice, George," he said. "Your voice has very compelling vibrations. I'm sure I'm not the first one to tell you that. And your head. It's an imperial head. It could be stamped on coins."

"Flattery will get you far," I said, "but I don't believe it. Not half. What exactly do you want me to sales-manage?"

He told me about the cable franchise and how they would need a good, aggressive crew of men and women who would go out and sell the cable service to the public. I knew television and had just the qualities needed to organize and manage such a sales force.

"Really? What qualities are those?"

"Well, there's the voice and the head to begin with," he said. "Frankly, George, you've always made me feel I would buy anything you were selling"—then he added with a smile—"if I happened to need it."

"Seriously," I said.

"Seriously, it's a hunch, but a very strong hunch. I've played these hunches in the past and they've worked out very well. People pay attention to you, George."

"For the wrong things," I said.

"Perhaps," he said. "I think I'm paying attention to the right things."

I asked him what it would pay, and he laid out for me the plan of a base salary plus an override on sales. Unless he was very much mistaken, a man could do extremely well. I knew damn well that Vince Taylor couldn't be very much mistaken about his own business.

"I have a family," I said.

"I know you do."

I wasn't sure what he knew, but it seems to me now he was saying what any good businessman would say: *I'm making you an offer. The domestic arrangements are your own affair.*

Ellen thought it might not be a bad idea. We needed something. A temporary separation might make clearer what it was we needed. It might be that the temporary separation itself was the thing needed.

I agreed.

I called the number Vince had given me and told him I would take the job.

"Which is better, to believe there is no God, or to believe there is one, but that He's not particularly concerned with us? In fact, couldn't care less. Totally indifferent. And not because He's mad, but because He never did care. All the incense-burning and hand-waving was an attempt to get His attention, but the crying fact was that He never turned His head. Something else had caught His attention after setting up this little scheme here."

I put the matter to Vince Taylor as we sit at lunch in a crowded restaurant high above the city. This one offers another view of the mountains. This one reveals the mantle of brown *shmutz* lying along the foothills. The moment a high-pressure system pokes its nose into this section of the country, the gases begin to collect and thicken, and, if it lasts long enough, it will form a dirty soufflé whose grit you can almost grind between your teeth.

Vince smiles his slow smile. He says, "To be quite honest, I've never really considered the question. I'm sure you wouldn't want me to rush an answer on that one."

I can talk this way to Vince. I like Vince. In some peculiar way, I feel sorry for him, which is ironic in view of the fact that he is by any going standard an enviable success while I am no younger than Vince and have no more than this job, a patchwork past, and a dim future. I would say that Vince is worth several million by now. I don't have several million. I know that Vince is married and has two kids—a son who is a rising architect and a daughter who is even now appearing in a repertory production of *Summer and Smoke* in Chicago. Why do I feel sorry for him? Because there's something incomplete about the man. It may be strictly in the eye of the beholder, but one sees what one sees. His slow smile and his watery, pale-blue eyes make me feel that he is in a perpetual state of semimourning for some aborted ambition or abandoned desire. I'm probably dead wrong about this, but in life (as in art, I suppose) we build on what we perceive, wrong as our perceptions may be. The truth is hard to come by.

I say, "My own sense of the thing is that God is maturing. He's in the process of dropping some of His childhood friends and concerns. At one time, when things were new, God liked to hang out with the neighborhood gang, rather liked the ritual and the worship, but He's outgrown that schoolyard stuff."

"What do you think He's interested in now?" Vince asks.

"Astrophysics."

"Then He should be able to find some interesting company back in the old schoolyard. That's the latest game the kids are playing."

"But it's gotten too messy. The place is littered with all kinds of crap."

Vince smiles again. We both look toward the mountains, the "brown cloud." I said I like Vince, and I do, but I don't feel close to him. If I stayed in Denver for the rest of my life, I doubt that he and I could become good friends. I don't know what it is, exactly. We laugh at the same things but not to the same degree. There's an intellectual affinity but a different order of priorities. We touch at many surfaces but the core dynamics are different. And something else, which I think I perceive, can't be sure of, and that is that he regrets this more than I do. He wants more than I do to transcend these differences and be good friends. I envy the internal organization that has brought him a considerable, if lugubrious, fortune. I'm not sure what he envies in me. He talks about my head and my voice, my cello voice, but that's all camouflage. It may be nothing more than the eternal imbalance of things.

"Did you have a nice visit with your daughter?" he asks.

"Great. We went skiing a couple of times, weathered one blizzard, talked up another. She's just coming out of a no-dice love affair, and she thinks the world stinks. She's as beautiful as two dozen roses. She's intelligent, and she sees absolutely no future for the world."

"Ah," says Vince, "therefore all the speculation about God's current interest in His handiwork."

"Something like that."

"Do you agree with your—Jessica, isn't it?—do you agree with Jessica's evaluation of things?"

Suddenly I remember something. I remember that when I first mentioned to Vince that Jess would be visiting, he had casually suggested that if it didn't interfere with any plans perhaps I might drop by with Jessica for coffee, or drinks, or anything. Possibly we might all go out to dinner. I thought at the time that Vince was just saying the polite thing, but I realized in that bleached moment that "casual" was the normal Taylor manner, and that in all probability that invitation had been sincerely and hopefully extended. After all, I had been to the Taylor home on several previous occasions, why not when my daughter was in town? Indeed. Once again, I heard the gates of another faux pas clang shut.

"I agree with Jess," I say, "but it doesn't much matter in my case. What depresses me is seeing the futureless future through her eyes. . . . Incidentally, I was planning to take you up on your nice offer to get together, but I was afraid we'd all be ass-deep in snow."

"I figured," Vince considerately says.

"How do you see the future?" I ask Vince.

He looks at his watch. I laugh. "I don't mean in the next five minutes," I say.

"I don't see the future," he says. "I just don't look."

Now that I've sidled my way out of guilt, I'm feeling a little more combative. "Sure you do," I challenge him. "You can no more prevent yourself from looking in that direction than you can prevent yourself from taking in one lungful of air after the other."

Vince considers the challenge and decides to tell me what he believes. He says that he believes along with Kafka that man's tragic condition is not that he must die but that he must live without knowing. Either you spend your life talking to the doorkeeper or you walk away and do other things. Fairly early in life he decided to walk away and do other things. He walked away and concentrated on making money and playing squash. (I'm very ancillary to the money-making, but we do go at it more competitively in squash. We play once a week, sometimes twice, and he almost invariably beats me.) "Which brings me," he says, "to the question that seems to be behind all of this. I may be mistaken, but I have a feeling something else is behind all these profundities. Shall I tell you what I think it is?"

"Shoot."

"You're getting restless," he says.

It surprises me to hear him say it, even though I know it to be a valid assessment. I thought I was being adroit enough to hide it, or that Vince wouldn't be paying that much attention. Instinctively, I turn the thing around, saying "Uh-oh, I don't like the sound of that. Restlessness is a two-edged sword. Are the boys getting unhappy with me?"

Vince smiles his laconic smile, letting me know that he recognizes the dodge. He says, "The boys are happy with you. I'm happy with you. You've done a fine job. And I repeat, you're restless."

"But, Vince, you know that restlessness is part of my nature," I say. "If you get right down to it, it was restlessness that brought me out here, and it was a kind of restlessness that went into building the sales force. You know that. Now that everything is in place, you're noticing what's always been there."

"Nice move," he says, "but I don't buy it. I'm the one who's doing the wondering. We're going to expand, I think you know that. It's pretty certain we're going to get the northern areas we're bidding for. That will mean an expanded sales force. More action, more money ... but I'm wondering whether you want it."

Our friendship goes back as long as any I can think of, even though our contacts have been sporadic, and even though it's stayed pretty much at the same level. He has a right to ask, personally and professionally. He brought me out here to do a job, and I've done it. What happens next depends on me. I can see that. Do I want to stay here, or do I want to go back to New York? That's what he's asking, and I've more or less been anticipating the question.

"I've been thinking about it," I say.

"Do you know what you'll be facing when you go back to New York?" he asks.

"I have an idea," I say. "I've always managed."

"You've always been younger than you are now," he says.

"Are you worried about me?"

It comes out that he is worried about me. I always figured him to have a mild nostalgia where I was concerned, and perhaps a mild envy for qualities he didn't himself possess, but I find out now it's been more than that. He does put greater weight on our connection than I do. He doesn't exactly say that, but I gather it from the concern he shows. He says he's always been aware of that streak of discontent in me. In a way, it's part of my attraction. But what I had really better keep in mind is that if I go back to New York, I'll be facing realities I never had to face before.

"Such as?"

"Your age."

"What is my age?"

"Fifty?"

"Give or take."

"Getting a new job, George. It's going to be difficult."

I nod. I resent his saying it, but I realize he's not trying to score points. He's telling me what I should have told myself. I've told him something of the situation between Ellen and me, and I think he's hinting at having my wife join me out here and leaving old scenes and old troubles back east. My own thought is that I could linger on in Denver for a while yet, putting money in the bank, getting a start on my man-woman project.

"My plan for the present is to stay where I am," I tell him. "I don't rule out the possibility of going back east, but if I did decide to do it, you'll know in plenty of time."

"Well, if you do decide to go back, I have some contacts that may be of use."

"You're a gentleman," I say.

He smiles.

The rest of that day I carried around an indefinably heavy feeling, as though I had ended something, when in fact it was agreed that things would go on as before. I kept going back to it, pressing nerves here and there until I found the right spot. What that lunch and conversation with Vince had confirmed was the long disparity of our friendship.

What to do about that? Nothing. That's an area not subject to too much scrutiny. One feels as one feels. I think of poor Marie Angelini. There was a situation about which I could do nothing. Not so Ellen. I could have done something about that. That was a bad mistake, perhaps a fatal mistake. But going over it in my mind, as I have done, countless times, I still wonder how unnecessary a mistake. There may have been some necessity in it, as it was necessary for Ellen to do as she had done.

8 I've been back to New York enough times in the past two years to assure myself that nothing has changed for the better. Some new buildings have been crammed into familiar streets, but the general condition remains the same. The last time I was there—it was summer, I was taking my vacation, hungry for my city, wanting to see Ellen, Jess (whose academic year had ended), some friends, some relatives—I stayed at a hotel near Lincoln Center.

I would have preferred staying at my house, in Forest Hills, but I was informed by Ellen that that was off limits. "No, George, you can't stay here," she said. "It's just not a good idea. Not the way things are."

"The folding bed," I said. "In the living room."

"No, George."

"Save me hundreds."

"You can afford it."

True, I could afford it, but I had hoped—well, I wasn't quite sure what I'd hoped—no, that's not true, of course I knew what I'd hoped—I'd hoped to test out the possibility of our being together. I could have, would have, kept it an absolutely chaste arrangement.

"I'm not going to quarrel with your decision," I said, "but I would appreciate a little glimpse into your reasons. I may not be entitled to it, but I would appreciate it."

"I should think my reasons were self-evident," she said.

"What's self-evident I can see, but I have a very strong hunch that there's something beyond the self-evident part of it. I've said that before, Ellen. You know that."

"It's not that you had sex with another woman," she said. "That's not the most important thing, although you probably think it is. That's only a symptom."

"Symptom of what?"

"Well . . . of your selfishness."

"First time I've heard that."

"I know, George, but it's not material things I'm talking about. You can be generous about *things*, but you don't have a generous view of life. You want—you've always wanted—a very conforming world. You're made very unhappy when it doesn't conform, and you make the people around you unhappy, as well."

"And you?" I asked. "How about your unhappiness? Was it entirely linked to mine, or was there something going on with you, as well?"

"Yes, there was something going on with me," she admitted.

"That's what we have to talk about, work out, the goings-on in both of us."

"So why can't we begin?"

"Because I'm going back to Denver," I said. "I can't quit cold, just like that. I've got to make arrangements."

"Yes, I know," she said.

I stayed in the city, in a hotel near Lincoln Center.

Quite a few things impressed themselves on me during that last visit. I remember a kid stalking along that broad street fronting the Center. He was a black kid, or half black, with the copper-colored hair often seen on kids of mixed blood. He was moving at a pace just short of a run, his face almost beatific with rage. It could have been self-induced, it could have had cause, but whatever the reason the result was a whole line of city trash baskets shoved over, contents spilling in front of oncoming traffic. He charged south, fleet as a wide receiver, knocking off one can after the other, then dashing across to the east side of the avenue and proceeding to knock over all the baskets in a northerly direction.

I witnessed that on the second day of my summer sojourn in the city. A cameo quickie for my benefit. I've seen worse, but that little presentation epitomized the city I'd been thinking about, missing.

On another day, on one of the many corners of 72nd Street, I saw a man sitting on the ground crying "Help me! Help me!" in the most hopeless, abandoned way I'd ever seen. I looked for something that would explain such a public display, but I could find nothing. Not one of those little wheeled platforms used by legless men, or the pinned-back sleeve, or sleeves, of an amputee, or the opaque shades of the blind. Nothing. He was freckled, all limbs intact, seemingly healthy, genuflecting as in prayer, or at a beheading, and simply wailing his want to the world. A young woman, horror on her face, hurriedly opened her pocketbook and extracted a dollar. She held it out to the man, who took it with magic swiftness, folding it into the pocket of his sport shirt and continuing his hideous supplication as if the two actions had nothing to do with each other. The wail had issued from a soul in torment; the bill had been plucked by an efficient clerk.

I suggested to Ellen that she invite just a few friends, people we both knew, for dinner, at the house.

"No, George."

"Not a good idea?"

"Not a good idea."

"I don't see why."

"Because," she explained, "it will look as though we were having some kind of a . . . *reunion*."

"Well, we are. I mean—"

"We're not, George."

"I don't mean a permanent reunion, but a temporary—"

"No, George."

Of course, she was right. I might take it as a convenience, but everybody else attending such a "party" would take it precisely as Ellen thought they might. Unless we made a deliberate announcement at the party that things were thus and so between the Lights, please not to draw any erroneous conclusions.

No, that wouldn't go down too well.

I suppose that somewhere in the cellar or attic of my unconscious, the wish was being father to the thought. I'm not really sure that's the case. One of my lifetime troubles is that I've never taken sufficient sweep of the landscape, assuming that what I see is all there is to see.

If I wished to come over to the house for dinner, that would be fine. Ellen said she would check with Jess, who had a summer job with a trade publication. Jess would want to be there if I had dinner at home.

"Ellen . . . Ellen, perhaps it would be best if we all went to a restaurant," I said, suddenly filled with the bleakness of being in my own house as a *guest*.

"All right," she agreed.

So we did. I asked Ellen to choose the restaurant, let me know, and I'd meet them there. She chose a restaurant in the east Fifties, the Swiss Something-or-other. I wondered if she'd been taken there by some horny head of a music department, or maybe a lonesome bachelor known to one of Ellen's nosy friends. She had every right, God knows! Hadn't I seen other women in Denver? But not lately. Lately I've become cautious. Scared, to be honest. I tell myself it's because of the AIDS thing, but I don't think that's really it. I think it's because I feel the time is coming to settle things between Ellen and myself. That's a place I must come to with clean hands.

There we were, the three of us, as in olden times. Well, not so olden. It wasn't that many years ago that we were doing this regularly. We had dined out often. But time is measured by more than months. Events had given a wrong-end-of-the-telescope perspective to our last occasion.

"So how's life in Denver?" asked my daughter.

"Slower and less expensive," I said.

"Sounds appealing," Ellen said.

Keep in mind that we hadn't seen each other in almost seven months. The last time I had been back in New York was the previous Christmas. People don't change all that much in seven months, except in the first couple of years of life. Physically, that is. And yet there's a tension that results, I think, from the expectancy of change. Everyday proximity breeds blindness. Minor mutations—hair, cosmetics, pounds on, pounds off—are made to accommodate a set image. In seven months of separation, the image can become unsettled. Tiny changes creep into those memory restorations. The in-the-fleshness of meeting brings on a quick crisis of identification.

Ellen looked somewhat heavier, and her hair had been

tinted a different shade. I wondered if this was to mask the gray. But the identifying cast in the left eye, the cleft in her chin, and the distinctive composure of her face remained exactly as I remembered them.

Jessica was looking her blue-eyed best. She had a deep summer tan. The glints in her chestnut hair were darkly, richly different. She also had done something different with the style of it. It fell about her face more softly and voluminously than I remembered.

I told them about Denver—and this may have been one of the reasons Jessica later decided to pay that visit. I told them about my apartment and its splendid view of the front range. I told them about the spookiness of downtown Denver at night, an unpeopled metropolis without a theater district, without movies, without the multiform, restless poetry that I have always thought of as being the cachet of a big city. The downtown area closed up at night. Like so many contemporary American cities, its life was fragmented, spread out. The restaurants and movie complexes attached themselves to residential communities. There was Littleton and Lakewood and Aurora and Arvada. There were great shopping malls. People in Denver were outdoor people. They went into the mountains to hike and hunt and fish and ski.

"Sounds great," said Jess.

"Well, it is, it is," I said. "You've got to come out and see. You've both got to come out and see."

"I will," said Jess.

Ellen smiled her guarded smile.

We discussed other things. Jessica's plan to visit a friend in New Hampshire before going back to school. Ellen's plan to go out to Sag Harbor and stay with her friend Milly Jacobs for a few weeks. Milly had managed to wrest the Sag Harbor house out of her divorce settlement, and now her guests were strictly her own.

I wondered if Milly's situation had stirred something in Ellen.

"Do you have any idea how long you'll be staying in Denver?" Ellen asked me.

"That depends," I said.

Ellen nodded, giving no overt recognition to the clear indication that I meant it depended on *her*.

I arranged to see Jess in the city before I returned to Denver. We met at the fountain in Lincoln Center. I saw her before she saw me, and I took advantage of the interval to admire the white cottony coolness of her, the coppery glints the sun teased from her hair. Then she saw me.

I suggested we eat at one of those outdoor cafés, if that wasn't too touristy a thing to do. I saw by the careful smile on her face that it was a bit touristy, but so what? Everybody was a tourist in Manhattan. Besides, she was entering her senior year at the University of Michigan, was no longer fearful of being found *démodé*. She was free of that undergraduate nonsense. On the other hand, she did know a place on Amsterdam Avenue where they served a wonderful chicken-avocado salad, and where you didn't have the fumes and the flies to contend with. Swell. Let's do that.

We took a cab to the Amsterdam Avenue restaurant, and it was indeed pleasant, with checked tablecloths and a youthful buzz. I felt a shiver of ancient delight, as if I were at the beginning of something, a newfound friendship, a love affair. For a few moments, I allowed myself a causeless, free-floating euphoria.

Jess told me she was planning to visit a girlfriend in New Hampshire before going back to school.

"Who's the friend in New Hampshire?" I asked.

"Her name? Her name is Cindy Stowe—as in Harriet Beecher Stowe—but there's no connection."

"Have I ever met her?"

"No."

"And what is Cindy Stowe like?"

"What's she like . . . let's see . . . she's like my age . . . she has brown hair, brown eyes, like yours, and a tendency to overeat. I met Cindy at Ann Arbor. We took a couple of Lit classes together. We became friends. She's staying with her parents right now. They live in Concord. Her father owns a lumberyard."

I looked at Jess wryly. I said, "Why do I feel I'm being told a little too much too quickly?"

Jess smiled. "Because you are," she said. "Cindy's dropped out of school. She's pregnant and she's decided to have the baby."

"I see. Amazing how real Cindy suddenly becomes. Do you think she's making a big mistake?"

"I don't know. I *really* don't know."

"It sounds to me as though you're going up there to help her make a big decision," I said.

"God, I can't decide that for her."

"I agree. You can't. I'm glad you see it that way."

"But she's got only a couple more weeks to make up her mind. She'll be going into her second—whachamacallit—trimester."

"Getting the culprit to do the right thing, I take it, is out of the question."

"The culprit *wants* to marry her," Jess said. "She doesn't want to marry him."

"Then why want to have his baby?"

Jess sighed. Jess shrugged. Jess explained that that was the complex heart of the matter. Cindy was in all ways superior to her impregnator. He was just a happy jock, on the hockey team, with a beautiful body and a C average. Was it the beautiful body, then? Frankly, it was. Like her eating compulsion. There were times when Cindy would face any consequence for the sake of a ten o'clock pizza—or a Jack Boyle. The trouble was that Cindy couldn't take the pill. Doctor told her not to. So she used a diaphragm, but obviously not with the requisite care.

From feeling that I was hearing a little too quickly, I was suddenly aware I was hearing too selectively. It wasn't that Cindy Stowe's compulsions were of no interest—after all, I *had* asked—but that Cindy and her compulsions were being used as a convenient screen. While we talked about Cindy, we weren't talking about other things, and it seemed to me that this suited Jess. She would rather talk about Cindy than about other things. I couldn't abruptly switch the subject, but when the waitress came with the salads I asked how Cindy's decision to have the baby could possibly be the right one.

Jess gave a little shrug. She was prizing the fat white chunks of chicken with the tip of her fork. She put a chunk in her mouth and chewed.

"Hmm," she murmured, and then added, "Maybe by foreclosing all other decisions."

Despite the excellent salad, despite the fact that we were still on the subject of Cindy, I could see that the clear water of Cindy's problems had become roiled with other problems, other thoughts, thoughts closer to Jess's own life.

"Speaking of decisions," I said, "how's your mother?"

"You just saw her two days ago," she said.

"I know. I guess I feel very unenlightened about my wife, your mother, the lovely Ellen."

"I don't know what you mean," Jess said.

"What I mean is this: Do you know what's happening in the life of your mother that I would do well to know about?"

"Like what?"

"*Like*," I said, scolding Jess's evasiveness with a deliberate, syllable-chopping manner, "your mother going out with another man. *Like* your mother simply wishing not to be married to me. *Like* your mother having recently been to a doctor and learning that she has a raffis divoris . . ."

"A *what*? Has *what*? Dad, what are you talking about? Has Mother been to a doctor?"

"Wouldn't you know?"

"Not if she kept it secret. Did she say anything to you about having been to a doctor?"

"No, she didn't."

"Then why are you saying that?"

"To get your attention."

"Well, you've got it. Now please tell me what it is you're getting at."

I told Jess about the change I had sensed in Ellen well before the Kim crisis. Of course, Jess knew about Kim. At the time of its discovery there was no way of keeping it from her. She was sixteen and as bright and everywhere as morning. She told me at the time that she'd never forgive me for that, and although that fierce verdict was softened, I think there's still an undissolved core of outrage. But I had never before told her about the detachment I had begun to sense in Ellen long before the Kim thing. I told her now, trying once again to give substance to smoke. It was not anything done, but things withdrawn, and withdrawn so gradually that there was no particular time or circumstances at which I could jab my finger and declare, "There! That's when it happened!" It could have been the normal attrition of marriage. How would I know? I'd only been been married once. I'd read about it, heard about it from friends, but who attaches such distant rumors to one's own case? That's what I was asking Jess about. I wanted to know if *she* was aware of anything of that nature in her mother. In other words, did Jess know or suspect anything that would explain the past and throw some light on the future?

Jess probed and peered into her chicken-avocado like a sweet young augur looking for a telltale configuration. . . . *Ah! Two pieces of chicken lying athwart a slice of avocado! A sure sign of* . . . I watched patiently. I asked if she was having difficulty in remembering what it was I had asked, or if the answer lay somewhere at the bottom of her bowl. Jess gave me a quick glance, of which I could make nothing. It seemed both a warning and a plea. Was I pushing her? Was I asking her to inform on her mother? Yes, I suppose I was, in a way. I put out my hand and touched her. "Listen . . ." I began, but she had already begun speaking.

"I'm not keeping any secrets," she said. "If Mother had anything to say about that, she'd tell you directly. I mean, you know, she's that kind of person. If you're asking me do I know that there's another man in her life, the answer is no, I don't. She gives more and more of her time to the schools, to the musical programs. She's made new friends." Jess looked again into her bowl. "But there is something . . . I don't know what . . . a kind of detachment. It may be that . . ."

"That?"

"That this is Ellen approaching fifty."

"Absolutely," I said, wanting to close off this conversation. It had taken a curiously ominous detour. I had imagined a mother-daughter buddyship as tight and far back as the cradle, but in these last few minutes I realized that even the mother-daughter relationship doesn't stay static, and that it might have moved on in a way I couldn't have imagined, a way that might be hurtful to Jess. Or Ellen. New commitments, new loyalties. Others. My blunderingly blithe inquiries might have forced Jess into her own realizations.

"Enough of that," I said. "Tell me, do you still have that Ann Arbor checking account?"

"Of course."

"Then what do you use for money here?"

"Money."

"It isn't a good idea to carry around a lot of cash," I said.

"I don't. Dad, what are you getting at?"

"I'm going to go with you to a bank, and I'm going to buy you some traveler's checks."

That started a row. What was the idea? I sent a check every month and that check included her allotment. The traveler's checks weren't at all necessary. There was no reason for it, no occasion for it.

"How about the occasion of our being here together and my wanting to do it? How about that, huh?"

"But I don't need it."

"Good. I want it to be something you don't need. I want you to have it with you when you go up to New Hampshire. I want you to have it with you when you get one of those impulses that you would normally argue yourself out of. Okay?"

So we went to a bank and I had her buy five hundred dollars' worth of traveler's checks, feeling at once expansive and ashamed. Expansive in my fatherly largesse, ashamed of the guilt-relieving taint in this giving. Did I mention that she was wearing a white dress made of that rough cottony material they all seemed to be wearing? She took my arm as we walked south on Broadway.

"Thank you," she said.

"Enjoy," I said.

"I love you anyway," she said.

I smiled. I wondered how she would put to rest in herself the unspoken fear that I might be trying to buy votes.

Two days later, I returned to Denver.

9 The year has ended, a new one has begun, and I am sitting again at my window observing another gray aerial ocean flowing over the Rockies. It's only a little over a month since Jess was briefly here and quickly gone, but that visit has been caught up in the stream of time rushing past this compartment into which I have sealed myself.

It's going to snow again. The underbelly of the overcast has obliterated the upper half of the front range. Why shouldn't it snow? This is winter. The middle of January. This is mile-high Denver. The ski lifts at Arapahoe and Loveland and Keystone and Winter Park are extensive and expensive. Ski-lift tickets have gone up in price. The hordes must come if these heavy investments are to be paid off. I've not done much skiing since Jess left. In fact, I went only once, this time with a woman who works in the office, who skis much better than I do and who I feel sure has been trying to promote something between us.

I didn't enjoy that day of skiing. It was cuttingly cold and getting to the top of the lift was an ordeal. The wind swooped laterally across the direction of the lift, making the seat sway. Yvonne, my companion, sat regally on my left, actually pushing off from one of the steel pillars when we swayed close to it. Unperturbed. Suppose we had knocked against that pillar? Suppose we had knocked hard enough to derail the overhead thingamabob, sending us catapulting thirty, forty, fifty feet below? Christ, you couldn't even *see* below! To the ground, that is. The wind was roiling a white cloud beneath us. It looked like escaping steam. I wasn't sure how far we'd drop, if we dropped, but it was surely enough to put us both in the hospital or mortuary.

On the run down, I crashed, I mean, *crashed*. Visibility was just about zero, and my skiing instincts are far from keen. Added to which, Yvonne called "This way!" to me at some point on the slope where the path switched, I'm sure, from "Intermediate" to "Expert." It felt steeper. And there were patches of ice. I couldn't bloody see where I was going! Then my right ski slid across the ice, and I just gave myself up to gravity and fate in a kind of a half-smiling, white delirium. It seemed to be happening in slow motion, but it was fast. What *was* slow, slow and soft, was the way I said "Fuck it" to myself as I tipped over, lost a ski, and cascaded off to the right, where killer trees waited to claim *schlemiels* like me. I did hit a tree, but enough friction had been applied to keep it nonlethal. Nothing was broken except my confidence. I made it down the rest of the way by cautious inches, and at the bottom, I began to hurt.

Yvonne (her mother is French-Canadian) was composed throughout. "Are you okay?" she asked. "Do I look okay?"

I asked. She smiled and nodded. "You look like a wedding cake," she said. Yvonne has dark eyes and black hair. She had the kind of skin and bone structure that makes any guess between thirty-five and fifty-five plausible. High cheekbones, wide-apart eyes, small mouth. That mouth pressed itself to mine when we were back in my apartment, after she had, at her own insistence, massaged back, side, neck. I didn't say it aloud this time, but I did think *Fuck it* once more . . . and gave myself to this fall with the same inevitability. We slipped out of our clothes and into each other in another kind of delirium. Yvonne mounted me, saying I must avoid sudden moves, must let her do the saddle work, her two hands on my chest, directing a fine, slow orchestration, until we finally clutched each other and dissolved.

I guess we both wondered what would come of that. Nothing came of that. Yvonne must have felt my disinclination, so we went back to being employees of the same company, perhaps a little less congenial than we were before.

I didn't want to get involved, because whatever else might be in it, my heart wouldn't. I'm not sure whether it was the flop at Keystone or Jess's recent visit or my man-woman project, but once again I felt that the movement of my life was changing. I felt it as one feels it in a train when there is acceleration or when the brakes are applied. A straining against momentum.

I stayed in Denver through the months of March and April, playing squash with Vince, who kept on beating me with tiresome regularity. I'm bigger than he is, stronger than he is, every bit as agile as he is, but there's a vital difference in our games that translates into his victories. He measures angles more accurately, sees opportunities more quickly, and takes advantage of them more ruthlessly. I see the opportunities, too, but some idiotic scruple makes me hesitate, resist . . . *Here, you little bastard, I'll give you another shot at it!* . . . Vince doesn't give me another shot at it. He puts it away.

"Do you find that there's something basically wrong with my game?" I ask him.

"No," he says. "You play as well as you can. I just happen to be better."

"I have a different theory."

"Tell me your theory."

"My theory is that I don't take advantage of opportunities as quickly as you do. That's no small thing. There's a whole life history there. I hesitate, Vince. Something compels me to give you another shot at the ball. Now—tell me—do you think that that little idiosyncrasy spells out the difference between our two careers?"

Vince sits naked on the locker-room bench and looks downward at the line of hair that descends from his solar plexus to his groin. He says something surprising. He says, "So I was right."

"Right about what?"

"About your restlessness."

"Would you mind telling me how we got from point A to point Z?"

"By the usual detour," he says. "Am I right?"

"It surprises me that any evidence was showing. I didn't feel any restlessness—except possibly this past week."

"What happened this past week?"

"I realized I was a permanent exile."

"If you mean what I think you mean," he says, "why not stay put? A permanent exile should find where he is as good a place as any."

"That's occurred to me. The only difference is people."

Vince nodded. My feeling was that he wasn't so much

trying to change my mind as to get a test sample of its tissue. "Are you saying," he says, "that people here don't appeal to you?"

"I'm saying that I have people back east. Family. A wife, a daughter, a brother, a few old friends."

"Well," says Vince, "we'll be sorry to lose you. You did an excellent job."

Now he's retreating a bit behind the businessman shield. I had been thinking that when I parted from Vince this time, there was every chance that I might never see him again. He had made Denver his home. The paradox of our relationship emerged strangely against the background of that possibility. I became aware again of the central part he had played in my career and the marginal part he had played in my life. But the historical fact was that Vince Taylor had *lasted*. Others to whom I had felt much closer at different times in my life had long since disappeared, some making it into a whole new galaxy, some finding old faces too painful to greet after some raking defeat. But Vince had lasted, perhaps because circumstances had arranged it so that we remained at an optimum distance.

"I was thinking how long we've known each other," I say.

"It has been a long time," Vince agrees. "Since Germany."

"We seem to have found some kind of a balance," I say. "You said you find things to admire in me—my voice, my head, an 'imperial' head, a head to stamp on coins, that bullshit. But what was it really?"

"Maybe it was really that," Vince says, looking a little askance. "Your voice and your head."

"Hell, you can buy a record and hear the greatest bass-baritone going. You can buy a plaster cast of the head of Augustus. You didn't have to keep me around for that."

Vince smiles. He says, "I'd like to ask you something, George."

"Fire away."

"Did you ever in your whole life wish to be someone else?"

I could have given him an equally facile yes or no. Doesn't everybody wish he were someone else from time to time? Hell, who wouldn't want to be Cary Grant, or Joe Namath, or Leo Tolstoy? But there was something in the way Vince had asked the question that made me take it deeper inside myself with each passing second. I owed Vince. If all that I had thought and all that he had done were considered, I surely owed him a considered response. Had I ever really wanted to be someone else? That is, if God visited me at some timeless moment between midnight and eternity and informed me in Kissinger's voice: *"Thou mayst be other than thou art, George. Choose!"* would I willingly vacate the body and soul of George Light in favor of someone else? I know the answer to that one.

"Not really," I say to Vince.

"I wouldn't have believed any other answer," he says.

"And you, I take it, have?" I ask.

"Yes," he says.

"But why?" I ask. "You're not the highest or the richest, but you've done damn well for yourself. A hell of a lot better than I have."

Vince gives me a quick glance, then says, "I have the knack of making money, but beyond that I'm not particularly pleased with the person I am. I'm a walking paradox. I have very little respect for what I do best. I would have liked to create something. A poem, a picture, a song. You've created something, George. You did that thing on TV, that series, *The Search*. You wrote that book—"

"You call those accomplishments?"

"I didn't say they were accomplishments. I said you created something. Degree is a matter of luck. But the impulse was there and you acted on it. That's how I know when you're getting restless. That's how I know that you're pleased with the person you are."

"Pleased?"

"If not pleased, then wedded."

I think he's right. I'm far from pleased, but I am fiercely wedded to the person I am, warts and all. Vince hasn't been eager to play his hand, but I have. Even now, with full knowledge of the hour's lateness, with the heart of an exile, I'm intensely interested in seeing how I will play the cards I have remaining. Even knowing that I can't win, I'm already poignantly attached to the manner of my losing.

10 Besides Vince, there's only one other person to whom I must say a serious farewell. I haven't seen her in months, principally because she was no longer at the place where I always found her. Nor was she at the address or telephone number I had jotted down in my little book. Possibly she had returned to that little town in Pennsylvania Dutch country she told me about.

Her name is Dorothy Koontz, but she is known as Terry. She prefers Terry because Dorothy was the girl in *The Wizard of Oz*, and Terry had once confessed to me that she would rather be dead than carry around that identity. Terry was a name she had plucked deviously out of history.

I met her shortly after I had arrived in Denver. She worked in one of those food stores that specialize in all kinds of exotic imports and breads so full of grain that your bowels loosen just at the sight of them. Dates, figs, dried fruits.

Health heaven. This was during my city-exploring period. I wandered in because it reminded me of other health-food stores I had known: a touch of home. I bought some healthy things, including an eight-grain bread to which I swore allegiance after my first bite. No other store seemed to have it, so I had to keep coming back to this one.

Terry was one of the girls behind the counter. I can't say I was attracted to her in the sense of a libido-pull, but I was drawn to her presence. She had agate-gray eyes, a pug nose, freckles (which reminded me of a childhood Jess), and a mouth that appeared, always, to be struggling with a smile. I told her I was an out-of-towner. She told me she was, too. I joked about the social attractions of a health-food store, to which she laughed and said I ought to hang around and see some of the characters that staggered in. I said—after about the fourth visit, when it was clear that we were both lighting up at the sight of each other—that maybe we could have lunch sometime, and she could tell me about the characters. She said that might be nice.

We had that lunch, a restaurant near the store where she worked. She told me that she came from a small town just south of Allentown. She asked me where I was from, and I said New York, and she said she planned to go there one day before she died as sure as her name was Terry. Her father had told her that Satan had established outposts in certain cities of the world—you could always tell by the number of Catholic churches and synagogues—and New York was surely one of the capitals of Satan's kingdom. He had told her that if she wished to hasten her journey to hell, she should go there.

"He was sure that's where I was headed," Terry said.

I asked if her father was one of those with the beard and the black garb and the horse-drawn carriage, and she said that his mind was bearded and black-garbed, but that he went around in the disguise of a businessman, which he was, in Allentown. He had a big building-supply store.

After several lunches, Terry invited me to have dinner at her apartment, an apartment not far from where she worked. It was a fairly bare place, just a few pieces of furniture and a mattress on the floor that was covered with a large paisley spread and surrounded on two sides by a rampart of pillows, double and triple deep. She had many books stacked on brick-and-board shelves. Her dinner was a concoction of meat and rice and vegetables with time-bomb spices that went off three or four seconds after impact.

"I've never had sex with a man with whom I didn't also have trouble," she said. "Could we keep it sexless? At least for the time being. If you get real horny, let me know. I'll decide then. You're not real horny now, are you?"

"No, I'm not."

And that's the way it was left. Terry was sexy in a diminutive way, but I was at a stage where I was perfectly willing to take no for an answer. As I've said, the AIDS plague was making prime-time news every night, and since I was being given a choice I'd just as soon not worry about it. Possibly I would have found out just as much about Terry if we had lain down on her floor-level mattress, but once we had made love she might have decided on a different strategy . . . or on *a* strategy.

More than likely, it would have made no difference at all. Terry was a young woman—twenty-five, twenty-six, twenty-seven—who had already made some remarkable personal decisions and had come to some remarkable conclusions. She believed in reincarnation. She wasn't loopy on the subject, but since I had asked her about the occult nature of so many of the books on her shelves she admitted believing in the everlasting journey of her soul. The one connection she was sure of was the Empress Theodora. She'd never even heard of the Empress Theodora, but the way she'd found out about her was itself proof of the reincarnation principle.

It happened when she was still living in Pennsylvania. Just a few days before she had gone into that library in Allentown, she had at last admitted to herself that there was an identity in her unconnected with her parents, her location, her time. It was difficult to describe, but she'd been feeling it for years, like her body was a sheath and this other thing was perfectly fitted inside it. There was the tiniest separation between the two, and it was this separation that caused the whisper she had heard for as long as she could remember. Anyway, she had gone into that Allentown library with a friend. The friend was looking for a book on vegetable gardening. While her friend looked for what she wanted, she, Terry, sat down at one of the reading tables to wait. On the table lay an open book. She just started reading—and then she read over what she had read, transfixed. She found a scrap of paper and wrote it down. It was about the Empress Theodora, who was the daughter of an animal trainer and who became the wife of the Emperor Justinian, after having been herself an entertainer and a high-class prostitute. Terry claimed that she knew, absolutely, whose soul had passed through the centuries and found its latest repository in Dorothy Koontz. It was in that moment of her life that she changed her name from Dotty to Terry. She had simply given an American spin to Theodora.

"Can you believe that the book about the Empress Theodora lay open by accident?" she asked me, her eyebrows raised, that incipient smile on her lips.

"Well, I can," I said, "but that's no reason why you should."

She had been married, to the boy she had dated in high school, and the baby was on its way well before the wedding. She was once Mrs. Dorothy Aldrich (although she thought of herself as "Terry"). She knew she wasn't going to stay in this marriage even before the baby was born, so she began looking around for another wife for Bobby, one whom she thought would make a good mother for the baby as well. She decided on Lucille, the girl she had accompanied to the library the day she discovered her Empress Theodora incarnation. She had worked it all out with Lucille before approaching Bobby. Bobby was a nice-looking boy who worked as a lineman for the utility company. He played on a company softball team and watched every athletic event on TV—baseball, football, hockey, golf, tennis. He would wonder some, but he would adapt very quickly.

"But *you*?" I asked. "How did you feel about leaving your child?"

"Lucille would make a better mother than I would."

"That may be, but there's still the *heart*."

"I would always feel connected with my baby, and with Lucille, and with Bobby, because we're all part of the same continuum."

Continuum . . . That was her word. She had others like it, part of her occult lexicon. What kept me spellbound was the hallucinatory shimmer of Terry's story. What was true (and I was sure that some of it was true) had been worked into a form that would harmonize with the purely fantastical. What was invented, or dreamed, or read, had been transmogrified into reality and made part of the Dorothy-Terry saga. These colored stones were turned in the light of her imagination, forming dazzling kaleidoscopic patterns.

Had she actually shopped for another wife for her husband, another mother for her child? I believe there was a marriage, I believe there was a child, but the abandonment, the flight, whatever it was, was covered over in a Walt Disney shower of stars because Terry was a woman who would live in no world but one of her own making. She had picked up somewhere the notion of reincarnation, and like a bird she had found a twig here, a string there, and had constructed her fabulous nest.

"How did you get to Denver?" I asked her.

"Some fellow I knew was driving to Denver, and I asked if I could go with him."

Was that true? Had she simply shacked up with this guy for the sake of the passage?

"Are you waiting for the Emperor Justinian to come along?" I asked.

"What do you mean?"

"What are you going to do with the rest of your life? Are you going to get married again? Are you going to go on clerking in a health-food store?"

"Oh, no. This is only temporary. I don't know what I'm going to do next. I have to wait for a sign."

It was like watching some eccentricity of nature—an electric eel, a glowworm, a fly-eating plant. It was eerily comical, but at the same time it left me with a feeling of dread. I wanted to grab that luminously giddy head and give it a shake, yell, "Enough! Stop it! You're headed for big trouble!" But that wasn't for me to say. I was neither her father nor her husband nor her brother nor her lover. Besides, when you're dealing with a fabulist, how much of the past can be believed, and therefore how much of the future can be foretold?

Then she disappeared. She was no longer at the store, and although her phone rang, no one answered. After some weeks, I stopped trying.

Since I had last seen Terry—almost a year—I had conceived my man-woman project. I was curious about Terry from that perspective. Was there something peculiarly feminine about her fabulosities, or was she a weirdo whose gender was irrelevant? I was curious about her, but more worried than curious. That fey feeling she engendered.

I was enormously relieved when I saw her behind the counter in the old health-food store. I caught her eye, and for an instant I thought she was going to avoid me, duck in the back somewhere. But then she smiled and waved. She looked different.

"Where have you been?" I asked.

"Oh . . . up in the mountains."

"I'm leaving Denver," I said. "Could we have lunch?"

"Okay. Same restaurant?"

"Fine."

She must have lost at least ten pounds. There were bluish puffs of distress under her eyes and her face looked positively shrunken. Her freckles looked anarchic. But still the suggestion of a smile.

"Been sick?" I smiled.

A quick shrug. No, she hadn't been sick. She'd gone to live with this guy up in Breckenridge. He had a cabin. He hauled supplies from Denver up to the smaller towns in the mountains. His name? Oh, what difference? His name was Dick—Dick Lattimore. He was crazy, to tell the truth. He got into a fight at least once a week, and he drank himself into a stupor every night. She didn't think it was possible to drink a fifth of bourbon every night—every night!—and wake up every morning as hideously sick as that. Why would anybody do that to themselves?

"Why would anybody go up in the mountains and live in a cabin with someone who would do that to himself?" I asked.

"He could be very nice," she said.

"He sounds nice."

The reincarnation of the Empress Theodora looked at me accusingly, as if I had betrayed some trust, an understanding we had; and to tell the truth I felt as though I *had* betrayed something. I was asking her whether this was the "sign" she had been waiting for, and this was a betrayal. I was challenging the self-myth she had created. Why such an elaborate self-myth if all you're going to do with it is run off with a Dick Lattimore and supply an audience for his sick behavior?

"Did he hit *you?*" I asked, my indignation having turned to pity.

"He pretended we were boxing."

"What?"

"He would say let's get some exercise, let's just pretend, and then he would start slapping me, and then he would start punching me."

"Oh, Christ!"

Something distant signaled my attention, but I was too appalled by the spectacle before me to be distracted. Ridiculously, I was disappointed in Terry. I hadn't believed more than half of what she had told me, yet I had accepted the fairy-tale shape of her edifices. I guess I would have preferred a fabulist who stuck to her fable.

"When are you going back to New York?" she asked.

"In about a week."

She looked away, then back to me, her eyes serious, pleading. "Can I go with you?"

I wasn't too surprised. I thought I had seen something like that coming. A corner of my consciousness had stirred, rummaged, and now gave me the equivalent image. Marie Angelini, she of the burnt sienna complexion and the haunted eyes. Maybe Terry was right, after all. Maybe souls are reincarnated. The fright, the forlorn hope, the utter fatigue.

"That wouldn't be a good idea, Terry," I said.

"Why not?"

"Where would you stay?"

"With you."

"Terry."

"We can have sex."

"No, Terry."

"But why? I'll drive with you across the country. We'll share expenses. I have some money."

"And then?"

"Then we'll see. When we get to New York, we'll see. I can find a job there."

It seemed as though the Marie thing was going to happen again—*was* happening. This woman would earnestly plead with me not to leave her life as I had found it, and I would have to refuse, because I didn't want the burden, the responsibility. I told Terry that in some respects her father wasn't wrong in describing New York as "Satan's capital." If I took her with me, I would be responsible for her, and I wouldn't have the time or the resources for that. No, it was no good arguing that I wouldn't have to be responsible. Whatever she may do or say, I *would* be responsible.

"I can go on my own," she said.

"Yes, you can, but I would beg you not to. You just have no idea how expensive it is, and you'll find yourself doing things that will make a mess of you and the Empress Theodora and everything."

"*She* hustled," Terry pointed out.

"I think it was safer then," I said.

"So—okay—have a nice trip."

"Terry, we're friends. Friends can help each other. Would you let me give you something?"

"What? Money? Sure."

I still had my checking account. I had left instructions to

close the account and send the remaining balance after a certain date. The address would be forthcoming. So I wrote a check for a couple of hundred and told Terry to cash it as soon as possible.

We said good-bye outside the health-food store.

"Why are you going back?" she asked.

"Unfinished business."

"Do you have my address?" she asked.

"I do."

"Write to me."

"I will."

When I was having the U-Haul trailer hitched to my car, I spotted a public telephone booth outside the rental lot. I thought of phoning Terry but quickly canceled the impulse. I wasn't going to dissolve the guilt with another telephone call.

And there was guilt. Guiltless, I felt guilty. Should I not have spoken to that friendly freckled face? In the case of Marie, it was she who spoke to me. But with both women there seemed to be an implied promise I hadn't fulfilled.

PART II

11 It doesn't make much difference which of the interstates you take, there are interminable stretches of boredom on both. Getting out of Colorado itself is a discouragement. All those hours of driving through only half a state. I listened to the music out of Denver as long as I could, and then plugged my portable tape deck into the cigarette lighter. I had prepared a bunch of tapes. The first one I slid into place was a 1930s eclectic. A Christmas present from one of the jazz buffs on the sales force at Allied Cable. He'd heard me say that I sometimes hungered for the Big Band sound, so he put together a tape from a Smithsonian album he owned.

That infectious tom-tom introduction by Gene Krupa to one of the famous Benny Goodman numbers. The lyrics, of course, made no sense, but then the lyrics to most songs make no sense. Not when they're set out bare, as mere words, unaccompanied by the music. Except Gilbert and

Sullivan. And maybe Cole Porter. There was a period when Jess was very fond of Cole Porter. He made great romantic sense to her at that super-romantic time of her life. . . . Come to think of it, even some of those divine Mozart operas had some damn silly librettos.

And what's that? That's another Benny Goodman number. It's one I danced to, I think . . . I'm looking at a 1980s landscape—which is pretty much the same landscape one would have looked at in the 1930s. Nothing then, nothing now. Just land as it undulates down from the 5,000-plus elevation of Denver to the Nebraska plains.

I can't tell whether I'm having these thoughts simultaneously or consecutively. I'm remembering my life back in the Benny Goodman era, and I'm also thinking that I haven't told either Ellen or Jess that I'm ridin' east. I'll have to handle that when I get there.

I did make some preparation toward my getting there, however. I had to have a place to stay, since my own home remained off limits. I had made a few telephone calls to friends in New York, asking them to nose about and see if they could find a sublease in the Village, or anywhere for that matter, but either they weren't trying very hard or there was nothing to be had. I had rented most of the furniture I had been living with these past two years, and the same problem would be facing me when I arrived in New York. Whatever it was, it would be temporary. A furnished place would suit me best. Go find!

I recalled my brother Henry mentioning something about properties he either owned or had a piece of, I wasn't sure where. I got in touch with him.

"Could I ask you a favor, Henry?"

"Of course."

"I've decided to come back east, at least for a time. I'm not sure it's going to be permanent, but however long, I'm going to need a place to stay. I don't think it's quite time for me to move back into my own house. So I was wondering if there was someone you knew who might be helpful in finding a furnished place somewhere . . . if there is such a thing."

"I'm sure there must be," Henry said, "but offhand I don't know of anything. Let me make a few inquiries, and I'll get back to you as quickly as I can."

"I'd appreciate it."

Henry is older by three years. We don't look like brothers at all. Henry resembles neither of our parents, while I have features of both. When they were alive, my parents played the game of trying to link Henry to old-country branches of either family tree. No luck. Henry remained an atavistic puzzle.

He's about half a head shorter than I am, began losing his hair in late adolescence, and became a balding, serious, older-than-his-years businessman. The business was the family trucking business, a business that was intended to have been shared by Henry and me, equal partners. When I was certain that I wouldn't be going into the trucking business, I let Henry buy me out. Henry was very thorough and legal about it. Two proposals: one, a lump sum and total quits; or, two, a small, continuing, nonparticipatory interest in Aaron Light & Sons. The latter figure would vary according to the profits and losses in any one year.

It was the dumbest and smartest move I ever made. Dumb because Henry now operates one of those coast-to-coast fleets, dozens of rigs, mainly refrigerated. He's made that his specialty. Food or anything else that needs a cold journeying. He's worth—Christ, I don't know what he's worth. He owns a forty-foot boat that he keeps in a marina in Larchmont. I would have had a smaller but still sumptuous piece of a very large pie if I had hung on to my interest.

In the long run, I think I was more smart than dumb. "Nonparticipatory" brothers, even the closest, inevitably revert to the roles of Cain and Abel. A clean break is the best. I opted for the lump sum, which was paid out over a three-year period, I put each of those lumps in a "growth" fund and let it grow. It's been the Flexible Flyer of my life, allowing me a generous margin for error, removing me from the specter of gaunt options. If there were two things I wanted—or wanted done, or wanted to give—I rarely had to make a choice between the two—I could usually have them both.

I don't imagine that the relationship Henry and I have fashioned is too peculiar. I'm sure there must be many like it. There has never been anything vitally active between us, neither hostility nor fraternity. Henry and his wife, Phyllis, enjoy the good life in their fashion, which includes the boat, golf, membership in quite a few organizations—business, social, and religious.

Perversely—or is it *humanly*?—enough, the thing that has saved our relationship from total calcification is the tragedy that fell like a blight across Henry's sunny acres. They have a daughter who is bright, attractive, married, and more or less living their kind of life. They also have a son who has been institutionalized most of his life. One of the organizations Henry belongs to is one that he helped found: a home for the multiply handicapped. A sizable chunk of the Henry fortune has gone into that home.

I don't envy Henry—and he surely doesn't envy me. We've been able to meet in that shadowed zone all our adult lives.

Henry contacted me while I was still in Denver, telling me that he had been in touch with some real estate people he knew and one of them located a furnished apartment in New Jersey. It was so near the bridge that you could almost consider it an extension of Manhattan. In fact, many people who worked in Manhattan lived there. Very reasonable rent, for a fully furnished apartment. Seven-fifty a month. He drove over himself to take a look at it. It was in a clean, safe neighborhood. It was not the sort of place I would choose for permanent residence—the apartment, that is—but it was certainly decent enough for emergency quarters.

"If you want it held, I must put a deposit on it," Henry said. "Shall I?"

"Sure. Yeah. That would be great. I do appreciate it."

A wood-frame house opposite a stand of trees. I rejected it instantly. That depressingly trim, little front lawn. The windows of the place seemed to stare at me with the same xenophobic gloom that I felt in staring at them. But here I was, so I might as well look at it.

The owner of the place—Mary Speros—showed me the upstairs apartment. Every room had some part of its ceiling angled in conformity with the many angles of the roof. Mrs. Speros—heavy on the makeup and with a Melina Mercouri voice—told me, "I'm not in the house much. I have visitors once in a while, but you can't hear upstairs."

"That's all right," I said, knowing that the possibility of minor disturbances was as nothing compared to the major disturbance of the place itself.

"I'll let you look around," Mrs. Speros said.

"Yes. Thank you."

The furniture, the view from any window, everything about the place was so unrelieved in its dreariness that I began to detect some kind of negative virtue. It might be the very place to house my present mood. It was convenient, temporary, and in some moral way the retributively right place for me to be.

I went downstairs and asked Mrs. Speros if I should make out the balance of the first month's rent to her.

"You like the place, huh?" she said.

"Oh, yes. Yes, indeed. It's perfect."

The next morning, I followed Mary's directions to the nearest shopping mall. I stopped at a coffee shop for breakfast. I ordered orange juice, my usual bran muffin, and coffee.

"You want butter or jelly with the bran?" the waitress asked.

"Butter."

"You can have both, if you want."

"Do I have to pay extra for both?"

"Nah, no extra charge."

"Good. I'll have both."

"You didn't say which one you wanted, so I thought I'd tell you."

"I appreciate it."

"Enjoy."

"Thanks."

It was a beautiful day in early May. I was home.

A telephone was installed after the necessary paperwork and payment. I was able to start making contacts. I phoned Jess in Ann Arbor. She answered on the fourth ring, sounded fuzzy. It occurred to me she might have been dozing. It was early evening, but this was May, and my guess was that she was heavily into finals.

"Did I wake you?" I asked.

"No, I was studying."

I thought I heard a voice in the background. Male? Should I ask?

"You with someone?"

"No. Why?"

"I thought I heard . . . Look, if this is an inconvenient . . ."

"This is fine, Dad. There are voices all over the place—but none within these walls except mine, at the moment. How are you?"

"I'm fine. And you?"

"End-term grogginess. You know. How's Denver?"

"I'm not in Denver."

"Where are you?"

"New Jersey."

The next few seconds wrinkled in silent inquiry. I explained that I had taken temporary residence in a nice little upstairs apartment in New Jersey. Uncle Henry had been helpful. The idea? Well, there was no single idea, but all the ideas going were going in this direction. My job in Denver had become largely routine. Cushy but dull. And, frankly, I was heeding the advice I had received from more than one source: Get back east and settle the unsettled. But not to get the idea that I was about to rush madly around making ultimatums and demanding quick solutions. I was all for caution and care. Really. Very, very tentative. This was going to be more a voyage of discovery than resolution. I stopped talking long enough to give Jess a chance, but it was, I guess, a bit too heavy for a quick response. I took advantage of the interval to revert to the matter of Jessica Light in her final semester.

"Actually," she said, "I'm working on an honor's paper."

"On what?"

A little seething sound, as if she had sucked air through

her teeth. "As usual," she said, "I decided to make things as hard on myself as possible."

"Come, come."

"You think not? I always do. Anyway, what I'm attempting to do is to compare the news broadcasting of the three major networks and the MacNeil–Lehrer show. I started back in January, shortly after the holidays. . . ."

What she was doing, she explained, was taping one of the shows when it was simultaneous with the other, or else watching consecutively. She had her own TV set and her own VCR, and she was borrowing another set from someone who didn't watch at that hour. She was even getting the hang of watching two shows at once. How did she manage that? "Oh, it isn't difficult. You put them both on, get the gist of what one is saying, lower it, then turn up the other. . . ."

"Toward what end, might I ask?"

"That's the stupid part. The killing part."

"Maybe I can help. I've had some experience."

"I know," she said. "I don't know how many times I've picked up the phone to call, then put it down."

"Why put it down?

"Because I have a hunch if I don't feel it myself, understand it myself, it will all go down the drain."

"Well, that makes sense," I said. "All right, I promise not to be the bull in the china shop, but give me an idea."

The idea was indeed an ambitious one, a killing one. My immediate instinct was to warn her away from it, but I gathered there was a large investment in it. Tossing a rock at this point might produce large, concentric circles of discouragement. It was this: The way Americans get the news, perceive it, depended to a significant degree on who gave it to them. Newspapers were one thing, radio another, but TV brought with it the enormous factor of *personality*. That is, the per-

sonality of the anchorman/woman brought a certain empha-
sis and play to the raw facts . . . Jess stopped talking. I waited
for her to gather her thoughts. I heard her sigh a weary "Oh,
shit!"

"I think I understand," I said.

"What do you understand?"

"That you're fighting smoke, evaluating abstractions."

"You're so right!"

"Take it easy, Jess. Don't let it throw you. May I ask a
question?"

"Why not?"

"In just what way do you want to make this evaluation?"

"If I knew that!"

"Okay, wait a minute. Let me offer this suggestion.
Sometimes it doesn't help to keep pressing in on a problem.
Sometimes you've got to stop pressing, move back, walk
around, approach it from another angle. Are you trying to
say that the personality of the individual anchormen actually
conditions the news, or that a relationship is set up between
the viewer and the TV person that gets in the way of a clear,
objective understanding of the news—you know, the way
the relationship between any two people very often gets in
the way of their understanding each other?"

This time the quality of the silence was positive. Possibly
I had indicated the other angle. Or had I indicated too much?
Had one of my bullish horns sent crashing a line of delicate
crystal, crystal of her own design? Pacing these considerations were thoughts of my own life—my life with the mother
of the girl to whom I was speaking. How much had *our*
relationship stood in the way of a clear understanding?

"How do you find measures and standards for such a
thing?" Jess asked.

"Ah!" I said.

"Ah *what*?"

"Ah, there I can't help you," I said, although an idea had already occurred to me.

"Unless . . ." she said.

"Unless what?"

"Unless you use yourself as the measure and the standard."

Which was exactly my idea. I said that what she had just said sounded promising. I said that the nature of the project made a certain amount of subjectivity inescapable. What I was feeling at the moment was the riot of my own subjectivity, a feeling full of sun and pride as I saw the *connectedness* between Jess and myself at this new, adult level. In the midst of so much dislocation and anxiety, this sweetness!

"Look," I said, trying to keep some of what I was feeling out of my voice, "I'm not going to kid you. This is a tough assignment you've given yourself. My opinion, for what it's worth, is that this is important and infinitely worth doing. I think you'll find that others have already made inroads, but the subject is boundless. I expect that you won't get more than a piece of it, but so what? You'll try for another piece another time. You can use the first paper as a platform. And then a third and a fourth. Just don't get too ambitious and don't get too discouraged—and don't let it get beyond you this first time. Okay?"

"Okay," said my Jess, already distanced in thought. "Are you going to get in touch with Mom?"

"Of course."

"Dad . . ."

"Yes?"

"Thanks."

"Why didn't you give me some advance notice?" Ellen asked.

"Why, are you about to leave town? I mean, why would

you need advance notice? It isn't as though you're going to have to make any provisions for my being here. I've got this apartment in Jersey, near the bridge."

"Do you have a job here?"

"Not exactly."

"I thought you had such a good job in Denver," she said.

"I did, Ellen. I just ran out my string on that. It was getting very routine. Besides, I was under the impression that you wanted to get things straightened out."

A measured silence. I don't believe in telepathy, but I do believe there are patterns that reveal themselves to people who have known each other for a long time. It has to do with the mix of words spoken and words withheld, with tempo and tonality. It seemed to me I was hearing a very wary Ellen. That "advance notice" business was a way of saying she found my sudden appearance inopportune, which puzzled me. Why should it be inopportune? I had already made clear that I wasn't here for a quick, definitive show-down. I had already told her that I would be preoccupied with certain plans of my own. She couldn't know that these "plans" were as nebulous as mist.

"Does Jess know you're here?" she asked.

"Yes."

"Well, what *are* your immediate plans?"

"To go about my own business."

"I mean," she said, "as far as I'm concerned."

"Ellen, I think I've conformed to some kind of an agreement we had. It was admittedly an unspoken agreement, but I do think there was an understanding. I put two thousand miles between us, which is what I think you wanted. We agreed that time and distance was needed. I think on the whole I've behaved as you wanted me to behave. My contacts with you have been held down to a minimum, wouldn't you agree? So, please, don't treat me like a door-to-door salesman. If there's something you've got to say to me, then say it. If there's something going on—I don't know what—another man?—then for Christ sake, tell me! We can settle this very quickly."

"I'm sorry, George," she said—and she sounded sorry. I soaked that up like a sponge. It surprised me how dry for a little Ellen-moistness I had become.

Then she began to tell me about *her* project, which had been in production since the beginning of that year. *West Side Story*. Kids recruited from all over the city. Singers, dancers, musicians. They had been rehearsing for two months. The show was going to be put on in a nearby high school—the one that Jess went to, as a matter of fact. She was living this thing every waking minute of the day and dreamed about it at night. In one way, it was a glorious thing, the way the kids were giving themselves to it; but in another way, it was like one of those monsters beloved by Hollywood, growing fangs and hair by the light of the moon. She was afraid that too much TV had crept into it, too much *Fame*. The kids loved what they were doing, found hidden resources in themselves, but it wasn't purely a creative binge. They were playing out roles they had seen too often on television and in the movies. She found that distressing. Still, that was the world they all lived in, and there wasn't much one could do about it. The point was that she was overwhelmingly in it, and she just couldn't handle anything else at this time.

"Who's asking you to?" I asked.

"I thought you might be," she said.

"Well, I'm not. When's the show?"

"End of May. The thirtieth. A Saturday."

"May I come?"

"Would you really want to? I know that *West Side Story* was one of your favorites, but I'm warning you, you'll be seeing a very amateur version."

"Ellen! For God's sake! I haven't become a complete id-iot!"

"I'll send you a ticket. Give me an address."

I gave her the Jersey address. She apologized once again for her distractedness. We left things in a satisfactory state of suspension. Why do I say "satisfactory"? I guess because like most people I prefer moving crisis off to the distance of the horizon. Twenty-one permanent miles away. There was also amelioration in the fact that Ellen was so thoroughly engaged in the production of a musical. Indeed one of my favorites! And hadn't she chosen it because it was also one of hers? Favorite or not, it certainly occupied a special place in our lives. I'm assuming she's still aware of that even if she didn't mention it.

An occupied Ellen should be a happy Ellen. A happy Ellen should be a conciliatory Ellen. A conciliatory Ellen . . .

What I wondered now was whether that coolness and distance I thought I had detected in Ellen was really in Ellen, or was it something I had conveniently implanted in Ellen to justify my own behavior?

I think it would be fair to say that I love Ellen. I have only to think of the size of the hole that would be gouged in me if she were to remove herself from my life. I could never hope to fill that excavation with other attachments, memories, gratitudes.

12 Despite the number of times I've been back in the last two years, I haven't on any of those occasions *driven over the George Washington Bridge*! And in all the rest of my New York life, there weren't all that many times when I found myself barreling eastward in the late morning over the upper or lower decks of the GWB. Damn few times. I had an aunt and a few cousins in Jersey, but those rare visits were nighttime visits. So the maze confronting me was as scary as any trip through nightmare alley.

You didn't choose your lane, you were forced into it. Squeezed out of one of the toll booths on the western side, you go with the flow, and the flow is not a matter of choice. It's where the thundering streams on either side of you say it is. If you make the slightest move otherwise some charging monster with ninety wheels will blast you murderously out of the way. He who hesitates is courting death. If you find yourself in the wrong lane, rectify it somewhere in the Bronx.

And I was not sure. I knew I wanted the West Side Drive, aka the Henry Hudson—ah, there's the sign, off to the right—but off to the right there are two choices—I guess the one I want is the one all the way over . . . *Hey, fellers, gimme a break. I'm a native. Just lemme edge over there* . . . a savage horn-bleat and a quick look of murderous contempt.

I made it to the West Side Drive. It was a bright, windy day. The river glittered. It seemed to me that the Jersey escarpment was as thick with buildings as some of those crowded European cities that slope into the Mediterranean. I can remember a time when scarcely a window or terrace peeped out of the cliffs that stretched from the GWB to the Hoboken docks. So what? So nothing. I just remember it, that's all. A man must be allowed his memories, else what's this life for?

I'm thinking of Ellen, of meeting her on one of those Village evenings, past wondering whether I was in love, waiting for her to appear at one of our arranged meeting places. We were going to have dinner, we were going to a movie, or possibly to shop. It was getting on toward Thanksgiving, and although it wasn't all that cold, there was a nice spice in the air, that peculiar American spice made of seasonal ingredients—foliage, football, upcoming elections, pasteboard turkeys in every shop, pasteboard Puritans. It was cheerful. That was definitely part of it: the good cheer.

And part of the feeling I'm recalling was being alone. Embracing whom or what you love is natural and gratifying, but *anticipating* can spiral you upward to a dizzying joy. That's what happened to me on that evening, an upward spiraling ecstasy that sucked up into its funnel cloud passing strangers, stores, traffic, the necessary past, the obtainable future. It still lives in me, that vortex, spinning away, a tiny tornado of happiness.

There are several garages on the West Side that I've always used, depending on the purpose of my visit. This time I headed for the garage on 58th Street. I noticed they were doing something with the West Side Drive, a demolition of some docks on the waterfront. I spotted the U.S.S. *Intrepid*, the navy museum, scarcely a novelty on the New York scene, but which still juts prodigiously. I turned into the city, went north on one of the avenues, saw the jam-up of traffic and the eternal utility island that had cordoned off a piece of the street. This part of the city looked more or less the same. The serious changes had taken place elsewhere.

After parking my car, I walked east, waiting for whatever sensation the sights would bring. I felt nothing in particular. Why should I? I hadn't been away that long. But time isn't measured by months alone. I had been away in spirit, and that isn't easily calculated. Superimposed on the familiar screen of Columbus Circle and the park was an image of Denver's front range with that aerial ocean of clouds flowing overhead. The first time in my life that the landscape of another city had competed with this one for dominance.

I had telephoned Larry Graff yesterday, and he had arranged this lunch at a Chinese restaurant in the east Seventies. Just opened. Splendid reviews. He'd already been there. The food was indeed sensational. Their shrimp Grand Marnier! I told him a sensational lunch wasn't called for, and he said of course it was. Old friends called for sensational lunches. That was one reason. The other reason was that any reason would do for a sensational lunch.

That sounded like the Larry I knew. A sensational eater. Loved food and looked it. He had once said to me, "With me there's always been a fat man trying to get in." The characterization was eerily accurate. Some men wear their fat sloppily. It sags, distorts their features, impedes their movements. Not so Larry. It was hard to imagine Larry *not* massively himself. His proportions had a creaturely naturalness. The wide face with its azure-blue eyes and brassy beard was almost a Hollywood cliché of feudal exuberance. Roaring over his cups with Henry VIII. Only Larry never roared. He sipped his white wine and ate his shrimp with, if not delicacy, then constrained relish. He asked if that was not simply unbelievable, the taste of that, the texture, the tang. I agreed that it was choice. Larry looked heavier than ever. Or perhaps it was the way his head had settled between his shoulders—like a nice round boulder in soft earth. If his liege lord had gotten pissed off at him, there'd be quite a mess at the beheading. No slim, trim neck to take a swipe at. God, what a thought! Some latent hostility? Perhaps. A bit. Nothing serious. I have known Larry, off and on, for almost as long as I've known Vince Taylor. Larry got started in TV some years after I did. His interest was always in news. "One of the pioneers in TV news gathering," it was said at one company function. So I guess there is some latent hostility. The hostility of a vagabond for one who had built his solid castle high on a hilltop.

I noticed that the Graff beard, that burnished emblem of good health and good fortune, was laced here and there with silver. But the eyes were as cannily blue as ever. Perhaps a little more recessed.

"I'm sure you know what's going on in TV," he said.

"Only what I read," I said.

"What's written usually has some foundation in fact," he

said. "General fragmentation. In one sense, it's bigger; in another sense, it's smaller. The total audience is bigger, but the individual share is smaller. Do you see?"

"I see."

Larry gave me his hooded blue gaze. "Of course you do," he said. "Your problem was never not understanding."

"What was my problem?"

"You tell me."

"I don't think I've got a problem," I lied. "I did what seemed right at the time, and if it didn't work out as well as one might have hoped—well, hell, that can be said of crossing the street. Getting to the other side would seem a simple and safe goal, but there may always be some crazy fucker rounding the corner against the light at eighty miles an hour."

Larry nodded like a Buddha, in full agreement with the vicissitudes of life, but his next remark came from another part of the forest. "Listen," he said, "how about some ribs? Jesus, they're good here. An order apiece, okay?" He caught the waiter's attention and ordered the ribs. His attention to food was wonderful to behold, but it didn't entirely mask other attentions. He was listening carefully to everything I said. The metaphor I had aimed at his armor hadn't entirely missed. It had bounced off, leaving, I suspected, an interior gonging. Whether he bought my explanation of my fate was debatable, but the quickness and assurance with which it was given wasn't lost on him. Whether or not I believed it myself also didn't matter. The point given and taken was that there was nothing lost or limp in the manner. I had never had the mark of a loser, and I believe Larry had been trying to determine if it was still true.

"So what's gonna be?" he asked. "You back permanently?"

"Definitely."

"How'd you like living in Denver?"

"It was swell. It had its drawbacks. Denver is not a city in the sense of this befouled place. Centrifugal forces working there as elsewhere. Things flying away from the center. Malls and movies in the suburbs. London and Paris have history. So does New York. New York also has an ocean. Denver has the Rockies. Some great natural phenomenon always adds a dimension. I had an apartment that faced the mountains, and I used to have my breakfast watching the morning light catch the snow-covered peaks."

Larry continued his Buddhalike nods to signal interest. I couldn't tell whether he did or didn't give a damn about the "great natural phenomenon," but it wasn't a matter of content but of form. I knew he had more than a suspicion about why we were having lunch. He wasn't sure whether it would come on this occasion, or if I was just priming the pump, but he would have given heavy odds on the ultimate purpose.

Did he owe me? No man owes another in business at the risk of sound judgment. When I had some clout, I had recommended Larry for a job in the news section. Larry had written an "in care of" letter praising my series, *The Search,* saying he'd become a fan, wouldn't miss an episode, wanting in particular to praise the script. Nice, crisp dialogue. Fast-paced, believable action. He gave a return address, so I answered gratefully, asking a few questions on my own. He answered, and we had the first of our many lunches, and then I learned he was working in radio and wanted to get into television. But I wasn't to think he'd written that letter for that reason. The letter was sincere. I had no doubt that it was, and I had no objection in principle to the marriage of flattery and expedience. When I heard of that opening, I spoke to the right person and got the interview for Larry. He got the job. He should have. He had the qualifications and the potential. Look at him now. Top banana. A man who ate his choicely flavored ribs with constrained relish.

I'm eating them, too, and they are indeed delicious. I'm sure the sauce in which these ribs were basted is a vault-enclosed secret. Smokily subtle. Subtly suggestive. Which qualities form a link to the man with whom I'm sitting. He, too, has been subtly suggestive, and elusive, in all those years since that letter and its happy consequences. What do I mean by that? I'm not sure. I mean something as subtle as the flavor of these ribs, and as Larry Graff. Larry was grateful for my help and he said so. More than said: He sent me on the following Christmas a little crate of fine French wines. But there has always lingered the feeling that I had acted only as an agent of the inevitable. I had done him a favor, yes, but if it hadn't been me, it would have been someone else. And *soon*. And I have no doubt that he was right.

"So you worked in cable," he said.

"Not exactly 'in.' Sort of around the edges. I organized a sales force. I was the manager."

"You know what's happening here, I'm sure," he said.

"Layoffs, cutbacks, reorganization, cracks in the earth."

"You got it."

"If I was looking for a job, then, you'd say forget it?" I asked.

"No, I wouldn't say that. If you're looking for a job, you're looking for a job. Are you?"

"Not at the moment. At the moment, I'm on a project."

"Oh, what's that?"

"I'm writing a book, Larry. Another book. This one's about women."

"Heh-heh." He laughed.

"Funny?"

"Isn't it?"

"What in particular is funny?" I asked. "The idea of writing a book about women, or the idea of *George Light* writing a book about women?"

"I'm not sure," he said. "I'm not sure that's a subject any man should tackle."

"Why not? Why not one man's opinion? Or perplexity?"

"What specifically?" Larry asked. "The way they think? The way they feel? The way they fuck? I've always assumed you were a man like me where women were concerned. I've always assumed you took women as and where you found them—and as often as you could. I've always assumed that you took them as they are."

"But that's it, Larry, I don't *know* how they are. Since you're assuming so much, I'll confess to you one of my own assumptions. I've always assumed there was some sort of ideal toward which one worked. An ideal relationship. Now I'm not at all sure that's true. Now I believe that the ideal has been *imposed,* if you see what I mean. The courtly love ideal. The Victorian ideal. I'm not sure what ethos is operating now, but whatever it is it's gotten badly out of whack. It needs new definition. It needs looking at. It needs talking about."

"Are you sure this is a book?" Larry asked, giving me a fat man's scrutiny: a sharp glance without body language; the body was too immobilized by fat to participate.

"Well, I thought of it as a book," I replied, catching sight of the same odd form that (I believe) Larry had seen flit by.

"Do you have a title for it?" he asked.

"Not yet. The working idea is that there ought to be, there *must* be, a better way of being together. For men and women, I mean."

"It's a subject of general interest," Larry said. "Marriage, sex, infidelity, divorce, therapy—as an industry, aggregately speaking, it must run in the billions. I'd say a question of general interest. I can see something like that on the tube."

I let an indefinite but fecund few seconds pass. "That wasn't my original idea," I said.

"You're a TV person," Larry said.

"A book person, too," I said, more reflectively than insistently.

"*A Better Way,*" Larry mused.

"What?"

"The name. Of the show. *A Better Way.*"

"You mean guest panelists, that sort of thing?" I asked. "A different group each week?"

"Interesting," Larry said.

"A better way of being together," I mused along with Larry. "Men might wonder the same things, but each one would put it differently."

"Basically," Larry said, "I see it as being constructed around questions that men would want women to answer, and conversely. . . . One week a panel of men, the next a panel of women. Or perhaps both. Or is it every day?"

I waved the question away. Everything too premature to consider.

"We'd need some very good MC-ing," he said.

(I marked the "we.")

"Because," Larry went on, "the quality of the show would depend almost entirely on the mind guiding it. The questions. The lead-ins. The break-offs. The way I see it, you'd need a synthesizing genius."

"That wasn't my original idea," I lamely repeated.

Larry gave me his Buddhalike smile. He said, "What I particularly like about it—I'm sure you must have had this in mind—what I particularly like about it is the self-generating source material. Questions on sex, sports, clothing, jealousy, aging, affection, conversation, mixed religions, no religion, children, no children. A sort of dialectical gold mine. Each statement breeds a counterstatement. Every male challenge evokes a female response, and vice versa. . . ."

Larry's thoughts didn't so much break off as begin to run underground. He sat in huge contemplation, absently licking the rib sauce from his fingers. "Have you spoken to anybody else about this?" he asked.

"Do you mean as a—? How could I have? It's existed in my mind as a *book* up till now. Naturally, I've talked to people—mainly women—with my book in mind. Well, not really talked to them in an investigative way, rather *listened* in a somewhat different way. More acutely. More disinterestedly."

Larry gathered these extraneous crumbs as a waiter would, sweeping them together and disposing of them. What I had thought I wanted to do was of no importance. Of importance was what time, ripeness, and Larry Graff had made of it.

"I think you've got an idea there," he said.

"It's still gestating," I said.

"That's good," he said. "That's what it should do. We ought to speak about this again. In a couple of weeks, say?"

We ate our fragrant ribs and considered the strange mutations of fate.

Why did I do it? Because it occurred to me, I guess. The particolored bird of inspiration—green for jealousy, red for aggression, blue for calculation. It went something like this: We were in truth sitting there and devouring shrimp and ribs because I was testing the waters for a possible job. I didn't need one immediately, but having worked all my life, I knew I wouldn't be able to handle unemployment for long. Even brief unemployment. I was like the alcoholic who can sit for hours, gabby and placated, as long as that drink is within fingertip reach. As I say, I didn't really need a job, but I had to feel one was within reach.

And then there was Larry himself. He was sitting so pretty, that mountain-hump of a man, top of his field, while I (who had given him a boost up) was in a very real sense starting over at fifty. I had tried on a half a dozen postures—straightforward, breezy, tough, and so forth—and none of them fit right. So when the moment came, I threw a switch and frantically groped for something to ride on. My "project," of course. But my project not as it had seriously backed and filled in my mind, but as it might interest Larry Graff. As a possible TV program. Clever George had something up his sleeve that he wanted to tease Larry with.

So it wasn't really a job, and it wasn't really a book, but a slab of real meat for the real world. So Larry thought. I could see it in the slide of his eyes. I could see that his mind had found something to concentrate on other than his enraptured taste buds. He wasn't himself a producer of such shows, but he knew who was, much better than I did. I had come to him because he was my best contact, and therefore I had already considered him as co-author of the whole idea. I could trust him. He owed me, and here I was giving him a chance to owe me again. What better way to generate trust? We could get our heads together, our hopes together, our lawyers together. After all, I knew what was happening. It was not out of the question that Larry himself had felt tremors deep in the rocks of the Avenue of the Americas.

We split after lunch, Larry going back to his office, I walking to the Plaza. Cool today. And windy. The cab horses adjacent to the park drooped woefully. Where did they get those pathetic nags anyway? They all had such a disconsolate air, standing in their little gardens of horseshit, waiting for the just-married couple from Ohio to take that fabled ride around the park. . . .

The fact is that I do have money enough to see me through. Through what? I don't know. Through to Social Security. I've paid for decades. I'm entitled. Even when I was on my own, I continued my payments to Social Security. Also a pension plan. I haven't contributed to the plan since I left the network, but I had contributed for years. It's been lying there accumulating interest and dividends. I put quite a bit of money away during the lush years of *The Search*. Not New York money. They say these days that a millionaire is someone who earns a million a year, not just has it. A *million*! Dear God! It used to—well, never mind what it used to be. The point is that there's a margin of safety. Jess can go to Europe, if she wants to. Ellen has her own income, but there'll be enough if she ever wants to pack it in. Besides, I'm going to be earning money. I'm an earner. I've got a hunch that Larry is going to get back to me as that idea of *A Better Way* simmers away in his clever, capacious head. I've got a hunch he's going to find a job for me just to keep me handy and well disposed.

Let me state one more truth: Despite everything that has happened this day, I still feel as seriously engaged in my "project" as I ever did. In a sense, I was like those cab horses around Central Park, standing in my little garden of horseshit, waiting to take a trip through the park. I'd like Larry to be helpful in getting me a job, and the soil around that project had to be fertilized, but my trip around the park is the important thing.

13 Maria and Tony, the star-crossed lovers ... I thought nothing of it at first because that catchy musical was so perfect for high school kids to get into. So many ensemble numbers. So many singable songs. I wondered about permissions, but I was sure Ellen had gone into that, done what had to be done, paid what had to be paid—although I seemed to recall reading somewhere that most of these Broadway classics were free to school groups.

I put that ancient keepsake on my turntable and listened to the scratchy evocations. It brought back that time more than adequately for me. Surely it must have registered on Ellen that working with that musical would bring back a very particular time! Unless it was someone else who had chosen the show, presented it to Ellen as a fait accompli. But in that case she could have turned it down, told whomever that for personal reasons, etc. Or, simply, that she knew that working with *West Side Story* would cause no emotional clogging. One man's nostalgia can be his wife's finger-snapping, toe-tapping release.

We met at the time of *West Side Story*. The logo that ran for years in the newspapers and magazines—a boy and a girl running toward their unattainable happiness—was the emblem of our meeting, because that was the occasion of our first date. By that time, the original cast had gone elsewhere, but the genius of the thing was that it needed no special star. The music and the lyrics and the theme and the choreography, like any other musical work of art, lived through generations of performers.

The melodies of *West Side Story* did take on a meaning beyond their own excellent musicality. I mean—Christ!—you don't have to be a sentimental slob to find in certain songs personal, permanent significance.

Ellen had been working at the time in a record store on Ninth Avenue. I had been working nearby in one of those early barnlike places that the networks had acquired throughout the city—old movie houses bought up, gutted, and made over into television studios. Ellen attended classes at the Mannes School of Music during the morning hours and worked at the discount record store starting at noon. Her boss allowed the arrangement because he was a music lover as well as a smart businessman. He was getting a twofer in Ellen. Ellen could play the typewriter as competently as piano keys.

I had my first TV job on the very corner of the avenue where Mr. Discount had his store. I also had an apartment on Jane Street in the Village. Young man about town, with a secondhand car, a fold-out sofa, and all the latest electronics. A TV set, of course. I was in the business. A Fisher radio-phonograph. I had gone to Brooklyn College for two years after my army stint, and had quit when I realized that my future depended on full-time apprentice training. For which I've never been sorry. Subsequent disorder had nothing to do with my choice of career. The same things, or comparable things, would have happened if I had taken my place in the Light trucking business, or had gone in for law, which, for some reason, was my father's fervent wish.

I was all set for serious seduction, which I was more or less attempting at every opportunity. And succeeding, here and there. But they turned out not to be serious. Or too serious. Amazing how quickly recriminations set in when there isn't the spellbound heart to keep them at bay. One was already married with two children. This I learned later. She despised her husband. He was the merchandise manager for a national chain of retail stores, and he spent more than half his waking hours in airports or airplanes. The other half he spent in one or another of the athletic clubs that kept him in shape with handball and swimming. The only companionship he wanted was that of other business types with hard muscles and heavy schedules. She wanted to divorce her husband. She would take the girl and leave the boy with him. She had a flair for interior decorating. She could set up her own small business to augment our income. We'd be very happy. We were sexually compatible, weren't we?

Yes, we were, but I also thought I was in danger of catching this dangerous lunacy. She had decided what she must do with her life and had decided to enlist help. I was the help. Aside from our sexual compatibility and the demolition of her present marriage, she liked to go to movies and talk about the lives of the movie stars. She was interested, that's all. Men follow baseball and football, don't they? Know the names of the players and their stupid averages?

This time I was determined not to repeat the Marie Angelini thing, with taffylike excuses and withdrawals. The penalty for that kind of hypocrisy was too heavy.

"I'm not the one," I said.

"Why?"

"Love, I guess. I'm not in love with you."

"You don't have to be," she said. "Skip love. Most people do when they get married. Love is for kids. Good bed fun is for adults. Be smart. I'll be good for you. I've had more experience. Trust me."

There was a moment—say five moments—when the argument, the woman, the sheer perversity of it pulled at me with a dangerous downhill pull. It would be like letting myself go on a sand embankment, sliding, tumbling, just for the giddy hell of it. *Was* she so wrong? Weren't my notions of true love just as much tripe as the tripe she read? Maybe. Maybe not. Time would tell. But to knife an ideal while it is still warm and breathing is murder, even if the victim proves to have been only a shadow.

"No, I'm not the one."

"Damn you!" she said with disgust. "I hope you get what you deserve, you stupid, time-wasting shit!"

In one respect, she was right. I had wasted her time. She had a purpose and a plan, and I had set her back. This last scene was enacted in a restaurant, and I quote her words verbatim. To complete this candor, I must add that the words were uttered loud enough for everyone in that smallish Italian restaurant to hear.

I'm not happy to be recalling this, but it's just as well that I do. It pins in place the fact that being called a shit doesn't necessarily make you one.

The other girl did set off Marie Angelini vibrations. She had a bit part in one of the shows filmed at the studio where I worked. She had a natural bouffant of kinky hair and sang pop songs like "Que Sera, Sera" and "Whatever Lola Wants" in nightclubs and at any special event her agent could book.

Weddings and Bar Mitzvahs. Even at a stag party where the entertainment slid from lively to lewd with each sweaty hour. She sang a few songs and left. One of the other girls had informed her of the rest of the evening's program. It would involve, she was told, a large collie.

Laurie had a voice perfectly suited to the songs she sang, and a complete set of gambols to go with them. Facial and body capers as unimprovisational as breathing, little tweaks and twists that were either sexily right or dismally wrong. Hers were right.

But in spite of her rightness, and in spite of the fact that she was more often than not displaying them, she was wretchedly unhappy. *So* unhappy. I spent a whole evening with her in my apartment, hours, trying to get at the source of those ceaseless tears. What? What? She was not good enough, she despaired. She would never get to the top. Did she have to get to the top? Yes, she did—*did*—because she had the talent to be at the top, and not to be at the top when you've got the talent is like starving in the midst of plenty, like being forced to walk with a crutch on perfect limbs. Well, give yourself time. No—*this* was the time! She saw other no-talent slobs getting *leads* while she couldn't even get in the cast. What was the matter? Huh? Please! Tell her the truth! I was smart, had a good eye, so please be honest with her and tell her what was missing.

I didn't think anything was missing—except possibly a cachet, a distinguishing something, that always and heart-breakingly gives the laurels to truly lesser talents. And I suspected she knew this, and that was why I would never say it, because to say it would be poison in the wound. So she went on grieving and doing her bit in large casts or small functions. What little there was between us tapered off. I learned that someone else had taken over the role of consoler. Obviously, she never made it big. I would have heard.

But when I recall the Laurie period, I find a parallel to Marie Angelini. The person and the circumstances couldn't be more different, but the pathos was the same. The prettying up and the deep lament.

It had also demonstrated to me, for the first time, that a woman's frustrated ambition could be just as maddening and mangling as any man's.

I suppose it could be asked why I needed that demonstration, and the short answer would be because I was born when I was.

I bought a recording of *West Side Story* as soon as it came out. The very first record in the set had a glitch. I brought the record back. The clerk said he couldn't exchange it because that was the policy of the store: no exchanges once the record had been taken out of the store. After all, I might have been the one who scratched the record, so, you know . . . etc.

"I've been buying records here for a year," I said. "I don't know how many records I've bought here. Never brought a single one back."

"I'm sorry, store policy."

"Hey, come on. I'm a regular customer. Haven't you got a policy for regular customers?"

Back and forth, until the clerk took me into the glass-enclosed office where sat the bald-headed, horn-rimmed Mr. Discount.

"Ellen, write the man a credit, please," he said.

"I don't want a credit," I said. "I want the recording, believe it or not. I just want a *good* recording."

"We have to make out a credit anyway."

So the girl he called Ellen began to write out a credit slip, which I was to take back in the store to obtain another album.

"Thanks," I said. "I don't usually look a gift horse in

the mouth, but I'm curious. How come you changed policy for me?"

"I've seen you in the store."

"Yeah. God! You must see a million people passing through here in a year."

"A million I wouldn't remember. A half-million is my limit."

Perhaps it was the occasion that brought it on, but it ended with my dating the girl he had called Ellen. I never did that sort of thing, move in on a girl with little more than a name to go on, but, as I say, there was that little happy spin for excuse.

"Can I believe him?" I asked her.

"You can believe him," she said.

I liked her face. There was a hazy something about her glance. Later I learned that the left eye was slightly off center. Esotropia, it was called. But what I saw in those initial moments was the narrow obliqueness she gave to her glance to compensate for that eye defect. And those finely wrought features. Not delicate. Ellen was not a delicate girl. But there were those clean lines and a certain *composure* to her face that made me want to ask what it was she knew, had done, or foresaw, that would account for such serenity.

"Where do you eat lunch?" I asked her.

"In places that serve food," she said.

"Do they have names? Give me a name. Better, give me a day, any day, and I'll be there."

She shook her head and gave me that narrow glance again. Then she said, "Call me."

"Where?"

"Here."

"Your name is Ellen," I said.

"Yours is George," she said.

We had an early lunch at a place near Carnegie Hall, a

publike place with very hard seats. After lunch, we walked back to our respective places of employment, a March wind buffeting our backs.

"I haven't seen *West Side Story* yet," I said. "Have you?"

"No."

"Don't you think we ought to see it together?" I said. "Seems like the auspicious thing to do."

She gave me her hazy glance. "Are you planning to buy tickets for both of us, or are you asking me to meet you there?" she asked.

"Hey."

"It was a little ambiguous."

"In the future, I'll try not to be ambiguous. I'll buy the tickets—for *both* of us—and I'll pick you up at your house, apartment, whatever, and drive you to the theater in style. Modest style, but style. Actually, I'm an old-fashioned gentleman. Where do you live?"

She lived in one of those giant complexes on the East Side. Stuyvesanttown. With her family. A mother, a father, a younger sister.

I remember announcing it to myself aloud, as one announced to oneself other life milestones, like "I'm no longer a virgin!" or "My God, I'm thirty!" This was equally profound. I said, "If she'll have me, I'm going to marry this girl!"

This after the transition of sex. I say "transition" because I believe that the relationship between a man and a woman does change after sex. I'm aware of everything said and thought to the contrary, but I still believe it. As my near-fatal (perhaps fatal) friend Kim said, "Sex just stands there, like a cranky child, getting in the way, until it's put to bed." It wasn't exactly that way with Ellen. In fact, it wasn't at all that way. I would have been willing to go along in our dry state of courtship for as long as Ellen thought proper, or wise.

I enjoyed being with her—her with clothes on—with lingering kisses in cars, in hallways, in my apartment. She did come to my apartment, but such evenings (or afternoons; I do remember a smoky autumn Sunday of drizzle, fireplace, and the Mozart recordings she had brought, her favorites) were more chaste than others, because the opportunity was too great. When she did it, *if* she did it, it would be not by default or surrender but by design. She never actually said this, but this is what I came to understand.

Patience? More effort? Less? Not that I was hotly in pursuit of that goal. As I said, what was was enough. That slightly off-center gaze. The esotropic haze. Go figure! There was removal, sorrow, mystery. The upward-tilting composure of her features. And a little tic, something I discovered on our second date, the *West Side Story* date: Her way of touching her tongue to her upper lip at moments (it seemed) when she was about to say something but decided not to; just an instant of hesitation, then that quick touch. All of it may have been trivial, meaningless, or a means of discovery. Like the Rosetta Stone.

"I'd like to hear you play," I said.

"Shall I strap a piano to my back?" she asked.

"I'll buy one," I said.

"That's very nice of you, but I'd wait if I were you," she said. "I'll try to arrange something."

What she arranged was not what I expected. I expected that she would arrange a visit with her family. Mama, Papa, Sis, that sequestered trio in Stuyvesanttown, about whom she said surprisingly little, although I asked, and she answered, but sparingly. I knew that her father was a union official in the garment trade. Arnold Feldman. I knew that her mother, Lily, was a hygienist in a dentist's office. I knew that her sister, Grace, was still going to school, studying English. She wanted to be a teacher. I saw the Feldman family in an ambient glow of intellect and forward-looking purpose. Children of the Haskalah, the Enlightenment. In any event, I was not yet invited to Stuyvesanttown.

I was invited instead to the school where Ellen studied. This was on another drizzly Sunday afternoon. She had obviously asked for permission, and she was given permission, but with a very definite time limit. At two-forty-five in the afternoon. For fifteen minutes. We walked into a room with a piano and a few chairs. I sat down in a chair. Ellen went to the piano. Without any introductory remarks or fidgeting, she began to play. I love music, but I'm no judge. That is, I haven't the training—nor, I suspect, the natural ear—for nuances, for the subtle ground between competence and excellence. She played (I later learned) the first movement of a Schubert sonata. It was soft, melodic, haunting. I allowed myself to imagine that she had chosen that movement because it best expressed what she was feeling . . . about us?

When she had finished, she closed the lid of the piano and got up. We walked wordlessly out of the room, out of the building, into the drizzle. It was part of that day's plan to see a movie. I hailed a taxi and told him where to go.

"That was very beautiful," I said. "The music and the way you played it. I wish I had the knowledge to tell you in just what way you were good, but I don't. I've tried to imagine you playing and all I ever got were three separate images—you, your hands, and the piano keys. There was never a sound accompaniment to my imaginings. Now that I've heard, you're more complete. It thrilled me. I'm not trying to be flattering. It did. I haven't got the language to say how or why it thrilled me, but it did."

She turned to me with her eyes all but closed and sought my mouth with hers. I took her hands. They were cold. It was a cold day, but I knew that the coldness of her hands had an inner source.

We went to the movie and then to an Italian bakery that served espresso to go with their pastry. It was only late September, but the weather was like late fall.

"Not a day for walking around," Ellen said.

"No."

"You're not far from here, are you?"

"No."

We went to my apartment on Jane Street and made love. I knew that the day had been planned toward that end. I also knew that Ellen was not a virgin. We made love a second time, and it was the second time that was successful for her. When I withdrew, she said, "Take that thing off." I did as she asked, dried myself with the sheet, and then she touched me there, a benedictory touch.

There was so palpably a story in that little ceremony that I said, "Tell me," and she understood.

She told me about her previous affair, her only affair, with a young man who had just completed his Ph.D. in history. His specialty was Jewish history. His problem was sex. He had only to touch her and he was more than halfway toward orgasm. He had only penetrated twice, and then more in a condition of completion than commencement.

"Were you in love with him?" I asked.

"Yes."

"He with you?"

"I think so."

"Then?"

"He became a Hasid," she told me. "He wanted me to marry him, but I would be a Hasid's wife—the *mikva,* the *shaitl,* everything."

"Did he think that would straighten things out sexually?"

Ellen turned in my fold-out sofa and looked at me in a thoughtful way. "Do you think that's what might have been behind it?" she asked.

"I don't know," I said. "Did you consider his proposal?"

"Not for long."

"Because?"

"I could accept the sexual period of adjustment," she said, "but not the other."

It was an indoors love affair. The streets that winter were painful passages from work to restaurant to movie to bed. It probably isn't true, but in retrospect it seemed as though it snowed every other day. The desire for warmth paced the other desire like a pair of eager runners. The lovemaking began long before our clothes were off, wherever we were, with looks, with touches, with quick, surreptitious kisses. We seemed to be engaged in a perpetual process, where each orgasm only punctuated the sexual narrative we were writing.

We invariably made love twice—at least twice, sometimes more. I didn't know until Ellen told me that she rarely achieved orgasm in that first round and that she rarely failed to achieve it in the second.

"Why's that?" I asked.

"I don't know, but please don't worry about it," she said.

"I'm not worried. I just want to know."

"I can't tell you why. It's just so. Don't you feel the difference?"

"I can't say that I do. What's the difference?"

The difference was that there was *something like* an orgasm the first time—a ghostly precursor—but it was the second time that the real thing happened.

"Why can't it happen the first time?" I still tried to get out of her.

Ellen was silent for some seconds, then said, "Let it be."

"Look, is there someone else?" I demanded.

"Of course not."

"What's so 'of course' about it? I don't know what kind of game I'm involved in here. Everything seems to be on hold. Is it me, my prospects, or you? I'm not asking you to become a Hasid, but I am asking you."

"You know there's no one but you," she said.

"Exactly! No one but me! But people usually come with other people. You've mentioned a few. You have a mother, a father, a sister. I've got the same set, only a brother, not a sister. People are curious. 'What are you doing with yourself these days, George?' I tell them I'm occupied with a girl by the name of Ellen, and they nod, and they look, and they wonder."

Ellen did that thing she always does under stress: She touched her upper lip with the tip of her tongue, and she veiled her eyes, and she allowed her features to settle into that Ellenesque composure. I had thought of it at the beginning as a mask to hide another Ellen, but I had seen it come and go with such frequency that I must have consigned that other Ellen to permanent oblivion. I decided there was no other Ellen—there was only this one with variations.

"Are you sure you want to marry me?" she asked.

"That's a question that's asked by someone who isn't sure she wants to be married," I said.

"It's true," she said. "I'm not sure. But not because of you. It's marriage itself. What will it be like, George?"

"I don't know. Maybe more sex. Maybe less. In any event, no going home after sex. Maybe the end of restlessness. It should get rid of a whole package of questions. Like, what am I going to do with my days? Like, who am I going to spend them with? Don't you want those questions settled?"

"Yes, I do. But you know what you're going to do with your days. What am I going to do with mine?"

"Whatever you want."

"Is that the way it will be? Can I be a pianist if I want?"

"What a question! You *are* a pianist. I would expect you

to go on being a pianist. Is there any question of that in your mind?"

"Yes."

"Why?"

"Because women bear children."

"Does that cancel everything else?"

She shook her head slowly, musingly. "No," she said.

I met her family and she met mine. We planned a marriage, and we were married, and the strong chemistry of these doings seemed to dissolve the question of what marriage would be like. It would be other days like these. Preparations and doings. Consultations and decisions. Gratifications and frustrations. Ellen insisted on a rabbi.

"If we're going to have a ceremony, let it be done by someone in the tradition."

Our honeymoon was an autumn tour of New England. I got rid of my secondhand piece of junk and bought a new, jade-green Plymouth. We drove up through Connecticut and Massachusetts, then through New Hampshire. Then we swung around and came back through Vermont and New York. We stopped at inns, hotels, and motels. We ate chowder and cheese and blueberry pie. We had baked beans and brown bread. We browsed in stores full of rust and time. We looked at the massed yellows, browns, golds, and blends too in between for naming. Ellen picked up one such leaf and turned it on its stem, tears in her eyes.

We stayed one night in an old house whose owner rented rooms to tourists. It had lacy curtains over the windows and lampshades like tutus. We tried to make love in the bed but the softness of it gave no support to our purpose. We sank and sank, and it became a kind of burlesque. We wound up on the floor, adding muffled laughter to the other noises we were making.

The next day, driving somewhere through the Green Mountains, Ellen said, "I can have a job in the city school system if I want."

"How come?"

"I made application some time ago. I can begin after New Year's."

"Would you want to do that? Teach? High-schoolers?"

"They told me they were eager to expand their music program. I have my certification."

I wonder if other men felt the way I did about the reality of marriage. I found something oddly charadelike about it, as if Ellen and I were trying to act out a situation known to us by hearsay. The marriages we knew, our own parents', didn't count. They were too well into their marriages to imagine what they might have been like as newlyweds. Besides, their histories were so different. The settled engagements of life weren't questioned. Ellen and I were the postwar, post-Holocaust generation. Something had become uncoupled in the line of inevitabilities. Marriage as yet seemed the only reasonable arrangement, but the inevitability was being questioned.

We bought a house in Forest Hills, because Ellen wanted to be free to practice at any hour, as fortissimo as she pleased. A brick house in Forest Hills, with a VA mortgage.

I suppose it would have to be called a period of adjustment, but I can't remember it as such. We were both very busy, that I do remember. I was by that time working in the main studio of the news division. I started out as an assistant to the director, but I asked for and got the opportunity to do research and writing. I was making good money. Ellen had her entry-level salary. We could easily afford the house. We could afford the Broadway shows, the concerts, the frequent dining out, the trip to Europe, the child we tried for, hoped for, got.

I asked, "Does this mean you're giving up the idea of being a concert pianist?"

"I gave that up a long time ago."

"No, you didn't. You never said you did."

"I didn't know I was obliged to make an announcement. Besides, it should have been apparent."

"In what way? How? You practice, almost every day."

"Oh, George."

"What?"

"A concert pianist doesn't practice *almost* every day. A concert pianist practices *every* day, for five, six, seven hours."

"I didn't know that."

I don't know why it was such a bemusing moment, but it was. I felt as if I were juggling several mental balls, a few of which floated up into the overhanging mist and got lost. I wanted to ask if it was her own sense of not being talented enough or of having to make deliberate choices. I wanted to ask if there was a residue of resentment about the choice she did make. I wanted to ask if there had been a moment of conscious choice or whether it was the usual putting off of decision until time itself determined fact.

"Did you know that when we got married?" I asked.

"Of course," she said.

She was like that. She would make decisions and then absorb them into her life without marking the time or place of their making. For her, it was like drawing a line in water. She didn't dramatize herself. When Jess was born, Ellen took over the motherhood role as if she'd been preparing for it all her life, when in fact I hadn't heard an apprehensive or anticipatory word throughout her pregnancy. I can't recall specifics, but during Jess's infancy it became clear that Ellen had read somewhere all the necessary information on feeding and bathing and handling. I saw her once expertly dunk an elbow in the baby tub before inserting the baby. I hadn't noticed her doing it before, but of course she had been doing it. Curious, I asked. I learned the name "Dr. Spock."

Ellen took a leave of absence after Jess's birth and then returned to her job in the school system, which she has kept ever since. Mrs. Schaeffer, a refugee who lived in an apartment house in the next street, became part of the family. Much more than a baby-sitter, Mrs. Schaeffer was governess and tutor. She inserted small portions of German and French in Jess's daily ingestion of language. Mrs. Schaeffer had lost several families in Germany. She was never clear about it—perhaps couldn't be—but her delicate, waving hands conjured scenes of carnage. She died the year those Arab terrorists killed the Israeli Olympic athletes. A surprising brother showed up at the funeral. A wealthy man. Something to do with animal glands and pharmaceuticals. We thought that he must surely be the source who made up the financial shortfall in Clara Schaeffer's marginal existence, but something he said that day denied it. She had made it on her own somehow. Doing odd jobs, with us, with others.

I think of Mrs. Schaeffer now because she was the one who had suddenly emerged, sibyllike, to warn me to be "careful." . . . "Now you must be careful, Mr. Light," she said one afternoon when I was at home working on my private eye, Nazi-hunting serial.

"Careful about what?"

"About your wife. About Mrs. Light."

"What are you talking about, Mrs. Schaeffer? Careful in what way?"

"You know, you know."

I didn't know, I didn't know, and all my efforts to get it

out of Mrs. Schaeffer were unavailing. There was no other woman in my life. Christ, I was at home a hell of a lot more than Ellen was. I was the thoroughly domesticated male trying to make money for his family. So I kept at Mrs. Schaeffer about her cryptic remark, but all I could get were little moues and headshakes and utterances about "Keeping one's eyes open" and "Not to take things for granted."

"Are you by any chance having an affair?" I asked Ellen.

"If I were, it wouldn't be by chance," she said. "Why do you ask? Are you having one?"

"You know damn well I'm not. It's just that Clara is full of strange warnings these days."

"About what?"

"Well, about you."

Ellen thought for a moment and then put on her own enigmatic, inward smile. "Maybe it isn't me she's warning you about," she said.

"Is she warning me about me?"

"Possibly."

"But what am I doing that I shouldn't be doing? And who the hell is Mrs. Schaeffer anyhow to be setting up shop as family counselor?"

"Now, George—"

"Christ, this is really 'Now, George' season, isn't it!"

We were going through a bad time. My book on television had bombed badly, but that hadn't posed any threat to family security. There was more than enough money put away, and I could tell by the back and forthing going on at the network that my private eye series would be taken. It hadn't been yet, and knowing TV, I knew the pitfalls. There was always the chance that someone in those endless upper chambers would shoot it down, but the rumor in my bones was that it would go.

That didn't make me content. I kept turning to Ellen for

encouragement, but it wasn't there for me. Not this time. Pressed, she reminded me that I had myself said that TV trivializes, must trivialize, and this was not a subject for trivialization. I said I was planning to get some moral bite into it, and she said she hoped I would. Of course, I didn't. As soon as it was accepted, the seriousness was quick-marched into mindless violence and the moral bite into sexual nibbling.

Nevertheless, it has always seemed to me that Ellen understood the margins within which I must work. There is a wide practical streak in her. One must make money. She never argued with that. She did everything to assist me in my money-making activities. During the early days, she listened intently to my tales of the organizing and politicking around the shows on which I worked. I had much to tell. Interesting stuff. Guest stars, well-known names, the astonishing vulgarity of some, the kindness of others. When I rewrote the script of a courtroom drama that had just about drowned itself in its own forensic spaghetti, Ellen said that this is what I should be doing. And I did. When I decided that my career needed a turn, that I wanted to write a book about TV, Ellen encouraged that, too, understanding the risk, but sensing along with me the excitement and the lure in the wind that was taking me.

Never demonstrative. Never shrill in her approvals or disapprovals. That angled, hazy glance of hers that had so drawn me that day in the discount record store became the distinctive, elusive emblem of my marriage to this woman. Those nice, precise features, the careful listening, listening to every word I was saying, touching her upper lip with her tongue, considering her words before speaking, that has become the domestic frieze engraved by time.

I suppose that says something. Sure it does. My talking, her listening. Was it that she *chose* not to say much about her own career, her own progress, her own doings? I don't know. I can't remember a single occasion—in hot conflict or cool reflection—when we consciously commented on the state of our marriage. I do remember pulling at Ellen from time to time, urging her to tell me more about the kids at school, the programs she was involved in, the incidents. She remarked that I did so only when I thought there was some material I could use. Was that true? Yes and no. Not *only*. The fact that some utility had crept into the impulse didn't entirely debase the impulse. It's true that in the moil of my own activities, I often lost sight of Ellen's, but when reminded I sincerely wanted to know, insisted on knowing. At times, she told. At other times, she seemed reluctant to say. I put it down to our different natures. Dear God, people *do* have different natures, even husbands and wives. I put it down to the intrinsically different natures of what we were doing. Mine was a more talky kind of business. Mine did excite curiosity, gossip, intrigue. Hers (she so often declared) was so repetitive that talking about it would be more work than pleasure.

"Maybe you ought to get out of it," I said more than once. "Practice more. Be with Jess more. Maybe find a job outside of teaching, outside of music. You could, you know."

"What makes you think so?"

"You have charisma. People instinctively trust you, easily relate to you."

"Do you?"

"Why would I say it?"

"Perhaps because you *watch* other people."

"What does that mean?"

"Oh . . . nothing. George, it has its compensations. It can be fun. Occasionally I feel sorry for myself. Don't take it too seriously."

I didn't take it too seriously. Everybody is entitled to a

self-pitying jag. Didn't I know? I didn't take it too seriously because it was clear to me that she didn't want to do anything else.

Was it *The Search*? Truly, I don't think so, although it was when I began writing that—sometimes in the office, sometimes at home—that I began to feel the removal. *But there was an explanation for that!* Ellen didn't like it. It was as simple as that. At least that's what I told myself. She couldn't get with it on moral grounds, and therefore it was just as well that we didn't talk about it. She didn't want to hear about it and she had no suggestions to offer. We talked about Jess and the madness in Vietnam. Plenty to talk about.

After this therefore because of this? After the distance Ellen had put between herself and me, therefore *because* of the distance did the restlessness set in, the discontent, the affair with Kim?

I don't know. If there was ever a time for me to be honest with myself . . . for how am I ever going to say a meaningful word on men and women if I don't allow myself to see things clear and whole? As if I could ever say the definitive word on men and women!

But that's the mission, isn't it? So I might as well face the fact that the Kim thing might have happened in any event. Not because of the distance between Ellen and me, but because of the long-kept image of me . . . and me. *The Search* had been alchemized into a weekly serving of shit. I had stopped writing for it. I was writhing around at the bottom of a self-deprecating pit. I didn't like my image. Worst of all, I had begun to sense my limits.

I don't remember even thinking it to myself, but somewhere in the unexamined files was undoubtedly the stupid notion that a conquest of some kind might polish up an old illusion.

14

"When did you get home?" I asked Jess.

"A couple of days ago."

"Did you graduate?"

"I told you—I still need four credits."

"When am I going to see you?"

"Whenever you want."

"How about a visit here? Come out here. See my *pied à New Jersey*."

"Okay. Tell me how to get there."

"You got the use of a car?"

"I use Mom's. You know that."

Jess found my Jersey dwelling funny, particularly the slanted ceilings. She said it reminded her of that silent movie, *The Cabinet of Dr. Caligari*. I said that it had its virtues. For one thing, I could never fall out a window when I was sleep-walking. I would bump my head into one of those slants before doing so. "You never sleepwalk," she said. "How would you know?" I said. Beyond the comedy was a grotesque but accurate symbolism. This canted hutch truly reflected the way things were: a cockeyed burrow for a time out of joint.

The weather had turned warm and Jess was wearing one of those white puffy outfits that look cool and unpressable. She looked wonderful in it. Most things look wonderful on her. How can things *not* look wonderful on you when you're young and slim and pretty and—what?—radiant? Was there something radiant about Jess? It seemed so to me.

I took her to dinner in a restaurant I had found in the neighborhood, an Italian restaurant whose excellence I had already sampled. Terrific lasagna and a veal parmigiana without blemish.

"I think you're going to like this," I said. "I can wholeheartedly recommend the lasagna and the veal parm."

("Parm" was a family trinket. I had coined it light-years ago and Jess had adopted it, made it standard.)

So what about the four credits? How was she going to make them up? Jess (buttering a chunk of crispy bread) wasn't sure about that. It seemed ridiculous to set up shop again in Ann Arbor just for four lousy credits. Agreed, but how else can it be done? She was working on that. She was in touch with the professor and had suggested several other themes for an honors paper. She was waiting to hear from him. If he approved one of the themes—she was sure he would approve *one* of them—she would work on it through the summer.

"Won't that screw things up?" I asked.

"How so?"

"That year abroad."

Jess shrugged, tipped her head, lightly dismissed "that year abroad." Well, well. Yesterday's heartbreak, today's insouciance. How about that? Since she had to make up the four credits anyway, she couldn't go abroad this year, and now she wasn't at all sure that she wanted to do graduate work. She said all this with the downward-gazing, hand-busy abstraction of a hungry young lady working on a yummy plate of antipasto. I decided at last that there was a bit too much abstraction.

"What's going on, Jess?"

"What do you mean?"

"I mean that I thought that the graduate work was settled. I thought you were going to sign on for that in any event, European trip or not."

"I don't recall that it was a settled thing," she said. "It was just an option."

"That isn't the way I recall it," I said. "I'm more than a little puzzled about the way you're giving up on that TV idea. I thought that you were really on to something there. The effect of personality on the news. That's high-grade stuff. That was a challenge, I thought, worthy of Jessica Light. You were pretty gung-ho about it last December."

The antipasto still usurped her attention, so that she wasn't looking at me when she said, "You know, I'm surprised you didn't kill that dumb idea on the spot. You must have seen the impossibility."

"I didn't think it was a dumb idea," I said. "I thought it was a smart, ambitious idea. I saw there would be difficulties, but I didn't think it was impossible. I thought I made it clear that I didn't think it was impossible. What's the matter, cold feet?"

"A clearer mind," she said. "First of all, the intangibles of personality can never be given any statistical evaluation—"

"So it can't. So what? Who says it has to be evaluated statistically?"

"—and secondly, even if one *could* evaluate it in any way, subjectively or statistically, how would it differ from any other kind of reporting? Once you get past the style of the individual, there's the event itself, and each viewer's predisposition toward that event cancels out personality."

What she was saying made sense of a kind, but it didn't sound like *her* sense. Nor was the *sound* of that sense her sound. In the past when Jess gave up on a thing she usually became peevish, sounding slightly nasal, slightly whiny. It didn't last very long, but Jess in defeat was not a Joan of Arc. Like that time in Denver, when she told me about Bryan Daniels. The suspicion of another hand at work had been implanted, but I couldn't say anything about it. I wasn't absolutely sure. Besides, Jess was getting more sophisticated by the day. Richer in reasoning and expression. What I was hearing now might be the latest Jess.

But something other than words was making me think that Jess was into a new dispensation. No more year abroad, no more TV news analysis, no last semester for those four credits. Something was going on. Just look at her. Jessica Light at her very best. Clear eyes, sun-tinted cheeks. And what else? Definitely something else. Confidence? Yes, definitely. A confidence you could almost weigh in your hand. A settled reserve. She looked like a cardplayer with an unbeatable hand.

I had ordered the veal marsala, just to see if the excellence was menu-wide. It was. I sopped up the superb sauce with some bread. Jess had gone for the parm. Obviously a hit. I said nothing. More veal, more bread. Jess glanced up at me. She caught my eye. She knew I was waiting.

"Have you seen Mom yet?" she asked.

"Wouldn't you know if I had?"

"She said something about your coming to the *West Side Story* thing."

"I've received a ticket."

"And will you come?"

"Certainly. Are you going to be there?"

"Yes, I will . . . with a friend."

Ah! A friend. The enigmatic cloudbank began to roll away like reverse, speeded-up photography. I could see all of last winter's projects fast-folding their petals.

"And who is this friend?"

"His name is Andrews—Neil—Neil Andrews."

I looked at her, half smiled at the way she had fumbled the name, like an expert juggler pretending clumsiness. She returned my look in the same inept way. What was going on? So she had a new boyfriend. So what? She had never been nervous about boyfriends in the past. Or *was* it nervousness? Maybe something else. Maybe it was a brimming agitation whose overflow looked like nervousness.

"So how did you like the parm?" I asked.

"Super," she said.

"And how's life, Jess?"

She put down her fork and knife and leaned forward, taking in a deep, audible breath. Here goes. She had hesitated because she wanted to see if there was any reaction on my part to the name. It was possible I would recognize the name. Should I? Well, Neil was active in politics. He had been on the New York Democratic Committee during the last presidential election. He had appeared on TV. He was a lawyer, but his main interest was in politics. Right now he was part of a team that was preparing the party platform for the next election.

"My goodness," I said. "Where did you meet him?"

"In Ann Arbor. In April. He was part of a panel sponsored by the Poli Sci department. He was sort of shuttling between Chicago and Detroit at the time, for both his law firm and the Democratic committee. I met him in Detroit a couple of times. That is, he invited me to some of the political functions there, because he knew I was interested. . . ."

"I see," I said, seeing perhaps more than she wanted me to see. "And was it Neil Andrews who set you straight on the effect of TV personalities in news broadcasting?"

"I did discuss it with him."

I felt a swell of resentment. My experience and encouragement were apparently very small candles in the sun of Neil Andrews. This resentment touched a button of memory that produced in sharp detail a TV program I had helped produce as long ago as the last election, a time before the Denver move. That, too, was a panel—a debate—and one of the debaters was a tall, good-looking, Waspy type who displayed what I thought was a remarkable storage tank of facts. Bills enacted, bills voted down. Names of officials, their past statements and voting records. I remember the man because I had studied him closely at the time, thinking how unlike him I was, how I had always disliked that kind of voluminous recall, thinking that people who committed that much to memory were somehow suspect. I remember also thinking that this fellow would probably show up again in the news because he had the kind of savvy and good looks that trades beautifully on the tube. Sort of in the John Lindsay style.

I didn't tell Jess that I had actually seen the man, had a few words with him, seemed to recall that he was married, seemed to have plucked out of the occasion the words ". . . any more than I would want my own children . . ." How young is young? Forty is still young. Quite young. These days. I said, "So you met him in Ann Arbor and now he's your companion at a high school musical produced by your mother. That's interesting. Wouldn't you say that's interesting?"

"Please don't be sarcastic, Dad."

"Please don't be devious, daughter."

She closed her eyes for an instant, and the smile on her face was so much like Ellen's that a psychic lurch almost derailed my sense of time. That secret-keeping smile that I had always imagined Ellen taking indoors for safekeeping. But this was not Ellen, this was Jess, and Jess had her own system of signals. Ellen's features conformed to her smile. Jess's did not. Jess's features were busily engaged in the job of containment.

"I'm not trying to be devious," she said.

"All right, then tell me what's going on."

I could see it: an elaborately fragile construct of resolves collapsing in on itself.

"We're kind of—involved," she said.

I said to myself: *Careful, careful, careful!* I said to her: "Are you in love with him?"

"I guess so."

"He with you?"

"He says so."

Then I told her that the name did ring a bell, that I had written the script for a panel show on which Neil Andrews had appeared, that I remembered him, that I had been impressed by him.

"Are you sure it was Neil?"

"Tall. About six-foot-three. Dolichocephalic."

"What?"

"Long-headed type. Dirty blond. Nice smile. Staggering memory."

Jess's blue eyes clouded even more with the smoke of incense. "So you really met him," she said.

"I really think so. I take away something else from that coincidence. Perhaps I shouldn't mention it, but I seem to remember that he gave some evidence of being a married man. At least was at the time."

"Yes, he's married," Jess said.

"And that he had children."

"Two."

"And with all of that he finds time to go to high school musicals."

"He really wants to see it," Jess said. "He's very community-conscious. He wants to see what's being done at the local level. He says if you don't participate in these things, you never think to talk about them."

"That's probably true," I said. "How did he find out about this particular local-level thing?"

"I told him, naturally."

"So his participations sometimes cover more than one base."

"Please."

"Aw, come on, Jess!"

We both retreated to zabaglione and silence. I regretted the outburst, but I didn't feel the least apologetic about the cause. What was she telling me? That she was involved with a man who was married and had two children? *Mazeltov!* A little *potchlein* for Neil Andrews. One man's meat was another man's daughter. I could accept that—but everything down the drain? Studying abroad, her TV idea, which I still thought exciting, challenging, doable. And there was more than a little bitterness that my own offering of seasoned judgment was kicked over so readily at a word from neat Neil, the dolichocephalic whiz kid.

"How come Jewish boys don't interest you at all?" I asked. "As far back as I can remember, they've all been *shagitzes.*"

"Dad! Are you serious?"

"I know, I know. I'm aware of everything I've ever said about stupid prejudices, and I know that we've done practically nothing to foster a special consciousness about being Jewish, but it's very strange. One hears so much about gentile girls marrying Jewish boys. The nice Jewish boy. The good provider. How come some nice Jewish boy hasn't crossed your path?"

"How do you know none has?"

"Good point. I don't know. Has one?"

Jess nodded, looking like a young woman who was confronting a peculiar truth about herself for the first time. "I've never really thought about it," she said.

"Is it worth a thought?" I asked.

Jess shrugged. "I'm not sure that it is," she replied. "Maybe it's just a case of circumstance. Really, Dad, how does one answer a question like that? You said yourself that you never made a point of it. Neither did Mom." She looked away, out the window of the restaurant, where car headlights dipped down, then up, following some deformity in the road. "And anyway," she said, "I believe the only hope we have is getting rid of all these separate clans. The religious clans, the racial clans, the national clans . . ."

"Are you saying you make your romantic choices for idealistic reasons?"

"Would that be such a bad thing to say?"

"Not at all—but would it be true?"

With her head still averted, Jess smiled. Now she turned, looked directly at me. "Jewish men can be overwhelming," she said, "particularly if they're ambitious . . . and clever . . . and if there's more than one career to consider."

"Like someone you know?" I asked.

"Like someone I know," she said.

"Did I overwhelm you?" I asked.

"I wasn't married to you," she said.

"Do you think I overwhelmed your mother?"

"You were a little overwhelming at times. Not in a tyrannical way ... Oh, look, this is silly. I really have no answer to your question. I'm not conscious of having deliberately rejected Jewish boys. I'm not sure there was anything unconscious working either. It's just the way things happened."

I nodded. I had grown uneasy with the subject. We were like two moviegoers—the *only* two—in a darkened movie house, watching the same film. But from what different perspectives? Drawing what different conclusions? Statistics were one thing, but Jessica Light wasn't being a journalist at this critical moment. She was being the daughter of George and Ellen Light, remembering her at times troubled but mostly happy, totally unstatistical, profoundly private life.

And would it have made any difference if Neil Andrews were Neil Abrams, rising young golden-tongued assemblyman, married, two children, member of the classy East Side Beth El congregation? Not the slightest. I would probably have been even more pissed. Possibly because the pretenses of Jewish virtue are more familiar to me. Ah, but what the hell! Who needs this? Shouldn't the George Light mess be settled before new ones are put into place?

"So what is it going to be?" I demanded, hearing more anger in my voice than I had intended. "Secret meeting in hotels? 'I love you, darling, and I'm going to divorce my wife as soon as it's politically, maritally, and financially possible, but in the meantime please be patient and available. And for God's sake, *discretion*! Remember what an important man I am. You wouldn't want to ruin my career, would you?' "

Jess removed her gaze again, looking off into a far corner of the room. She said, coldly, "Whatever gave me the idea you'd be understanding?"

More self-cautioning. I was in no position to take the high ground in a morality contest. "I *am* understanding," I argued. "I understand all too well how something like this could happen. And I understand, perhaps even better than you do, the complications. Two children, Jess. He may be truly out of love with his wife and truly in love with you, but there are those two kids. If he's at all what he appears to be, then he's a large paternal presence. The *kids*, Jess."

"It happens every day," she said.

"The statistics also show how miserably it happens. I'm thinking of you. How unfair to you."

"Why unfair to me?"

"Because it's addition for him and subtraction for you. It's got to be, even with the best intention in the world. He goes on being a husband, a father, an ascending, first-magnitude star. You have to put a stop to everything in your life in order to accommodate somebody else's. He moves, orates, meets people, does important, satisfying things. You wait, dodge, do nothing."

"Why do you say that?"

"Because it's true, isn't it?"

Jess kept her angry gaze riveted to that distant corner. Of course it was true . . . *but so stupidly, unfeelingly understood!* Those weren't blank spaces I was describing but bowers of anticipation, fragrant with honeysuckle and lilacs. Didn't I know? Yes, I knew, but not being in love with Mr. Neil Andrews, being the father of the unbride, I could also project myself onto that bare plateau for a hindsight look.

Impulsively, I reached out and put my hand on hers. It was cold. Ach! Penalties were already being exacted! She turned and looked at my hand on hers, then at me. I think my face reflected what I was feeling: regret and tenderness. "Listen," I said, "I know that if you weren't deeply into this thing, you wouldn't be telling me about it. But what shall I tell you, my Jess? Good? Fine? A wonderful life experience? I can't say that because I don't believe it will be. I hope I'm wrong. I don't know the man—and, I'm afraid, I don't really know you. I just love you. You had wonderful things lined up. If they've got to be put aside for the present, then so be it. You're young. All I'm asking is that you don't use yourself up making futile plans."

That reached her. I saw her eyes stare inwardly at potential sorrow. She put her hand on top of mine, then removed them both.

"Why do you say you don't know me?" she asked.

"Do you think I do?"

"You must or you wouldn't have said 'Don't use yourself up making futile plans.' I've thought of that. I do love Neil. It's true that you don't know him. He hasn't said any of the things you think he has. Hasn't even intimated them. But you do know me. I don't want to use myself up on futile plans."

"I hope to God."

"And speaking of plans," she said, changing her tone along with her subject, "what about yours?"

"You mean Mother?"

"Yes."

"I'm coming to the *West Side Story* wingding. I haven't seen Mother yet because—well—I guess because I wanted to give us both plenty of time to think about—what?—about what it is we have to think about, I guess. Like, here it is. We've been putting off something for so long that the intermission has become a way of life. It's peaceful, but so is death."

"What are you hoping for?" Jess asked. "What would you want?"

"That's an odd question."

"Is it? I don't know. I'd like to hear it from you."

"Hear what from me? That I would like to resume life with my wife? I would. But you must know something, Jess, or you wouldn't be asking these questions. Don't you think you ought to tell me?"

"I know that Mother has changed," she said.

"Haven't I changed, too?"

"Yes, very much."

"How do you see us? Two very different people with a shared history?"

"Something like that."

"Maybe that's the thing needed."

"Maybe," she said.

15

The role of Maria was played by "Dee Hurvitz" and the role of Tony by "Tony Zapapas." Hurvitz and Zapapas. The "Tony" was fate's gratuity. Miss Hurvitz was peach-ripe. Not exactly the shy, virginal Maria of the story. Nor was her voice the limpid, tremulous thing it should have been. But it was a voice—large, untrained, and unabashed. Tony was an engaging Greek kid with a pleasant, round face. He, too, had a nice voice. He sang with rock inflections and his own very distinctive body movements.

The racial tensions were black and white instead of Hispanic and white. Bernardo was Bubba. Instead of the Latin dances, the kids did disco. The dance numbers were raggedly impromptu and some of the lyrics were transposed into a rap rhythm. Two of the black boys did a great break number. The orchestra was sustained by two or three players who could hold a melodic line, while the rest of the strings and brass pumped out a rhythmic accompaniment.

I enjoyed it. It was done with amateur enthusiasm and a marvelous use of available means. The audience was on its feet at the end, applauding the effort, the effect, the sheer ebullience of the thing. The kids took their bows and then signaled for Mrs. Light to come on stage. She did. This was the first time I'd seen her since last summer. She was wearing a blue suit with a corsage. Not mine. The kids in the cast, I later learned, had chipped in for that. Was she heavier? Yes, she was. And she was doing her hair differently. Longer but simpler, gathered in the back.

Although I had given myself plenty of time, I had arrived when the orchestra was starting in on the overture. The traffic over the Triboro had held me up. I didn't have a chance to scout the place before the show, and there was no intermission. A little over one hour of raw but infectious showtime. I began to look as soon as the lights went on. Oddly enough, I spotted the spottable Neil Andrews before I saw Jess. He had the kind of height and presence that suggest recognition before the fact. Good posture, a vaguely old-fashioned way of arranging his hair: modified F. Scott Fitzgerald. And there was something Fitzgerald-ish about his clean-cut face. I asked myself whether this was a man my Jess could fall in love with, and I replied that I was an ass.

There was Jess, not exactly by his side, but close by. She was wearing a loose, light outfit. Whatever it was, I didn't think it was ideal for her coloring. But what do I know? I began working my way toward the front, finally reaching Jess.

"Well, how'd you like it?" I asked.

"It was *fun!*" she said. "Didn't you think so?"

"You bet I did. Great fun."

It was one of those long, sweaterlike things she was wearing. Pale yellow. And a skirt. Her hair seemed more than usually shot with coppery glints. I could see she was hesitating. Finally she reached for something that materialized in the person of Neil Andrews.

"Neil, this is my father. Dad, this is Neil Andrews."

"Hello, Mr. Light," he said. "I understand we've met before."

"Not seriously," I said. "I only handed you a paper."

"Well, I'm pleased to meet you again."

I said I was pleased to meet him and we shook hands. His handshake was masterful, of course. Large, warm, dry, hinting at all the distinguished games he played. Tennis? Golf? Sculling? Lacrosse? I don't know when it began, but as far back as I can remember I have examined a man's tie (if he was wearing one) on first acquaintance. Naturally, Neil Andrews was wearing one. It was a blue tie of generous length and discreet pattern. Small, overall dots on blue silk. I could wear a tie like that. From the tie, I go to the man. This man was wearing a pin-striped suit and a checkmating smile. He was handsome, all right. Not the kind of handsomeness I thought Jess would go for, but, as I said, what do I know?

That smile. It wasn't just the smile itself but my knowledge of what that smile contained. It contained *his* knowledge that he was having an affair with my daughter, that he was married, that he had two kids, that he was a man with political ambitions who must cover his public ass because his private life was, or could be, a matter of remorseless scrutiny. Politicians talk a clean line, and when the dirty linen shows up, it's all the more shocking. So I must say, in all fairness, that Neil Andrews's smile was a work of art. It admitted everything with perfect candor. It concealed everything with perfect discretion.

"I'm trying to get over to Mom," Jess said.

"I'll join you," I said.

Ellen was surrounded by students in the cast who were happily and ostentatiously still wearing their makeup, and by the parents of the students, who were just as ostentatiously wearing their excitement. I saw that the black kid who played the role of Bubba was wearing a sprinkling of silver dust on his blue eyeshadow. I also gathered from his speech and gestures that he was gay. Odd that it hadn't come through during the performance. I heard Ellen say, "I'd love to do it again, and I know the kids would, but where?" Her voice was the same, measured, cool voice that had sporadically escaped my memory these past two years. Jess, Neil Andrews, and I had to stay on the outer perimeter of that congratulatory crowd for many minutes before we finally got to Ellen.

Jess kissed her. Neil shook her hand. I didn't know quite what to do, so I just stood there and smiled. Then, moved by her own smile, I said, "That was a winner," and I kissed her.

"Hello, George," she said. "Tell me the truth. Was it awful?"

A bubble of pleasure rose in me. She had always valued my judgment, had always admitted valuing it, even in the worst of times. She had once said to me, "It's amazing to me that you've never tried to play an instrument. You have such a good ear." She had valued my judgment in other things as well. It was in the area of human relations that she had lost faith. Not too trustworthy there. I remember something else she had once said: "You have trouble imagining other lives."

I wonder if that's true. Sometimes I think yes, sometimes no. I can imagine other lives, all right. Perhaps what she meant was that there was a want of empathy for what I had imagined. And speaking of imagining, I know I could never have imagined this scene: daughter with her tall, new, married, insuperable lover. And this woman, my wife, who (as Jess had warned) had changed, and who had indeed changed.

"Everyone is so reluctant to go," Ellen said. "I think I ought to make the first move. George, will you come over to the house? Neil?"

"Thank you, Mrs. Light, but I really must be getting on," Neil said. "But I do want to thank you. That was a treat. It really was." He shook her hand again, then turned to me. "I'm very pleased to have met you, Mr. Light." He gave me another large-handed shake.

We made our way out of the auditorium. Ellen leading, the rest following. A lobby, through one of those push-handle doors, into the parking lot. Jess went with Neil to his car. I stayed with Ellen. I felt as if I were being taught the first moves of a new game. I was being informed of the rules as I went along. Do I leave my car here and go with Ellen? Is Jess going to vanish with Neil Andrews? If so, where? He has a family, for Christ sake! Isn't he expected home? Shall I go find my car and just drive back to my slanty-roofed, precrisis rabbit hutch?

A spotlight from the school building threw an inadequate cone of light over the lot.

"Is Jess coming back with us or . . . what?" I asked.

"She's coming now," Ellen said.

There she was, with her own fine composure and an invincible smile. She said, "Why don't I go with Dad? There's that big detour because of the broken water main. You can get fouled up in the dark."

"Good idea," said Ellen. "I'll see you back at the house."

I got into my car, Jess next to me. I started my car, pulled out of the lot. I know this neighborhood cold. I've lived in it since before Jess could speak her own name. Not very likely that I'd get lost in it. But quiet. Go along. Maybe Jess wants these few moments alone with me. And why am I not triply pleased that Jess chose to go with me rather than with her mother? I guess because it violated the scenario I had been intermittently creating for days. Alone with Ellen. Talking to Ellen. Finding out what there was to find out from Ellen. Two characters only. Ellen and George Light.

"Well?" Jess asked.

"The play? Your mother? Neil Andrews?"

"Any," she said. "All. Start with Neil first."

"Ask me a question."

"What did you think?"

"I thought he was tall, handsome, and very self-possessed. I thought he managed a complex situation like the Secretary General of the United Nations. I thought he was wearing a nice blue tie."

"Dad, did you like him?"

"Ah, Jess, don't ask me a question like that. I could very well have liked this man—yes, I'm sure I could—under different circumstances. I think he would be my kind of man. Direct, sincere, courteous, considerate. All good things. But I can't see him in that kind of light. I see him as the man who, with the best intentions in the world, with love and gentleness, might hurt you. That gives me a very skewed image. Do you see what I mean?"

"Yes," Jess said. "Take a right at the next corner."

"Please don't be mad if I can't celebrate this thing as you'd like me to, Jess. May I ask a question?"

"I know your question," she said.

"Well, what's the answer?"

"He's been married for twelve years. His wife is a snob. She comes from a very wealthy family and she has nothing to do with Neil's political life. She hates the people he associates with."

"Including you?"

"She doesn't know about me."

"That's what I was trying to find out," I said. Then, after about five preparatory heartbeats, I asked, "So what? A divorce?"

"Not yet," Jess said. "Not now."

"But you'll stay put in the meantime," I said.

"Yes."

I would need a surgeon's skill to separate out the tangle of nerves I took with me into the house, my former house, my former life. The first recoil was against the sight and sound of the place. A party! Of course! No one told me there was going to be a party, but what more natural thing? And why should anybody have bothered to tell *me*? Life goes on in your absence, buddy. People make their own plans. There was a stereo blaring and about a dozen strangers with glasses in their hands and smiles on their faces. Ellen put on her own semisurprised smile. I saw her do that thing with her lip and a heavy visceral something moved inside me.

Lots of introductions. Mr. So-and-So and Miss So-and-So, the school principal and assistant principal. And this was Mr. Whozis, from Grants Development down on Livingston Street. . . . "Did you do something there, George?" . . . Yes, I did, indeed I did, a news program on education when there was widespread fear that schools were becoming fortresses of organized ignorance. And this was Katie Delgado, who taught Spanish and French in the same school where Ellen taught music.

I learned that this party was taking place tonight because there was going to be another party tomorrow, by and for the kids in the cast, and Ellen would be attending that, too. Tonight's party was strictly in honor of Ellen, the work she had done, the tireless organization and coaching that had culminated in this wonderful evening. At first, a single large celebration had been planned, everybody together, but older and wiser heads (Ellen's among them) thought that the kids had best be given a day to cool off. They would want to celebrate themselves, and rightly.

"Did you know there was going to be a party here?" I asked Jess.

"I helped arrange it."

"Then why didn't you tip me off when we were in the car?"

"Because I wanted it to be your party, too. A homecoming party."

"Was your mother aware of that aspect of the party?"

"Of course."

I'm not sure whether it was the strange moves of the evening or Jess's sweet planning that accounted for the sting of tears. I kissed her.

It's a curious business to look at a chair, a coffee table, a lamp, a sofa, one thing after another, artifacts that annotate your life, and while knowing the history that surrounds each piece, feeling estranged from that history. It was a sort of bankruptcy, all your goods impounded, awaiting auction. You're like the citizen of a defeated nation, your property occupied by the conquering army . . .

Hey, come off that shit, Light! You're talking about wood and fabric! That a fact? Well, it so happens that I made love to that woman, that one there, the one with the light-blue suit and the orchid, the one who's spoken about half a dozen words to me all evening, right there on the carpet—there!—right in front of the coffee table. I remember the occasion very well. Big party on the publication of my book. Not here. In Manhattan. Got home at three in the morning. We'd forgotten to draw the curtains. Moonlight streaming through the front window. Stripped down right here, in this room, letting our clothes scatter and fall like leaves in a high wind, doing it right there, an authentic second-time orgasm on the first booze-and-moon-drenched try. . . .

"Aren't you going to eat something, Mr. Light?" asked the woman whom Ellen had introduced to me as—what?—Kitty Donegan?—no, it wasn't Irish—she didn't *look* Irish. "The quiche is wonderful," she said. "I made it myself. And those Swedish meatballs."

"Thanks, I will, a little later. I'm having too much fun with this drink. Were you at the show, Miss . . ."

"Delgado. Katie Delgado."

"Right! Katie Delgado."

"Yes, I was there," she said, "but I left a little before the end so I could get things started here."

"That was nice of you. Have you known Ellen long?"

"Oh, about six, seven years."

"You teach at the school?"

"Spanish and French."

"Right, right. Ellen said that."

She was a fairly attractive woman, with tight-knurled hair (somewhat reminiscent of Laurie, the sorrowing girl who couldn't reconcile her talent to her fate). This woman's hair was a sort of autumn mulberry. She had broad features and one of those light, anticipatory smiles. A look of friendliness, a look that encouraged contact, that promised that things were a bit brighter than you thought them to be. But it was the tinge of her skin that stirred something way back. It didn't take me long to place: Marie Angelini. That burnt sienna tincture that had seeped permanently into time. And what did that mean? Nothing.

"I understand you've been living in Denver," she said.

"That's right," I said, thinking that if she understood that, then this was someone whom Ellen trusted. Ellen was not a woman to go around handing out her private life like calling cards.

"I have relatives in Denver," Katie said. "My mother's brother and his whole family. They live in Lakewood. Do you know Lakewood?"

"I sure do."

"I visited them a couple of years ago. In the summer. I was surprised at how hot it was there. I had the mistaken idea that Denver was up in the mountains and therefore would be cool. Did you enjoy living in Denver?"

"Very much. It's a lovely city and I had a nice apartment with a view of the mountains. My daughter, Jess, visited there recently."

"Yes, I know."

"Are you a dancer, Miss Delgado?"

"*Katie*, please. Why do you ask?"

"Something about the way you carry yourself. You have a dancer's build."

"That's very perceptive of you, Mr. Light—"

"George, *please*."

"George . . . Yes, I do dance. I love dancing. Thai dancing—" and she performed one of the Oriental head movements, that sinuous side-to-side maneuver.

"Are you teaching my husband royal ballet?" Ellen asked as she joined us.

"I didn't say a word about dancing, and he guessed that I was a dancer," Katie said. "Did you tell him?"

"I've scarcely spoken to him all evening," Ellen said.

"Well, now, here's your chance," Katie Delgado said, waving and walking away.

So there we were. Ellen asked if I had had something to eat, and I said not yet but not to worry, I would, later. I looked around and saw Jess in another corner of the room, looking softly incandescent in that yellow outfit. She was talking to the school principal, Mr. . . . what's-his-name? . . .

"What's the principal's name?" I asked.

"Charles Krauss."

"Krauss. I find my recall mechanism getting creakier by the day. Is that happening to you?"

"More and more."

While all else was going on—the show, the party, Jess, Neil Andrews, Katie Delgado—I had mentally and emotionally tried several possible approaches to Ellen. In my imaginings, it was I who approached her. I would say, "Now, Ellen, we must talk." But about what? About the past. About the future. But since reality pays no attention to plans, I said instead what came most naturally:

"You really did a splendid job with those kids."

"Thank you, George. I had a lot of fun doing it."

"You weren't the choreographer, too, were you?"

"No, Katie was in charge of that."

"Shouldn't she have been up there taking a bow?"

"Yes, she should have been. She left before the end to make sure she wasn't called up."

"Why's that? Shy? She doesn't look shy."

"It wasn't shyness. She insists the kids made up their own dance steps anyway. She says all she did was show them how to make it work a little better."

"Self-effacing, then."

"Not exactly. It's more a matter of character. She's like that."

"So . . ." I said.

I meant it as a transitional ploy, a signal to get on to something else, *us*, but it developed into a stretch of awkward seconds. I realized I hadn't been this close to Ellen in two years. I was aware of so many different things, things that came at me from all directions, that I was held mute and motionless, like a fixed hub. I was aware of the changes in Ellen, the substantial mottling of gray in her once-raven hair, the heaviness that had set in around the jaw, disturbing the clean lines of her face. The beginnings of a sag. Scoring around the eyes and mouth. Dear God! *No* exemptions? The off-center cast in her left eye was the same, and the sum of this quick inventory was an instant of such shattering poignance that, if I could have transferred it pure and undiminished to Ellen, it would have made my case with an eloquence I could never hope to match.

You see, the point is . . . the point is that I had before me living confirmation of what I had suspected in all the busy loneliness of the last two years. I loved Ellen. I wanted to live with Ellen. I wanted to catch up with her history and continue what seemed to me the inevitable course of my own. But instead of saying these things, intimating them somehow in a sudden flight of lyricism, or even shit-kicking clumsiness, I asked, "What is one to make of Neil Andrews?"

"Come, let's sit down," Ellen said.

All the chairs and sofas and hassocks were occupied, so we sat on the semicircular apron of steps that flared out from the staircase. I saw Jess glance at us. It seemed to me that most of the people here knew something about us, were staying discreetly away.

"What do *you* think?" she asked.

"I know so little."

"There's very little to know."

"How did it all happen?" I asked.

"Didn't she tell you anything?"

"She told me that she met him in Ann Arbor."

Ellen supplied further information. They had flown back to New York together, Jess and Neil. The plane landed at

La Guardia, and they took a cab together into the city. Of course, Jess *should* have taken a cab for the fifteen-minute ride from La Guardia to her home, but it was a beautiful afternoon, and no one had been specifically informed of either Jessica Light's or Neil Andrews's arrival. Ellen didn't know exactly what flight Jess would be taking. She may have kept it vague deliberately. She didn't want to be picked up at the airport, she'd take a cab. All the usual clandestine maneuvering. So Jess and Neil spent the day together and, as it developed, the night, as well.

"Have you had a chance to speak to the man?" I asked.

"Yes. Once. He took Jess to the ballet. Brought her home by car. He came in the house and stayed for half an hour."

I wanted to ask what he had said, how he had explained his position, how secret or open was this affair, but I checked myself, recognizing symptoms of pushiness, demand, the ancient complaint of being left out. None of that. Ellen was telling me what she knew.

"What do you think of it all?" I asked.

"It doesn't make me happy," Ellen said. "She's in love, that's clear, and I believe he is, too, but it's bound to be messy."

"I said the same thing," I said. "He's got two kids. How the hell can it turn out? I gather he's a serious politician, and a thing like this can be used to beat him to death."

"If anything is to happen," Ellen said, "it should happen quickly. Neil's private life is his own at the moment. He's an ambitious man. It will matter later."

"What bothers me is what Jess is giving up," I said. "Or having to put aside. Do you think Neil might be approached? I don't know, of course, but he seems like a fair man."

"I wouldn't do anything now, George," Ellen said, an edge of warning in her voice, but maintaining that perfect facial calm. "I really wouldn't. I think Jess must be left to work this out in her own way."

I nodded, feeling the sting of an awakened nerve. I wasn't exactly being told to mind my own business but to take into account certain truancies. I'd been out of touch. It wasn't a question of *right*—no one disputed my right as a father—but there had been a lack of continuity, of close touch. Ellen, in short, knew better than I what to do and what not to do.

"So there's nothing to do," I said.

"Nothing useful," she said. "Nothing one can be sure of. She could have kept the whole thing secret. I take some comfort in her willingness to share it with us."

"What do you suppose that means?" I asked.

Ellen thought about it for a moment, and a quick glance revealed to me that she was smiling her faint inward smile. She said, "Aren't you writing a book about men and women?"

"Are you being sarcastic?"

"Not at all. Tell me what you think."

"I think her willingness to tell her parents is evidence of trust," I said, "but I'm not sure whether it's you she trusts and lets me in on sufferance—"

"Don't, George."

"—or whether she's giving some other kind of signal."

"Such as?"

"I don't know, Ellen. She would have so much to explain or excuse—her plan to study abroad, graduate school—that it's probably easier to tell the truth. Or possibly she's saying, 'Watch me. I don't know if I'm doing the right thing, so watch me.' "

"I've thought that, too," Ellen said.

I looked across at Jess, who was now talking to Katie Delgado, both glancing our way from time to time.

"Have you thought about us?" I asked.

"Of course," she said.

"And what have you thought?"

"I thought it was time to tell you."

"I'd say so, yes. It's time."

"About Katie," Ellen said.

"Katie?"

"Katie Delgado. You see . . . Katie lives here."

"She does? You mean—as what?—renting a room?"

"She lives with me."

We might have been wired to Jess and Katie, for they separated on the instant of Ellen's words, as if at that signal each had some scheduled functions to perform. I almost turned to Ellen to ask her if this was so, but stopped in the realization that it couldn't be so, that I was only providing myself a necessary diversion.

I understood what I had been told, but I found that I couldn't *assimilate* the meaning. It remained outside, like some strangely colored bird on one of the wires strung along the backyard of the house. I had seen strange birds out there in the past, birds I had never seen before. I wished at such times for a guide that would identify the species. The regret I felt at not knowing the name of that off-course wanderer was a brief one. The regret that would follow *this* identification was likely to stay with me the rest of my life.

16

We imagine extremes, and the kinds of extremes we imagine say something about us. For instance, I've never been able to conjure myself into a state of poverty. I don't mean rag poor, but minimum-wage poor, nothing in the bank, no CDs, no IRAs to cash in. I guess I've always had, or thought I had, too much buck-making capacity in me to give a really ragged existence too much credence.

I have imagined sickness. That I have. Pain, debilitation, the stinks and ceremonies of the sickroom. Or death. Not my own, since that inevitability is canceled by the very act of thinking about it. Real death is *no* thought. But the death of somebody close *is* thought. Jess. Or Ellen. The cop at the door ... *"Mr. Light, I'm afraid I have some bad news for you."* ...

As a matter of fact, that did happen. Jess had been riding her bicycle around the block when her front wheel caught in a cracked pavement and she went over the handlebars. Knocked unconscious. The man before whose house it happened carried her inside. His wife recognized Jess as a neighborhood kid, and the man came to our door. . . . *"Mr. Light, I'm afraid your daughter had a little accident."* . . . I interpreted "little accident" as "dead," and all the color drained out of the world. I don't know quite how to describe it. Of course I could see the maroon trim and the blue door across the street, but the nerve that registers such values had gone dead, and it seemed to me that if Jess was dead, then my life would become a similarly dead stretch of unregistering time.

Ellen's announcement was something I *couldn't* imagine. It matched nothing in my gallery of extremes.

By the time I had reached my Jersey apartment, I had run through the whole spectrum of disbelief and rage, and I got into bed convinced that it was all part of a strategy, a cruelly uncharacteristic strategy, but one that circumstances had made necessary. I couldn't be expected to understand the circumstances, but time and a little more objectivity would allow me to see why it was necessary to handle the matter this way.

I slept. Amazingly, I slept. So often when events promise a sleepless night, I conk out. I don't know why that's so. Maybe shock itself turns an internal valve that releases a sleep-inducing chemical. I woke the next morning, Sunday, and stared at the slanting ceiling above my bed. The absurdity of that angle and morning light acted as a cold corrective to last night's hallucination. What had happened had happened, and if there was to be any strategy, it had to be mine.

I replayed the scene:

". . . You see, Katie lives here."

"She does? You mean—as what?—renting a room?"

"She lives with me."

At that point, I had looked across the room at the conspiratorial figures of Jess and Katie Delgado, watched them separate. Then I had gotten up and walked into the room where all the goodies were spread out, and I took a plate and I filled it with ham and shrimp and meatballs. Ellen was beside me when I did that, saying in a whisper, "Please, George. Please talk to me." Then I put the plate down somewhere, uneaten, and I walked back to the staircase, Ellen following. "Come upstairs," she said. And I climbed the stairs.

In the room that I had once used as a study, I turned to Ellen and said, "What are you telling me, that you're a lesbian?"

She said, "I beg of you, George, don't be abusive or crude."

I said, "Why did you tell me this tonight, at this moment, at this worst possible moment?"

She said, "I admit this is not the best time. I hadn't planned to say a word of this. Not tonight. But I had been living with it for so long, and suddenly I couldn't live with it another night. Not another night. I didn't know I was going to say it until the words were out of my mouth."

"What? That you're a dyke? Do you expect me to believe that, after living with you for twenty-five years?"

"I beg you please not to throw meaningless words around."

"Give me a meaningful word."

"Patience. Understanding. Will you come tomorrow, so that we can talk?"

"I don't know. I don't know how I'm going to feel tomorrow. All I know is that I've got to get out of here. Right now."

And I got out. I walked down the stairs. Jess was waiting for me there.

"Dad—"

"Jess, I can't talk to you right now. I want to talk to you but not now. Okay?"

"Okay."

"What do you understand?" I asked her.

"I don't know what I understand," she said. "I only know what's happening."

"I'll call you, Jess."

And I walked out of the house, my transfigured house, and walked to my ghostly white car, and I drove away.

The phone rang while I was having coffee.

"Will you be coming today?" Ellen asked.

"Is Jess there?"

"Yes."

"May I speak to her?"

"Just a minute."

Jess got on the phone. Her voice was small and harried. "Dad—"

"Listen, kid, could I ask you a favor? Could you meet me somewhere? Not in the house? Do you remember that diner we used to go to on Queens Boulevard? How about having lunch with me there?"

"What about Mom? She wants to talk to you."

"Tell her I'll be there in the afternoon, after we have lunch. Okay?"

"Okay."

God knows how many years ago it was since I was last in that diner. I wasn't even sure where it was. Somewhere between where we lived and the Queensboro Bridge. Nice pinpointing. I did remember that it was on the south side of the boulevard. And I was sure that Jess had eaten cherry blintzes and sour cream on that last occasion, and that she had crossed her eyes in ecstasy at the first mouthful. Blood-red cherries and snow-white sour cream. Maybe it was the colors that had stamped the occasion so indelibly on my mind.

I drove over the George Washington Bridge, continued on the Cross Bronx Expressway, onto the Whitestone, etc., etc. I listened to music on my car radio. It was somebody's Mass. Whose? Bach's? It sounded like Bach . . . *"Kyrie, Eleison . . ."* Lord have mercy on us . . . Yes, please do. . . . The question of *when* kept going round in my head like a headline announcement of war. *When?* During my Denver hiatus? Before? How much before? Before my affair with Kim? After?

Whatever else it was, it was as profoundly ungraspable as smoke, as a mirage. I had once taken an aptitude test—those tests were big at the time—and one of the things I had to do was trace the mirror-image of a line—have my hand do the opposite of what my eyes directed. I was feeling something of that gut-roiling perversity now. I had lived two years in exile, had taken myself away from home, child, friends, career, for the sake of doing penance, repairing a life. I had nursed guilt and remorse like sick children . . . *and was this going on all the time? Hey! Have I been played for a fool? Has everybody that I know and care for been privy to this howler? My own Jess? The Bernsteins? The Stockmans, the Viscontis, the Heilbruns . . . Hold it! Hold it!*

I took a deep breath and gripped the steering wheel firmly. This is what I had promised myself *not* to do. This roaring through the forest with pelt and club. Have I been kidding myself about the man-woman thing? Shouldn't this be grist for my mill? Yes, no doubt, but the stuff has to be fed in gradually, doesn't it? There is such a thing as *too much!*

"I don't think it's going to surprise you when I say that I'm rather hung up on the question of *time*," I said to Jess. "Do you know what I mean?"

"Not exactly."

"I mean the chronology of things. Like—did you know about this when you visited me last December?"

"By *this,* do you mean Mother and Katie?"

"Yes, Jess, that's what I mean."

"Dad, if we're going to talk, then please get that aggression out of your voice. Particularly if you're going to go and talk to Mother."

"Is there aggression in my voice?"

"Quite a lot."

"And have you been able to pick it up every time it's been there?"

"Without fail."

"And how many times would you say that's been?"

"Several million."

"Have I been a beastly father?"

"You've been a wonderful father."

"Do you care for me, Jess."

"I love you."

"Then imagine what's happening to me. *Did* you know?"

She told me that she knew that Ellen and Katie were friendly, had been for maybe a year, maybe more. Katie was staying frequently at the house when she, Jessica, visited me in Denver last December, but she hadn't actually moved in. Of that she was certain. That must have happened some time after the holidays, after she had gone back to school. . . .

I think it's important to see Jess in this context. The immediate world is real enough—nice diner, traffic on Queens Boulevard, her salad, my sandwich—but I also mean Jessica Light and her father sitting opposite each other for the purpose of discussing in full seriousness the fact that gravity had been canceled and that the oceans had become vast, dry sinks. She didn't look well. I hadn't expected her to look well. Distress shows quickly on her face, and she was in one of her sick-cat states. Her hair looked stringy and her eyes looked smudged. I was sorry for that, but I was not the author of this crazy crisis. But I *had* yanked Jess into it immediately, hadn't I? Nonsense! Jess was in it because of who she was and where she was. How could she *not* be in it!

"Jess, what's going on?" I asked beseechingly.

"It's best if you ask Mother."

"No, no, please don't palm me off like that! I *will* ask Mother, but I'm also asking you. After all, you're affected by it. This is happening to *you* as well as to me. I'm not asking you for a—an *analysis*—I mean like that analysis you had planned to do on news and the anchorman—which I still happen to think is a swell idea—no, what I mean is how are you laying this out in your soul? Are you *believing* all of this? That's really what I want to know. Is all of this some kind of an elaborate subterfuge? Is it that, Jess? Do you know if it's that? Do you suspect that it's that?"

"Please calm down," she said.

"I thought I was calm."

"You're not."

"Believe me, it's my prayerful intention to be calm. It may take me a little time to catch up with my intention. Jess—I repeat—what's going on?"

"I know that Mother and Katie are friends . . ." she repeated.

Jess told me what Ellen had told her about Katie. Katie had worked among the natives in the Andes before taking up her post as teacher in the New York school system. She had already been accepted as a teacher but had decided to do the Peace Corps thing first. At a school picnic, Ellen had described to Jess, Katie wore a native Andean costume and one of those little derby hats and she did a Peruvian folk dance.

"Has Katie ever been married?" I asked.

"She was. She's divorced now."

"But what exactly is the relationship?"

"Ask Mother."

"Are you saying that because you don't know, or because you can't bring yourself to tell?"

"I don't know for sure."

"Have you asked?"

"Yes."

"And what did your mother tell you?"

"That she was very fond of Katie. That Katie was very fond of her."

"And?"

"And what?"

"And—Jesus Christ!—are they *lovers*?"

Jess looked at me as she had once looked at one of her beloved lions or tigers, the cubs of whom she had once longed to take home and raise as pets. In her voice was an echo of my own when I had tried to explain the difficulty of rearing such a creature at home.

"I don't know," she said.

Naturally, Jess had to be elsewhere when I asked if she was coming back to the house with me. I refrained from asking if Neil Andrews had provided the excuse for her absence. That consideration lay like one coat in a pileup of coats in the guest room of the house I had just purchased. For that's what it seemed like to me: a new habitation. Through some mysterious process that had slipped between waking and sleeping, I had become the bemazed owner of a whole new set of nightmare rooms. They were full of known and unknown strangers, and while I held the deed, I knew that I could never move in until there had been a great sorting out.

So I didn't ask Jess where she was conveniently going. That would have to wait. One nightmare at a time, starting with the largest.

I drove to the old house—my house—*not* my house—*whose* house? Ellen's house? Who the hell held the mortgage anyway? I believe it was made out in both our names. No matter . . . *How dare she bring into my house her fucking dyke lover!* . . . Who, *Ellen*? Ellen of the hazy, off-center eye? Ellen who had encouraged me for so many years, encouraged the book I wrote, encouraged me each step of my career . . . except the private eye thing. She couldn't get with that. She didn't think the Holocaust was a suitable subject for entertainment. Immovable on that point . . .

"But I'm not writing about the Holocaust. I'm writing about the Nazis."

"The perpetrators of the Holocaust."

"Exactly! As hunted dogs! As the monsters they were!"

"Caricatures."

"Weren't Nazis caricatures as human beings?"

"That's the awful part of it. They weren't. The danger lies in making them look like caricatures. The lesson is lost if they're made to seem like anything other than human beings. Perverted human beings, horrible human beings, but human beings. There's comfort to be had in making them appear like a cartoon strip. False comfort. The human beings who will come along some day in the future with the hearts of Nazis will not be believed because they look like human beings, not cartoons. People mustn't be led to believe that the Nazis were something else. They were not something else. They were us."

I argued against it, of course. Had to. I couldn't have gone on unless I could make out a case. I guess what I could never forgive was the truth of her argument. I think her argument planted the seed of my alienation from the show. Was it also, I wonder, the outgrowth of another alienation—hers—from me? It was about that time that I had begun to feel a change of state. Hard to specify. Meals were prepared, clothes laundered, parties given, parties attended, everything in place. But if there had been a thermometer to measure such things, it would have registered a drop of at least ten degrees. A high level of attention but a lowering of interest. Cooperation without giving. Pleasure without passion.

"Wasn't your opposition to *The Search* happening about the same time as your opposition to me?" I asked her.

"I was never opposed to you," she said.

"Find a better word."

"For what?"

"For what was happening between us before the Kim affair."

We were sitting where we had sat so many times in our former life when we had serious discussions: the breakfast room off the kitchen with its bay window overlooking the back garden. I could see red and yellow tulips and the pink blossoming dogwood. The familiar colors provided a marginal throb of pain.

"I don't recall that anything in particular was happening before that," she said.

"You had changed," I said. "You were different. You were withdrawn."

"It's possible."

"Why?"

"I was unhappy."

"You never said you were unhappy. What were you unhappy about?"

"George, you're becoming nasty. This is not a court of

law. I want to answer your questions, but I won't be bullied."

"Have I bullied you in the past?"

"Yes."

"I would not have thought so. I swear to God I can't remember bullying. I've been angry, I've been frustrated, but I can't recall a genuine desire to browbeat you. Do you really think there's a sadistic streak in me?"

Ellen didn't answer immediately. She, too, reverted to the tulips and the dogwood, leaving me more a profile than a front view to cope with. She had become heavier, and in this light I could see how much gray had infiltrated her hair. But the line was still there, the line that ran from brow to chin, and the narrowed, nebulous look she had perfected to compensate for that esotropic eye. . . . *"Yes, I know, true beauty and its little imperfection. Thank you. I could have lived very nicely without mine."*

"No, you're not sadistic," she said.

"Tell me what happened," I said.

I could see that this was the telling she had thought much about, had possibly dreaded. I would keep my mouth shut. Mum. Silence. Let her take as much time as she needed to say what it had been in her mind to say for so long. But it was not many seconds into her meditation that I realized for the first time how separated we were. Something in the range of her considerations gave me a sense of it. I wondered if this would one day find itself in the book I intended to write. How? As a speculation on the degree of estrangement that can go on when all the semblances of married life continue routinely, numbingly?

". . . each behaved in a way that came natural to us . . ." she was saying.

Hurriedly, I reached back for the words that had preceded these, and I attended very closely to the words that followed.

She said that mine was the more extreme temperament and therefore she had had to do more adjusting. My job, my ambition, my talent. She knew that even before we were married. That was the reason for her long hesitation. She knew in advance that's what she would have to face—

"Ellen . . ."

"It's true," she said.

"How could you have known?" I asked. "I can accept what you discovered, and that you adapted, but did you really *know* in advance?"

"Not precisely, but I knew."

"Then what?" I asked. "What did you come to resent?"

It wasn't resentment. Well, perhaps some, but nothing that couldn't be absorbed in the normal round of things. There were many satisfactions, too. There was Jess. There was a real satisfaction in seeing me advance, succeed, do the things that I wanted to do. I must never think she begrudged the success I had. No, it was something else. It was the gnaw of hunger that became more and more insistent in her life. All our parties were with people who had something to do with television. There was fun and excitement, but she was always left with a gnaw of hunger. When we did anything together—nice things, mutually satisfying things—she was still left with that gnaw of hunger—

"But why?"

"Because I couldn't talk about *myself*. Because you set the tone, gave direction."

"I wasn't aware that I was doing that. What I was trying to do, perhaps unconsciously, was make the world pleasant and interesting, for both of us. I thought you preferred it when I gave direction. I thought that's what you wanted from me."

"I know you did. I did like it for a time, a long time, but the gnaw of hunger began, and it grew, and grew."

"Then why didn't you tell me?"

"Because it would have done no good to tell you. You weren't doing anything wrong. You were being yourself. That was the size of your ego, the need of your ego. It would have been like telling you to have a smaller foot."

"It might have been worth a try," I said.

"Perhaps," she said.

"What made that gnaw of hunger?" I asked her. "What would have fed you sufficiently?"

"Having the room and the freedom to be myself."

"Oh, God, how I hate those words! Ellen! *Be myself!* I don't know what that *means*!"

"I know you don't. You don't know what that means because you've always *been* yourself. If you had been prevented from being yourself, if you had to repress, compromise, you'd know what it meant."

"Why *didn't* you be yourself, push me aside, take the room and the freedom you needed?"

"Because I didn't have the strength."

"But that doesn't explain it," I said.

"Then I'm sorry," she said.

"I mean it doesn't explain . . . Katie."

"With her I have the room and the freedom. The gnaw of hunger is gone."

"But that still doesn't explain it, Ellen. It doesn't explain the basic thing, the gene thing, the blood thing, the matter of love, the matter of sex."

Ellen nodded, slowly, as if she were expecting this, waiting for it, certain that all else was minor and preliminary to this scorching question. And it was. Asked, I would have said yes, all else is minor and preliminary. So what about it? What about the basics and the blood?

"It seems not to matter," she said.

"Ellen, could it be that that gnaw of hunger is better explained and satisfied with Katie than with me?"

"Do you mean, am I a lesbian?"

"Yes."

"I don't think I am, George. Not in the sense that you mean it."

"What other sense is there?"

"The sense of humanness, understanding. The sense of being myself."

"Are you free of the gnaw of hunger now?"

"Yes."

"Then Kim never mattered at all," I said.

"Yes, she mattered."

"Why?"

"Because she proved to me what I suspected."

"What's that?"

"That if I made my demand known in some way, you wouldn't meet it, that you would turn to someone else."

It was her eyes I couldn't meet. I turned to the tulips and the dogwood.

While driving back to New Jersey, I remembered that Ellen had another party to go to that evening. Why should that cause me pain now? What did I think she was doing during the time of my absence?

Yes, but it's one thing to assume, quite another to see.

17

Mrs. Speros talks with her neighbor, Mrs. Gregorio, almost every morning. I can see them from my window. Different reasons bring them out of the house—the garbage, gardening, just gabbing—but they're well synchronized and on the best of terms. They stand on the sidewalk in their housecoats and comment on the weather or their children or (I suspect) local or national sex scandals. It gives them an excuse to get out of doors and survey the scene.

I keep my car parked in front of the house and must pass Mrs. Speros when she is thus engaged.

"Good morning," I say.

"Good morning," the ladies say.

Then Mrs. Speros excuses herself from Mrs. Gregorio and walks to the sidewalk side of my car. I'm already on the other side. We talk over the roof of the car.

"Listen, Mr. Light," she says, "I gotta ask you a question."

"Shoot."

"You got any idea how long you gonna keep that upstairs apartment?"

The agreement is on a month-to-month basis. She understands that it's only temporary for me.

"At least two more months," I say.

"You see, I got a couple—nice couple—they're interested in the apartment on a permanent basis. The man's got a job here in Jersey. Works for a food broker. It's not right away, but they'd like to have an idea when they could move in."

"I'll know better in a week or two. Okay?"

"Sure. Okay."

I drive to the stores and pick up a paper and some fresh-baked bagels.

Mrs. Speros's innocent inquiry brings everything into sudden focus. What, indeed, is my status? Where will I be two months from now? I returned east to resume a life, and I have no life to resume. I can't imagine the future because I find it impossible to accept the present.

Impossible!

I realize that my suspicion of some kind of elaborate strategy is a defense mechanism, but the fact is that I still can't take it in. Ellen is not a woman to construct Byzantine plots, but the truth can be just as incredible as any invented fantasy. I'm not saying I could have accepted a more conventional blow with equanimity, but at least I would understand. . . . *"I'm sorry, George, but I'm in love with another man."* . . . Would that hurt less? I'm not sure. Would it be less painful to lose out in an understandable way? The quick impulse is to say yes. Tough luck, old cock, but you had it coming. But—

goddammit!—let's do have the truth!—I find a saving grace in this craziness! It falls so far out of the defining limits of my fate pattern that I can't credit it with the same sword-thrusting, bloodletting reality that a male rival would have inflicted on me.

Egregiousness argues against permanence. It will pass. Maybe some sort of counseling is needed. For Ellen. For both of us.

The telephone was ringing when I stepped back into my Caligari apartment.

"Hello, George. It's Larry. Got a minute?"

"Absolutely."

"I've been thinking about your idea, and the more I think about it, the more I like it. Have you done anything about it?"

"Like what?"

"Like some sort of treatment. Something to present."

"I'm working on it."

"Good. You don't want ideas lying around too long. I'm not saying it's a shoo-in, but it should be protected. Get it down in a proposal. Have it notarized. Have it copyrighted, if that's possible. Do I have to tell you? As you know, there are programs similar to yours, but this one can have a range and depth. That's what intrigues me. I mean—*tie-ins*—like a panel of ordinary men and women shooting questions back and forth about sports, Sunday football, pros and cons, bites and backbites. And then the next program you can have a panel of pros, football players and their wives. One program you can have a panel of unmarrieds airing their wonderments, and then a panel of marrieds doing the same, and then a third panel of married men and unmarried women, and then reverse the order. What I'm saying—I guess what I'm saying is that there's a deep human itch that no amount of scratching can get to. Everybody suspects that everybody else has a piece of the action that they're not getting. Everybody suspects that others have seen a light they haven't. So what I'm saying is that played right a program like this could have a self-perpetuating . . . umm . . ."

"Dynamic?"

"Right!"

"You haven't by any chance talked to anyone about it, have you?" I asked.

"Talked to? No . . . I . . . well, I was having lunch the other day with Ted Samuels—"

"And he said why don't you get it in the form of a treatment."

"Well, yeah . . . something like that. George, I want you to know up front that this is your idea, that I told Ted that it's your idea, and that it's going to stay your idea. That's why I'm very eager to get this down in as much detail as possible. Ted agreed. He said pack it with ideas. Get at least twenty program ideas into it, and indicate very strongly the self-perpetuating aspect of it."

"I appreciate the interest you're taking in this, Larry."

"I'm sure you know it isn't entirely altruistic," he said. "I'll give it to you straight. It's your idea, George, but I want to work with you on it. As soon as you get the treatment written, I want to start working on individual programs. I'm jumping with ideas. Let's get started."

"I'm working on it."

"Good."

I sat down at my typewriter and began to work on a treatment. What the hell, rain or shine, sanity or madness, we'll all have to go on living. Will we? Sure we will. I've detected no fey signals, even in this eerie light. Things are out of hand, but as far as I can tell no one's out of touch. I can't believe what I'm being told, but the telling is coherent. There's disorder here, but it's a disorder of heart, not mind. That may be just as bad for me, but it leaves me free of the other worry.

I don't get very far with my proposal. I'm not thinking clearly. My mind is on other things. My mind is on two o'clock this afternoon, when I'm to meet Jess at the monument on Columbus Circle.

"Is she really living at the house?" I asked Jess.

"Katie? She sleeps over frequently, but she still has her own apartment, as far as I know."

"Are you in the house when she sleeps over?"

"Sometimes. Sometimes I'm staying with a friend."

"A friend like Neil Andrews?"

"Sometimes."

We were walking along a path in Central Park. Green had settled everywhere, but a delicate, young green, reminding me of other walks with Jess, not here, in Bronx Park, where caged cats paced and pissed and stretched out with measureless grace, their great eyes staring through steel and space into God knows what tawny covert. I felt it come on like a fever's chill, or an inexplicable rush of joy; and before I could begin the brake-pumping I've practiced so frequently in the last few days, I was rolling, not entirely heedless, but not in full control . . .

"I know you're not lacking in imagination or compassion, but I wonder if you can fully appreciate what has hit me since that pleasant party in Forest Hills. I mean like . . . well, take what just now passed between us . . . Katie Delgado sleeps over . . . Where? In what room? In your mother's room? . . . Do you see what I'm saying, Jess? Where are *you* when that happens? *Does* it happen? Are we walking along this path, you and I, discussing what we're discussing, or is this also part of the new dimension I seem to have walked into? I hope you understand the difficulty I'm having. Frankly, I don't understand . . . Your mother and I lived together for twenty-five years. I keep saying to myself that in twenty-five years if there was the slightest sign of some sexual disarrangement I would have known about it, wouldn't I? I mean, a man knows when he isn't welcome. I was welcome. Is this a crude way of putting it? If so, I'm sorry. I don't mean to be crude, but I'm being taxed these days to find adequate words. I know how unnerving a parent's sex life can be to a child. But this is almost a . . . I don't know . . . what would you call it? . . . a *medical* situation. I just don't see how one orientation can change into another. *That's* what I'm saying. And I'll admit something else to you, my darling, since I'm in an admitting mood: I don't quite see how *you* could dump all those wonderful plans. . . . All right, never mind that, that's another part of the forest. . . . But let me tell you something. Just this morning, I got a telephone call from Larry Graff—does that name mean anything to you?—yes, I thought it would—and Larry wanted to discuss further this idea I had about a TV show where men and women . . . No, that wasn't my original idea. My original idea, as you know, was to write a book, but Larry immediately saw it as a TV show where men and women, panels of men and women, would ask each other questions about what hurts and haunts and plagues and puzzles . . ."

I stopped, abruptly, sensing how far my rush had carried me, like one of those cartoon creatures, ten feet off the cliff's edge, gravityless for one crazy-eyed moment before the plunge down. I felt a sick surge of resentment against my Jess for being witness to my hysteria. I was on the verge of making some hurtful remark . . . about . . . oh, about having known all of this when she visited me in Denver, about her own reprehensible complicity, but fortunately I was able to check that in time. Enough!

"Well, that's enough spouting," I said.

Jess didn't say anything immediately. She took my arm with a breeze-light touch, so light that I had to look to see if it was there; and seeing that it was, I looked at her face and saw that she was crying. We stopped for a moment, and she leaned her head against my shoulder.

"Oh, Christ!" I heard her whisper.

"What?" I asked.

"I'm sorry," she said.

"About what?"

"About your having walked back into all of this. I'm sorry you're hurt. I really am. I should have prepared you better. I don't know what I was thinking. I was too occupied with my own life."

"You should be," I said, feeling lumpish, an emotional moocher.

"No, I shouldn't be," she said. "You've always found time for me. I don't like one-way streets. In any kind of relationship."

"Come," I said, resuming our walk. "Listen, don't berate yourself about who gives to whom. Water flows the way it flows. But tell me this, and tell me truly, do you understand what's happening?"

"I think I do."

"Then tell me."

"It's just that Mother is comfortable with Katie," Jess said. "They talk about school, they talk about music, they talk about cooking. Katie will read an article and tell Mother about it. Mother will read an article and tell Katie about it. I don't know if there's any sex. I swear I don't. I think of it as a kind of caressing, an extension of everything else they're sharing. I don't know about that part of it. I don't want to know. But I do see what's going on most of the time."

"A sharing," I said.

"Yes."

"As she could never share with me?"

"I don't know. Could she?"

"I thought so. Obviously, I was wrong. When you say you understand, I take that to mean that you accept."

Jess looked over at the chalk-white face of a pantomimist doing his jerky little routine before a couple of kids who were standing open-mouthed, not sure whether to be amused or scared. I saw that he was pretending to sew his fingers together with an imaginary needle and thread. I had seen that routine before, somewhere, but the occasion slid away into a time tunnel that narrowed into infinity.

Jess's calm, almost vacant statement brought me back. "No, I don't accept," she said. "I understand, but I don't like it. Why should I? I don't want to compete for my own mother."

"Are you having to do that?"

"In a way."

"Did you ever feel you were competing for her against me?"

"No," Jess said. "Then I was competing *against* her."

"*. . . Your mother and I lived together for twenty-five years . . .*"

The things I've chosen to remember in these last few weeks are the things that would help explain why Ellen and I are where we are. The Kim thing. That TV program she had rejected with such quiet vehemence. The tandem job crises of my career. But there were other times. My God, there were oceans of time during which we lived together as a man and woman should.

Am I kidding myself about that? Was what I look back on now as the halcyon years only compromises and concealments on Ellen's part? I don't believe it. I am indeed capable of kidding myself, but it's not a full-time occupation. When something blows in the wind long enough, I pick up the scent. Didn't Ellen admit I was right about the pre-Kim atmosphere? There had been withdrawal, a decided drop in the marital temperature. If I was right about that, why shouldn't I be right about the halcyon years?

When? According to my book, all those years between Jess's birth and that pre-Christmas walk at Radio City, right after Jess and I had seen that comedy with Walter Matthau and Glenda Jackson. One can't be dead accurate about things like that. Time bleeds off the page in the day-to-day progress of change. But I remember . . .

Well, I remember when we had a group of people over to the house for one of those Saturday night clambakes, the necessary nexus coupling one week to the next. A dinner party, the preparation for which made a high-walled fortress of Ellen's hours. Couldn't go near her. Couldn't talk to her. She was busy. She was preparing a dish out of *The New York Times Cook Book*. Craig Claiborne. Did she have to be *so* absorbed, for *so* many hours? Yes, she did. That was her way. So please . . .

And then the arrival of friends—the Viscontis, the Heilbruns, the Bernsteins, the Stockmans, sometimes the Graffs. We talked politics, TV, movies, the metamorphosis of New York City . . . and Ellen would signal me by a dip of her head when someone's glass needed filling, or when she could use a hand in clearing away dishes or getting coffee to the table. To all of which I think I responded willingly, gladly. Ellen wouldn't deny that.

The particular occasion that sticks in my mind does so not so much for the Saturday evening's dinner party—which was pretty much like hundreds of other dinner parties, those we gave and those we attended—but the pendant to that party, the next day, Sunday, a glorious day in mid-October. That was the day when, on impulse, we piled into the car and drove not, as one might expect, away from the city, north, where each turn in the road would present another burst of autumn foliage—but *into* the city, with Jess, to the Central Park Zoo, because autumn foliage is so distant and impersonal, while the eyes of a caged tiger burn with a thrilling brightness.

We parked on Madison and walked to the zoo—the old zoo—and we looked at the tigers and the lions and the monkeys and the elephants. We ate hot dogs and peanuts, and we put Jess on the little pony cart that at the time still trotted around a loamy, dung-strewn track. Ellen and I sat on a bench and watched.

It was late afternoon, somewhere between three and four, and the sun had gone below the Central Park West battlements. What I was seeing—or perhaps feeling—was a soft radiance. There are, after all, trees and bushes in Central Park, and they had joined the seasonal refulgence. I looked at Ellen, whose fine profile seemed etched into the golden air. To say that I was happy would be to say very little. I was very often happy—the smell of the Sunday paper, a freshly laundered shirt, a perfect fifty-yard pass—but what I realized in that mellow moment was that step by accidental step I had wandered into the *definition* of my happiness. Ellen, Jess, this day, last evening's dinner party, the friends we had, the work we did, the pleasures we could afford, the pleasures we could give each other.

As if I had framed it all into a single, silent statement, Ellen turned to me and smiled.

"So?" I asked.

"Yes," she said.

"Seriously," I asked, "what's missing?"

"I can't think of a thing," she said.

I know I've been guilty of solipsism, more than was good for me or the people around me, but I am as convinced of the reality of that day as I am of gravity or hunger. We were happy. *Both* of us.

I wish I could define as well what was happening to me now. Nothing is static. Stasis is a form of anesthesia. Grief can produce stasis as a means of limiting pain. You imagine nothing, neither the past nor the future, and in that way you avoid the memories and anticipations that flay you alive. Even while I moved through time, I was moving inevitably toward change.

In my secret chamber, I proposed scenes of reconciliation. This present unreality had ended, and Ellen and I were somehow repairing the damage. We sold the house and found an apartment in the city. No, that wouldn't do. Ellen wanted to continue working. There were plenty of apartment houses in Queens. My program—*A Better Way*—had taken off like a rocket, and we were rolling in it. Ellen could stop teaching and go back to playing the piano more seriously. No, she was too old for that. Too late to be a concert pianist. No TV program. Such a program would carry the same stigma as *The Search*. Superficial and exploitive. It will be a book instead. I'll write it, using my own life to light *A Better Way*. Would that also be superficial and exploitive? More than likely. God damn it, I'll make it deep and relevant! I'll be honest and soul-searching. . . .

There you have it! A future full of Georgics. *I* will do this and *I* will do that. Clearly, I've learned nothing. No, I've learned a lot. What? Well, if nothing else I've learned that the future can't be composed of my doings. So what will it be composed of? I don't know. It will be composed of whatever form my acceptance finally takes, whatever compromise Ellen finally accepts. But more than the certainty that it must come to this was a haunting reprise of our earliest days, the days when Ellen came to my room on Jane Street, the scene of our couplet lovemaking, and of my growing suspicion and resentment that I was not quite good enough for the Feldman family, that I was a sequestered stud, good enough for Ellen's major sexual experiment, but not good enough for marriage.

Of course that wasn't true. That wasn't the real reason for her hesitation. The real reason was what she had foreseen and I hadn't. The real reason was what had ripened into this strange fruit . . .

Katie Delgado.

18

It was surprisingly easy. I phoned the school and left a number for Katie Delgado to call. She called at three-thirty in the afternoon.

"Hello."

"Hello, George. I thought I might be hearing from you."

"Did you? Good. Could we meet? Could we talk?"

"Of course."

We arranged to meet on Saturday. She was free on Saturday. Where could we meet? Well, how about the fountain in the Plaza? She could meet me there about one o'clock in the afternoon. That would give her a chance to go to Bloomingdale's first. She seized every opportunity to go to Bloomingdale's. She would have no trouble recognizing me. I would have no trouble recognizing her.

I wondered if Ellen also expected that I would get in touch with Katie.

She seemed somehow—different. She had gone through so many metamorphoses in my mind that nothing in the flesh was likely to match. She had *café au lait* skin and light-green eyes. The hair was as I remembered it: tight-knit and reddish. She was a little shorter than I remembered. Maybe she was wearing high heels that night. Now she was wearing flats. A wide paisley skirt, a black jersey blouse, a jacket over the blouse.

"Shall we walk?" she said.

"Have you eaten?" I asked.

"I had a bite."

Frankly, I didn't want to walk. There are too many things to look at when you walk through the park. Too much evaporation going on. I wanted a more hermetic conversation.

"Let's have coffee, or a drink, or whatever, in there," I suggested, nodding at the Plaza.

"All right."

We went to the lounge and ordered drinks. Katie ordered a white wine spritzer. I ordered the same. I was thirsty. Nervous? As a matter of fact, yes. I had been through a warehouse of attitudes and none had felt right. I was essentially off balance with this woman. It didn't surprise me that I was. The reasons were obvious. But it was only when we were seated at a table that I became aware of a reason that had escaped me before. That one reason provided me with the opening I had been looking for.

"Katie . . . may I call you Katie . . . ?"

"I called you George."

"Katie, under other circumstances, I might like you. You

look like a person I might like. You can understand that my feelings toward you are, to say the least, ambiguous. . . ."

"Yes, I can understand that," she said.

"Yes, well . . . one of the things contributing toward that feeling is that you know a hell of a lot more about me than I know about you."

"Under the circumstances—"

"Exactly. Under the circumstances."

"But does it matter?" she asked.

"Maybe not, but it would put me more at ease."

Katie nodded. I didn't know if this was forced cheerfulness or if Katie Delgado always came on this way, but in either case she could carry it off. She was one of those eye-seekers who seem to beckon your gaze if it happens to stray for a moment. Her voice assisted, gradually slowing until your eyes were back on track, then resuming at her normal cruising speed. I can't say it was actually a smile, but the expression she maintained throughout was relaxed, as if to say our destination was both pleasant and desirable, so please sit back and enjoy the ride.

Her father was Peruvian, her mother was from New York, German-Irish. Her mother had worked at the American Embassy in Lima, where she met Katie's father, who worked at the Peruvian Embassy in Lima. They were married in Lima, went to the United States, where her father worked first in the United Nations, and then applied for citizenship. They moved to Philadelphia, where her father worked for a publishing company. They moved back to New York, where her father worked for another publishing company. They lived in the Inwood section, not far from the Columbia football stadium. She had two brothers, both older. One was living in San Francisco; the other had gone back to Peru. She had done her undergraduate work at NYU and had taken a master's at Hunter. She taught Spanish and

French. She had always been interested in folk dancing. She had been married, was divorced, no children . . .

"Why not?" I asked.

"I didn't want children."

"Don't like them?"

"Love them."

"Then?"

"I believe a child should have a mother and a father. I was pretty convinced I wasn't going to be able to keep a father around."

"Why's that?"

"I didn't like the arrangement."

"The sexual arrangement?"

Her smile increased as she shook her head. "I don't enjoy sex in the way I think you mean it," she said. "I never did. It can't be helped. I enjoy being with certain people, and when I enjoy it enough it becomes sexual."

"Did it ever become that way with a man?"

"Yes—a few times."

"Why didn't you stay with one of those rarities?"

"Because they didn't stay the same," Katie said. "Because they changed."

"Don't women change?"

"They do."

"Have you had affairs with women before . . . Ellen?"

"We're not having an affair."

"What would you call it?"

"A very good relationship. A very satisfying one."

I nodded and broke off, deliberately and perhaps a shade sarcastically, the persistent eye contact. She was not trying to be provoking, clearly she was not, but I felt provoked. Why? It was in the way she answered my questions. Quickly, unresistingly, as though all had been anticipated, and her purpose here was to satisfy me in every regard. I guess what

I didn't like was the sheer obligingness of it all. I felt I was being manipulated. I felt there had been a preparatory strategy session on "the best way to handle George."

"Ellen know we're meeting?" I asked.

"Not unless you told her."

"I mean . . . was there anything said between the two of you about the possibility of my getting in touch with you?"

"Yes," Katie admitted. "Ellen seemed to think you would."

"And of course there was a strategy session about that, wasn't there?"

"No," she said.

I laughed. "You're a liar," I said.

Now it was Katie who broke the gaze. She waited a few seconds before speaking. Then she said, "Yes, there was a strategy session. Ellen said there would be a point at which you would lose your temper."

I leaned back in my chair, not trusting myself to speak in the flush of anger and defeat that coursed through me. Christ, I was hot with it! I wanted to reach across and slap Katie Delgado across her brown, congenial face. *Hard.* Make her head snap. I hate being handled, and I was being handled. I couldn't remember ever feeling this much hostility against a woman. Particularly one this attractive. Because she *was* sexy in a compact way, all rounded and smooth.

"Shall I tell you what I'm feeling?" I asked.

"It might help."

"I'm feeling that you're taking advantage of your advantage. I'm feeling that you're a one-woman damage-control team."

Katie looked away again. "I'm not sure I know what you're talking about," she said. "I'm sorry if my manner bothers you, but that's the way I am. I agreed to meet you because I thought I could help explain the situation. If you're going to beat up on me, I'll leave."

"No, don't leave," I said, suddenly believing what she was saying. "I'm sorry. Does the situation include me?"

"What do you mean?"

"You said before that you thought you could help explain the situation, and I'm asking whether the situation you refer to includes me. You see, I'm having a bad time sitting here with a stranger who is going to explain my wife to me. Can you understand that?"

"Yes, but . . ."

"Go on."

"Your wife is not a stranger to me," Katie explains.

"Yes, I understand that. That's what I'm finding hard to take. But go ahead, please. I'd appreciate it if you would explain the situation to me."

That wasn't true. I wouldn't *appreciate* it. I would endure it. I liked Katie Delgado no better for her having put me in my place, but I figured (in my general snake pit of figurations) that I might as well try to find out whatever more there was to find out. As I've said, things progress, and I think by this time I was beginning to see the leading edge of what was to be. What was to be was not what was. Katie Delgado was the living symbol of that. All the minutes since that party when I sat on the apron of steps in my own house and heard Ellen tell me that this person (growing more familiar by the second) was "living" with her, was occupying her life as I had not occupied it for a long time, were minutes spent in mental restoration. I had wanted Katie and her attendant meaning obliterated and the past given back to me, even with all its structural damage. That was the whole idea: *I* was to do the repairing. What I seem to have overlooked was that some earthquake-damaged buildings must be torn down, not repaired.

Nevertheless, I listened. I listened as Katie asked me to believe that Ellen had never spoken ill of me. Ellen had told her—this other woman—Katie Delgado—how hard we had both tried to make our marriage a good marriage. There had been sincere and rewarding years. I noticed that she didn't say "happy," and I wondered if the omission was paraphrased or editorialized. I was going to let it pass, allow her to go on talking, but my curiosity got the better of me.

"Ellen ever use the word 'happy'?" I asked.

"I don't remember that she used that particular word," Katie said.

"Would you say it was implied?"

"Yes, I would,"

"Please continue."

Please continue, you dyke! You sleek, patronizing cunt!

Did that make me feel better? A bit. No, not really. Now that the breach had been made, I was being invaded by such heavy dejection that that kind of gutter spittle offered no relief. I was standing before a three-way mirror, the kind you find in men's clothing stores. I could look straight ahead and catch my reflection full on, at this moment, opposite Katie Delgado, or I could turn and see myself positioned in time, any random time that memory might provide, or I could turn in a third direction and try to imagine myself in some unimaginable future.

Katie was telling me that Ellen had made it clear that it was not my fault. I had inherited the same world that she had, and we had both made the same assumptions. Since I was finding reasonable gratification in my job, in my advancement, and in my marriage, there was no reason for me to change my assumptions. Since she was not, she began to change her assumptions—

"In what way was she not gratified?" I asked.

"She could have continued her piano lessons, become a concert pianist," Katie said.

"She could have," I agreed. "I wanted her to."

"Not really," Katie said. "You didn't really encourage her."

"How could I know for sure that such encouragement would be the right thing? She told me at the time that she would never be good enough to be a concert pianist. She knew music, I didn't. How could I encourage in the dark?"

"*She* did."

"How?"

"When she saw what it was you wanted, she encouraged you to go after it."

That was true, but so was the other. I *did* encourage her to continue her piano career. Ellen lied if she denied it. There opened up before me a great black blossom of deceit, and as quickly as it opened, it closed, withered, disappeared. I felt we were getting closer to the truth because it was getting more difficult to find. It was not to be picked up in pure form. It was buried in other material. Alloys had to be burned away. Ellen might have become a concert pianist, but she had made the deliberate choice to nourish a marriage instead of a career. That could have been an excuse not to face the frustration and heartbreak of professional competition. That was something that had occurred to me at the time.

And what I also knew at the time was that Ellen hadn't married me in the hope of repletion that most girls bring to their nuptial bed. There had been hesitancy and something less than joy and hope. There had been that curious double motif in our lovemaking. It seemed never to work the first time. Perhaps that was because Ellen's sexual imagination needed that much time to catch up with the heterosexual facts.

"Did Ellen ever tell you . . . ?" I began.

"What?" Katie asked.

"Nothing. Never mind. Please go on."

Nothing . . . nothing to be found or fostered in that direction. If there was some lesbian latency back then, it was, I was certain, unknown to either of us, so what was the point?

"What would be the point?" I asked aloud, without deliberation, speaking more to myself than to this woman, who was beginning to fade in and out of relevance as I engaged more and more of my own past, more and more of my own realizations.

"What point?" Katie asked.

"Is Ellen a lesbian?" I asked.

"I wouldn't say so," Katie said.

"Then why wouldn't she find what she was seeking in another man?"

"You assume that what must come first is the other sex," said Katie Delgado.

"Yes, I admit it. That's been my lifelong assumption."

"And you still don't see how—"

"That's right. I don't see how. Tell me how."

Katie told me that some women simply became tired of battling maleness. Part of the fatigue came from admitting that it *was* maleness. There was no use trying to put down the other sex, but it was equally useless to go on pretending that the other sex was what one wanted, exclusively, no matter at what sacrifice. It finally had to be admitted by some women that what one wanted was *peace.* Not a contest, not a conflict of interests, or moods, or desires, but simply peace and quiet. The peace of understanding. The quiet of compatibility. Not to have to pass endlessly through the brambles of not having received enough, or not having given enough.

One wonders sometimes how a conversation will end. A subject seems inexhaustible—and then suddenly there is nothing more to say. One can go on talking, but it will only be variations on a theme. There was nothing more that I wanted to hear from Katie Delgado. I had been right and wrong about her. I had been right in thinking her an adversary, but I was wrong in thinking her merely self-serving. I was right in thinking there had been advance preparation for this meeting, but I was wrong in thinking it had been merely for the purpose of outmaneuvering me.

"So what do you think?" I asked her.

"About what?"

"About Ellen and me."

Katie looked at me, thought for a moment, then shook her head. Nothing to say. Of course. What should she say? That was for me to decide, wasn't it?

"Do you think it could have been otherwise?" I asked.

She looked puzzled. How did I mean that? Since I meant that in more ways than could be condensed in a simple explanation, I said, "Never mind," and looked around for the waiter.

19 Did I mention that Ellen and I came back to that Jane Street apartment after our honeymoon? We lived there for about six months while looking for a house in Queens where Ellen worked and where she could practice. We had both decided that the Village was no place to bring up a child, *schlepping* up three flights of stairs, all kinds of human spindrift in the streets. That Village apartment with the high windows and the temperamental fireplace.

I can't say it was the best of times, but I don't think Ellen would deny that it was a good time. We had youth and money and freedom. We had the most varied city in the world to entertain us. We had friends, health, and (at least I thought so at the time) an ambitious sex life. By "ambitious," I mean that we seemed to be striving toward some higher level of attainment. I couldn't imagine anything better than what we had, but Ellen always suggested something beyond, a possible transcendence through the flesh. I put it down to gender differences, the difference in sexual tempo, and although I never really discovered *her* tempo, I believe I was a good and willing partner. I may have been kidding myself then, and now, but I did, and do, believe it.

Now I wonder if it had anything to do with tempo. Perhaps it was all gender. I wonder if even then Ellen wasn't trying to magic away a frightening discordancy with an Orphic ritual.

I remember once—strange that all these agitated hours hadn't released it before—when we had been to a party somewhere in the Seventies, one of those crowded parties with hired bartenders and ambulatory trays of food. Whose party? Oh, yes—Steve Singleton, an ad man whose client sponsored a program on which I had worked. The party was in celebration of Steve's recent promotion in the agency. He was being elevated to V/P of Something. During the evening, we learned that Steve and his wife, Sue, were getting a divorce. The divorce decision had been taken some weeks before the party, but since it was (so we were told) an amicable thing, they saw no reason not to have the party.

Ellen wanted to get out as soon as possible. I agreed. We walked to Second Avenue to find a taxi—finding a parking space for your car was well into its crisis stage—and when we had found one Ellen sat silently in her corner, staring out the window.

"Hey," I said, "if someone hadn't told us, we wouldn't know. Then it would have been just a party."

Ellen continued to stare out the window, saying nothing. I remember thinking: *Well, fuck it! Why the hell should I be iced for the queerness of others!*—and I returned her silence with my own, all the way home, to our apartment on Jane Street.

In the apartment, Ellen took off her coat and sat down before a dead fireplace. "Please," she said.

"Please what?"

"Please come here."

I went to her. She took my hand. Hers were frigid. I was still riding the wave of my resentment, not being very compliant.

"Did you see her face?" she asked.

"Whose? Sue's? Yes, I saw it."

"It was ghastly," Ellen said.

"Was it? I didn't find it so. I promise you one thing—we won't have a party for our divorce."

I said it because I felt I was somehow being *blamed* for the stupid affair, and that, it seemed to me, was as stupid as the party itself. What particularly irritated me was the inadvertence of the whole thing. Steve and Sue hadn't announced their divorce as the reason for the party. The divorce was something we had learned about by accident, by gossip. So I made no effort to get with the panic mood it had produced in Ellen. I should have, I suppose. I should have been alerted by, tried to probe, such an excessive reaction. But I didn't. I preferred nursing my own sense of injustice.

It passed, but it left a sediment that had stirred itself into other occasions. I'm not sure why. Perhaps because of Ellen's clutch of desolation, a presentiment, too distant to define.

And now as I drove toward Forest Hills, I caught a taste of that old sediment in the mix. Part of the mix was something that Katie Delgado had said. . . . No, it was something *I* had said . . . what was it? . . . Oh, yes, I had said that I was having a bad time sitting opposite a stranger who was explaining my wife to me. And then Katie had said, *"Your wife is not a stranger to me."* . . . which had seemed off center, since I hadn't said that *Ellen* was the stranger, but that she, Katie

Delgado, was the unwarranted stranger. Was that accidental or deliberate on her part? A Freudian slip? Whatever it was, it was taking on more and more significant weight.

The implication was clear. Ellen was a stranger to *me*. I didn't know her. I had lived with her for over twenty-five years, but I didn't know her. Is that something Katie guessed, or something Ellen told her? If the latter, was it meant figuratively or literally? In either case, what did I think about it? *Did* I know Ellen?

Well, let's see . . . I knew that Ellen could fall asleep flat on her stomach. That was something I could never do. But I could have known that of the soldier occupying the bunk next to mine. I knew that she rarely achieved an orgasm on the first trip, needed that second epiphany. But I'm sure her gynecologist knew that—and more—about her. I knew that she preferred Bach to Beethoven, Serkin to Horowitz, and a walk in the park to any athletic contest devised by man. I knew the incision in her left breast where a benign tumor had been removed. I knew that she preferred squeezing fresh oranges in an old-fashioned glass contraption to the quick, efficient whir of an electric juicer. Why? "Because I like a certain amount of pulp in it, and I can control the pulp in the glass thing." I knew the two Schubert sonatas that made her cry. I could go through a mail-order catalogue and tell you which dresses, skirts, blouses, sweaters, and coats she was likely to choose. I knew the kind of human company that would render her silent and the kind of company that could coax her into speech. . . .

I could go on and on, but I see what is happening. The lists I could accumulate are only accurate, not revealing.

"Was it a question of my not asking or your not saying?" I asked Ellen.

"I can't be sure," she said. "The two work together. One is willing to talk only after the other has shown sufficient interest. If there isn't sufficient interest, nothing is volunteered, after a time."

"But that's what I can't buy," I said. "It seems to me that I *was* interested. I can't remember a time when I wasn't interested in you."

"You were interested in me as a presence who would listen."

"Ellen, is that true? You're saying a very damning thing. It might be true, but please think carefully. Was it? Was I never interested for your sake, *just for you*?"

"Of course you were," Ellen said. "I never made you out to be a monster. There were many times when your attention was turned entirely to me."

"Can you remember a time?"

"Yes, I can remember a time. I can remember many times. There was one thing that always turned your attention to me."

"What?"

"Piano recitals. In the concert hall, recordings, on the radio. Whenever we were together and piano music was being played, you would turn to me. Sometimes you would say something, sometimes not, but I always knew you were thinking of me."

"With a guilty conscience?" I asked.

"No, I don't think so. I think you were genuinely concerned. I think you were wondering if I had made the right decision."

"And had you?"

"That's a foolish question."

"Why?"

"Because it is," Ellen said. "It's a question out of its time."

"You thought at one time that you didn't have enough

talent," I reminded her. "At least that's what you said to me."

"I didn't have enough something," she said.

We were sitting where we always sat when important things were said, positively or negatively. In the dining area, the one that gave out on the back garden. The tulips and the flowering dogwood were still there. Emotionally I had passed through a jumble of seasons, and it wouldn't have surprised me to see mums and marigolds out there. . . .

How strange. I remembered the girl—Kim—the immediate cause of our break, and she seemed to me now a piece of floating nostalgia, a fragment of the wreckage.

"You had withdrawn from me long before Kim," I said.

"It must be so," Ellen said.

"Anything I say—is that it?"

"No, George, I'm tired. I haven't slept for days. Not well. Not a full night's sleep for days."

"Am I the reason for that?"

She looked at me. She did indeed look tired, hollow eyes and that nebulous gaze gone almost blind. Her usually perfect hair looked dessicated and frayed.

"You've been so much a part of my life," she said, her voice near tears.

"I wouldn't have thought so."

"Then you've missed the whole point," she said.

"The point being," I said, "that you made it your business to know me, while I only wanted a presence who would listen."

Not completely, but enough—that's what Ellen's haunted look told me. And it was true. Arrange it any way you wished, to ease your conscience or your breathing (I was having some difficulty with mine), it was essentially true.

"So what shall we do?" I asked. "Divorce?"

"Wouldn't that be best for you?" she asked.

"Not for you?"

"It doesn't matter all that much to me," she said. "I don't intend to marry again."

"Will you want to go on living here with Katie?"

"No," she said. "I think we should sell this house. It's paid for. It should bring quite a lot of money. We can divide the money, if that's all right with you."

"That's all right with me," I said. "Ellen, I'm going to leave now. I realize that there's a mountain of details that have to be gone over, but right now I've no head for details. Later. We'll settle everything later. Okay?"

She nodded.

I could have said more, I could have said it differently, but it didn't matter. As a matter of fact, more was said. I'm giving only a summary here. The important thing is that I was truly having difficulty with my breathing. I had to be away from Ellen because there was a layer of subsidence lowering in my mind and it was smothering me. Like those layers of subsidence around Denver, under which gather the fumes and pollutants they call the "brown cloud."

Out of the house, into my car, where I could open all the windows and have the air rush all about me. That was good. It created an external agitation to balance the internal one. I hoped it would. It didn't really. It just set up a roaring and blew my hair about. I drove aimlessly, if not blindly, and wound up on the Queensboro Bridge. From there I drove downtown and got off somewhere around the Battery. I drove through the semideserted Wall Street area, and then made my way back to the East Side Drive. From there to the George Washington Bridge. Over the bridge—but not home—that is, that incidental, cubistic hutch I had made my temporary home. No, I couldn't go there. The prospect of walking around in those silent, hopelessly alien rooms, with the distant voice of Mrs. Speros hailing in her cheerfully harsh way one of her sons or daughters-in-law or sisters or friends was not to be contemplated. There was an indefinable danger in that. I wasn't about to do myself an injury—I'm not the suicide type—but it was conceivable that the binary fulminate of that silence and my tumult might blow the upstairs Speros apartment clean into the Hudson River.

Instead, I kept on going, turned off at a familiar turnoff, bought a ticket to one of those multiple movie hideouts where lunatics, lovers, and layabouts go to escape the glare of reality.

I saw a movie about a young girl who loved to dance, who did dance, wildly, acrobatically. When I could no longer bear that jittery fairy tale, I got up and left. I walked out into the large, more or less deserted lobby, saw there was nothing or no one to stop me, so I ducked into another of the movies. This was about American marines being stitched by Vietnamese gunners. Amazing what bloody gouts appear in a soldier's uniform when Hollywood does the shooting. The bullets don't appear to be going from the outside in, but the reverse, inside out, blowing open ragged carnations of blood. When that palled, I walked out into the same spooky lobby and entered a third movie house, where another kind of film was in progress. This one seemed to be about international intrigue, with quirky British and Soviet agents acting, I'm sure, as no British or Soviet agent ever acted. Homosexuality was involved. At one point, one of the agents shows someone a photograph of his son about to bugger another young man. I tried to concentrate. It wasn't that I was at all interested, but I felt that concentration on this flamdoodle would be both a challenge and a therapy. If I tried to figure out what was going on, it would take my mind off myself. It also bothered me that I was invariably lost in these spy intrigue movies. I can never figure out what's going on. Try as I might, I just can't figure out what's going on. And I don't think I'm stupid. . . .

Am I not? Then how is it that I couldn't figure out what was going on in twenty-five years of marriage? I asked this of myself in the dark of the movie house, and I repeated the question in the Jersey twilight as I got into my car and drove away into the dangerous traffic. I had delayed the critical moment, leaving it in a state of suspension. Now there was nothing to do but confront it.

Ellen was a stranger to me. It was as clear as the air on Milner Pass (and as difficult to breathe) that I didn't know the woman who had borne our child, made my meals, shared my bed, listened to my gaffes and griefs, gratified my body countless times in countless ways.

What do I mean by that? What does Katie Delgado mean? What does Ellen mean? Jess? ANYBODY! I mean, who is kidding whom? Isn't the eternal problem what I said it was: separate heads? There's just so much we can know about each other, and the rest is darkness. Isn't that so? I would stake my life on that dark verity. After all, I love Jess with as deep and selfless a love as is possible for egotistical George Light, and I really don't know what goes on in her heart or head. . . . But maybe . . . just maybe . . . I will find a way to compensate for that. . . .

I entered the house and climbed the stairs to my apartment. I heard Mrs. Speros fuss with her door, open it, call up to me, "You eaten yet?"

"No."

"I made this here moussaka. I got tons of the stuff. I got some salad. You can have a nice dinner."

"That's very kind of you."

"No problem. I'll bring it up."

Mrs. Speros brought it up, instructed me on how to heat it, told me I wasn't looking all that well. Sure I'm not getting sick? I refrained from telling her I *was* sick, but it was a sickness neither moussaka nor medicine could fix.

I heated the moussaka and ate large quantities of it. Then I sat down in front of the TV set and watched anything for hours. Around midnight, I went to bed, trying to make my mind a vacuum, thinking that sleep would be impossible tonight, and promptly fell asleep. I woke up the next morning with my mind still in a vacuum state. One by one, the happenings of my recent history filled the vacuum. The high school production of *West Side Story*, jigsaw chunks of foolish movies, Ellen, Katie Delgado, and the new reality I had carried with me since my meeting with that green-eyed, formidable woman.

I felt quieter about it now.

Ellen was a stranger to me. Too many secrets of heart and head had been left secret because she had spent too much time listening to me. . . . *"One is willing to talk only after the other has shown sufficient interest."*

I hadn't shown sufficient interest.

And the terrible truth that had been trying to reach me all day was that it couldn't have been otherwise. Even if I knew then what I know now, it couldn't have been otherwise.

Because I was what I was, just as Ellen was what she was.

And now that it *could* be otherwise, it was too late.

20

I am, I think, a responsible man. Have I said that before? No matter. I don't forget appointments or fail to pay my bills. I say (or repeat) this to give perspective to the next week or so. Frankly, I'm not sure how many days passed in that sunny fog.

I didn't want to see anyone. I told Mrs. Speros I had this TV project, and that it was a very exciting, time-consuming thing. Lots of hours up in my room, lots of trips here and there. Did she understand? Yes, she understood. Good. She mustn't be surprised at my comings and goings.

I stayed out a lot. The weather was very obliging. A bouquet of spring days, full of sunshine and greenery. I drove north, not really knowing where I was going, and wound up somewhere around Lake George. I stayed overnight there and drove back the next day.

"Your phone was ringing a lot," Mrs. Speros told me.

"I'll have to get one of those recorders," I said.

I couldn't let the phone ring when I was at home. Mrs. Speros would suspect something unkosher. I supposed I could have unplugged the damn thing, but some vague, superstitious fear prevented me from doing so. Cutting myself off that way would invite the evil eye. Something disastrous might happen and the frantic voice on the other end couldn't reach me. I counted on my instinct to inform me whether the voice at the other end was frantic or not. So I picked up the phone when it rang, partially muffled it with my hand, improvised a throaty, nondescript accent, and announced something like "Mister Light say he be gone coupla days. I'm repair man for Missus Speros."

I know I recognized Jess's voice. Ditto Ellen's voice. Larry Graff's voice. My brother's voice. The flurry of phone calls—answered or unanswered—reinforced my claim to great doings.

I drove into the city, parked my car in the usual garage, and went to museums and more movies. I passed rows of paintings, cases full of pottery, dully amazed how little seeing there could be with so much looking. I ate in museum restaurants and tried not to remember other times when I had sat in approximately the same place, feeling haughtily at home. My museum, my city, my future. I sat in another darkened movie house and saw a foreign film. Deliberately, I didn't look at the captions. I understood nothing.

I dropped into the liquor store I had patronized when I was drawing a regular salary. A well-stocked liquor store with imported wines cradled row on row.

"Mr. Spivack in?" I asked a clerk.

"Nnn—yeah—there he is."

I had already looked at the man indicated and hadn't taken him to be Mr. Spivack. The Mr. Spivack I knew was a round, bald man I used to call "Akim," because he looked so much like that old movie favorite of mine, Akim Tamiroff. This man was a stray wisp in baggy clothes shuffling toward the stairs that led to the upstairs office, the office where I had always been invited for a pre-Christmas drink by the prosperous proprietor.

"Mr. Spivack?"

The wisp turned. He recognized me—and then I recognized him. It was Mr. Spivack rehearsing his death.

"Ah, hello," he said. "How are you, George? Haven't seen you in a long time."

"Been out of town," I said, taking the hand he offered me.

His voice was a whisper and his hand was a little sack of twigs.

"Nice to see you," he said. "I'm sorry I'm not feeling too well."

"I'm sorry, too, Mr. Spivack."

"This Christmas I'm afraid I won't be here to offer you a drink," he said.

"Five will get you twenty," I said.

"Save your money."

I walked out of Spivack's Liquor wondering why the stupid fuss about love and the end of love when each of us was growing his death like a black pearl.

I suppose I could have packed my things and gone back to Denver. Vince would have found a job for me. I thought about it, but only as a respite from the more serious business of reengaging my life. The idea of total escape gave me a certain amount of malicious satisfaction. Let them all stew.

What I dreaded was the final acknowledgment. I didn't want to start over, I wanted to continue. But I couldn't continue because the people I had counted on continuing with had moved on in unimaginable ways. But I *had* to start over. It ached me to think of it.

"Honestly, Dad, that's the last thing I expected of you. That's childish. What was the point of it?"

"I just didn't feel like talking," I said. "I seem to recall there were many times in your life when you shut yourself away for hours and even days at a time. I don't remember that I ever accused you of being childish."

"But there was somebody in your room," Jess said. "Somebody answered the phone. Who was that clown?"

"Me."

"Oh, God! So where were you?"

I told Jess where I'd been. Around. No place. Doing things she would understand, like going from one movie to another. To museums. A drive upstate, to Lake George.

"And what did you decide?" Jess asked.

"Am I supposed to decide something? Is somebody waiting for my decision?"

"Please."

"What do you think I should decide?"

"Dad."

"I'm serious, Jess. What kind of decision is called for? A divorce? Does your mother want that? I'm waiting to find out if she wants that. There are things to look into. Property. I have to talk to a lawyer. I have to talk to her. I have to talk to you."

"What do you have to talk to me about?" Jess wanted to know.

"Oh, Christ, Jess!"

"What?"

"I'll tell you what!" I stopped, cleared my throat, started over, several decibels lower. "I'll tell you what. Where are you living? Where *will* you live? I don't want you in that house if Katie Delgado is there. I realize I have very little authority—"

"I have my own place," Jess interrupted to say.

"Good. Where?"

"On the West Side. Near Columbia."

"Can you give me an address? A telephone number?"

"Yes."

"Jess . . ."

"What?"

"I'm not going to preach to you. I'm in no position to do that, but I am going to ask if Neil intends, eventually, to leave his present wife and be with you."

"I don't know," she said.

"You said, 'near Columbia.' Was the choice of location deliberate? Are you planning to go to Columbia?"

"Maybe. I'm not sure."

"How about Europe?"

"No, I'm not going to Europe."

"You're going to stick around and be available for Neil Andrews, is that it?"

"I'm going to stay here and be with Neil as often as I can."

"Even though it may come to nothing?"

"How can it come to nothing if it's an enormous something every time we're together?" she said. "I love Neil. I love it when he puts his hands on me. Is there anything else you'd like to know?"

"No, there's nothing else I'd like to know. I'm learning my lesson—but good! It's George-bashing time and everybody is getting in on the fun. I didn't think I'd built up such a delinquent account with fate."

"Oh, Dad," Jess said. "This is not the way I had imagined things either. I don't know what to do about it except live from day to day. We were a family—and suddenly we're not—suddenly each is on his own."

Another failure of imagination? Why hadn't I asked myself how all of this must appear to Jess? Why was I so quick to assume that she was part of the conspiracy?

We were a family—and suddenly we're not!

"What can I do, Jess?" I asked, feeling almost drunk with helplessness. "I have money. If you need money, ask me. If you need my presence or concern, I'm here. I shouldn't have disappeared, but I did. It won't happen again. You know where to find me. If I can help you in any way, I'm here."

"Thank you," she said. "It's a rotten time, but we'll all live through it."

"Bet on it!"

"Why don't you drop over to the office?" my brother, Henry, said. "We can have lunch. They've opened up a new restaurant right off the parkway. I've eaten there a few times. It's quite good."

"That would be nice, Henry. I'd be glad to. But not right now. I'm working against a deadline. I promised to have a treatment very soon, and I'm working day and night."

A moment of phone silence. Harry teetered on his own brink. He jumped. "How can you have been working day and night when nobody answered your phone? No, there was somebody. I couldn't understand a word he said. But in any case, *you* weren't there."

"I do have to go into the city, Henry. That's where the people are who must buy what I'm doing. I do have to consult with them. Like you do with your customers. You know?"

"I don't see the need for this," Henry said. "It's not as if I were trying to pick up some gossip. I'm trying to find out what's going on, if I can be of any help."

"I know you are, Henry, and I appreciate it. There's nothing you can do. If there were, believe me, I would have come to you."

"Sometimes it helps to talk."

"How much time do you have to listen?"

Another short spell—this time of wounded silence.

"That was uncalled for," Henry said. "Have I ever cut you off? Have I ever indicated to you that I didn't have the time to talk?"

"No, you haven't. Please don't be offended."

"It's a little too late to tell me that. You've given me more than enough reason to be offended."

"If I have, I'm terribly sorry, Henry. It's true that I haven't been in touch with you much since coming back east, but I have been occupied. Very. I don't question your good intentions. I know you want to help, but there's no way you can help me."

"Why not? Why can't I help? I'm your brother. How many brothers do you have?"

"Henry, here's the way it is. Ellen and I have split because of who we are and the way our separate lives have developed. Since you know nothing about that, there isn't much good advice you can give me. You're about to say whose fault is it that you and Phyllis know so little about Ellen and me. I don't have a sure answer for that, but I'd be willing to split the blame fifty-fifty. It's unfortunate but there hasn't been much mutuality there. Just one of those things. Basically, you'd like to know what's going on, and that's not what I want to talk about. I want to talk about *why* it's going on, and I can't talk about that to you because I'd have to go back too far. Besides, it would take up too much of your time and my time. When something definite happens, I'll let you know. In the meantime, rest assured that I know that your intentions are of the best."

"I've been trying to get in touch with you, George," Larry said, his voice heavy with put-upon patience.

"I had to run up to Boston."

"What's in Boston?"

"The Charles River."

"Are you still interested in the idea you told me about?"

"What do you think I've been doing, Larry? I had to get the hell away from here so that I could do some work on it. The goddam phone was ringing all the time. I packed my typewriter, took some clean underwear, and drove up toward Boston, stopping in motels. I do my best thinking in the car. And in motel rooms."

"Did you get to Boston?"

"I got as far as Cape Ann. It's beautiful."

"Know something?" he said.

"What?"

"You're full of shit."

"Larry."

"You were right there in your Jersey hideout, making like a drunken Hungarian."

"That's not quite true, Larry. I have been in my car. A lot. I have been thinking. A lot."

"Ted Samuels wants to get together with us. Can you give me a date?"

"Next Tuesday?"

"Will you have something by then?"

"Depend on it."

Someone—I forget who—I think it was a lawyer—once said to me that it was amazingly difficult to get lost. Unless you changed your name, your country, your history. And even then, a determined investigator could track you down. I had no trouble tracking down Neil Andrews. I didn't want Jess to know that I was contacting him, so I couldn't ask her for his most discreet telephone number. I didn't want to speak to him at his home (which I found in the Bronxville telephone book), so I called his home when he was most likely not to be there, spoke to a woman who was probably his wife, told her that I was an old fraternity buddy passing through the city, would like to say hello to Neil. I knew he was connected to a New York law firm, but I didn't know which one. Could I have a number where he could be reached? I could.

"This is George Light . . . Jessica's father."
    "Hello, Mr. Light. How are you?"
    "I wonder if you could have lunch with me, soon. I realize you're busy—"
    "When would it be convenient for you?" he asked.
    "I'm the one with all the time. You say when."
    "Would this Friday be all right?"
    "Friday it is."

To say that I didn't know what I was doing, running amok, would be wrong; but to say that I had planned and was executing a course of carefully considered action would be even more wrong. Where I had only to respond, I responded as decently and noncommittally as I could. I tried to satisfy curiosity and concern without promising to do or not to do anything in particular. Where I had to take the initiative, I did so with no great certitude or sure direction.

My life had changed. Very well, my life had changed before. But this time I hadn't authored the change. I hadn't even co-authored it. It had changed without my knowledge and without my consent. It had changed because the people closest to me had been changing without my knowing it. I didn't know whether I wanted to, could, accommodate myself to these changes, or simply to tell the turncoats to get lost.

I make my own changes, thank you. Others accommodate themselves to me.

Is that being a responsible man?

I was riding between responsibility and survival, bouncing off one and into the other. Pride and anger. Belligerence and contrition.

More than anything else, I wanted to establish the identity of the guy being bounced around. How could I write a book on the man-woman thing if man had become as much a mystery as woman?

21 This restaurant features what they call French-Vietnamese cuisine. Apparently, the surest way into the cookery of another people is to go to war with them. I wasn't sure whether French-Vietnamese was an amalgam or a choice. I ordered a chicken dish that left me in doubt as to its nationality. Not its taste. It was delicious, in a hyphenated way, and that very hyphenation suggested an answer to a question I had raised before: why my Jessica went for the Bryan Danielses and Neil Andrewses of this world. It suggested that I might have the things backward—that the attraction originated with the Danielses and Andrewses. They were drawn to the hyphenated charm of Jessica Light. I could believe that. Those smoky blue eyes, that ecumenical smile. I could see how a Neil Andrews, with his liberal politics, his distinguished ancestry, might feel he was tasting the apple of a different Eden when he kissed Jessica Light.

That difference of background intrigued me so much that I couldn't resist filling Neil Andrews in on possible omissions on Jess's part. Had she told him, for example, that her grandfather and great-grandfather had come from the Odessa region of Russia, that they were draymen, truckers, in the Isaac Babel tradition? Had Neil Andrews ever heard of Isaac Babel? Had he ever read the stories of Isaac Babel? Neil Andrews confessed that he hadn't. Well, I could recommend Isaac Babel to Neil, because Isaac Babel was a splendid writer, one who could spell out for him in hilarious ways life in the Odessa region, particularly for Jews. Isaac Babel had described one of his characters as a man "with spectacles on his nose and autumn in his heart." Wasn't that catching a character in a line? Yes, it was.

As for the Light history before Jessica's great-grandfather, that was uncertain, as uncertain and itinerant as the Diaspora itself. The name, of course, hadn't been "Light" originally. Whatever its origin, it had undergone a German transformation, then a Polish, then a Russian, then an American. So in a very real sense, you might say the name is arbitrary, self-selected. But of the two great divisions of the Diaspora—the Ashkenazim and the Sephardic—Jess's line was definitely Ashkenazim—that is, it was culturally more connected with the eastern European enclosures than with the Spanish agonies. . . .

Why was I doing this? I knew why. I was curious to see how Neil Andrews would react to this thick impasto of Light history. What was I looking for? I guess I was looking for a faint flicker of Anglo-Saxon dismay at all the *shtetl* mud and pickel-barrel pungency. Oh, yes, I hadn't left out my grandfather's chief account in this great country—the pickle-maker—hauling whose product saw my family through the Depression.

If I was looking to make Neil Andrews's eyes smart with

all that pickle juice, I was mistaken. He hadn't made his way in politics by being a Wasp wimp. He was smart. He was educated. He had been indoctrinated into many ethnic ways. And he was wearing a tie to which, again, I could offer no objection. It was a rep. Nice. And a light-blue, button-down shirt. And a gray, pin-striped suit. Very nice.

"My family background is as dull as ditch water compared to yours," Neil said, as if he meant it, and he might have. "My father was a lawyer, and his father was a textile manufacturer in Massachusetts. I'm told that one of my ancestors was a friend of Henry Adams and that another had a cabinet post in the Monroe administration. He had something to do with obtaining Florida from Spain. My ancestors were born advantageously, and they held on for dear life."

"I understand you met Jess in Ann Arbor," I said, beginning to fear that this meeting might dissipate in mere pleasantries.

"That's right," he said. "I had been invited to be on a panel discussing politics and the media."

"I can see how Jess would be interested in that," I said. "That's her subject. Did she ever tell you about the paper she wanted to write?"

"You mean the one—"

"The one about TV and the news. The effect of personality on the news. You know, like the anchorperson's personality distilling the news through expressive eyes and charming smiles and a perfect voice. I was very sorry she gave that up. I thought that was really something for her to cut her journalistic teeth on. It would have been tough. God, it would have been tough. But I thought it was worth doing. Even if it failed, it would have been worth doing. You see, I've been in the business—"

"I know."

"—and I really felt that a failure like that would have been worth a half-dozen meager, conventional successes. Because she would have had to dig deep into herself to come up with a halfway decent analysis. She might not have been up to the task, but trying as hard as she could would have been an invaluable lesson. If nothing else, it would have taught her how to stretch those muscles."

"I see what you mean," Neil Andrews said, with a contemplative look in his clear brown eyes.

"Do you? What do I mean?"

Neil smiled. He had a very orderly smile—that is, it distributed itself over his fine features, no one part in excess or in deficit. Some people smile lavishly with their lips while their eyes remain unamused, apart. Neil Andrews smiled sincerely, and a little reflectively.

"I think you mean that you're sorry I was discouraging about that," he said.

"Yes, among other things, I mean that," I said. "Why did you? I mean, were you absolutely sure you knew what you were talking about?"

Neil shook his head, his smile turning wry. "Absolutely? An opinion is never absolute. It's only an opinion."

"I had encouraged her to go ahead with it," I said.

"I didn't know that until later," he said. "It was while we were on the plane going back east that she told me she had discussed it with you, and that you thought it could be done."

"So what did you say when you learned that?"

"I said that you would probably be better informed about such a thing than I would."

"No, I wouldn't," I said. "Why should I be better informed? You're a lawyer. You're a politician. I'll bet you're a hell of a lot better educated than I am. Where did you get your undergraduate degree?"

"Princeton."

"And your law degree?"

"Harvard."

"My prophetic soul!"

"Mr. Light—"

"I wish you would call me George. The nice thing is that you're as contemporary with me as you are with my daughter. If you don't mind my asking, how old are you?"

"Forty-one."

"Let's see . . . that leaves a twenty-year gap between you and Jess, but only a ten-year gap between you and me. Definitely. You and I are more contemporaneous. So please call me George. Why did you think Jess's idea wouldn't work?"

"I thought that the intangibles of personality would be too difficult to evaluate."

"I agree," I quickly agreed. "Hellishly difficult. Which I saw as a reason for the attempt. People are remembered for their splendid failures. Have you ever failed at anything, Neil?"

"I have."

"You see, the way I saw it, Jess would try this thing, she would be forced to consider things she hadn't considered before, and whatever the outcome it would have been an enriching experience. Sometimes poetry doesn't seem to make much sense, and yet lines are remembered and quoted long after statistics are stored away in computer banks. . . . 'Swept with confused alarms of struggle and flight, / Where ignorant armies clash by night'."

"George—"

"I couldn't tell you what else was doing at that moment of history, but I do remember that line."

The smile had faded from Neil Andrews's lips, and something steady and unfriendly now composed his features. I had a premonition about this. These handsome Yankee types, all civility and charm, can go rock hard when push finally comes to shove. I had been shoving him, waiting for this sign.

"I didn't have your understanding or your motivation at

the time that conversation took place," he said. "Jess and I had only just met. I was trying to give an honest opinion. I see now that yours was the deeper insight, the better one."

"Then perhaps you'll grant me better insight about other things, as well," I said.

"Perhaps."

"Perhaps you'll grant me a father's insight that you're fucking up Jess's life—but good!—with this affair."

"No, I won't grant you that," he said.

"Then for all your education and good looks and nice manners, you're rather a prick. If you were in my shoes, I think you'd be having my insights. You as good as admitted that you made a mistake before about Jess's project. Couldn't all of it be one lousy mistake? Jess was going abroad to study for a year—"

"I know."

"She was going to do that paper, start her graduate work—"

"She will."

"I mean, you can find playmates anywhere," I said meanly, aggressively. "Leave Jess. Let her get on with her life. I'm asking you, one man to the other, husbands and fathers, please don't put Jess through this wringer."

Neil leaned back in his chair. I was sitting on the cushioned wall seat. He had been leaning forward in a vain attempt to keep our conversation *sotto voce*. There were diners on either side of us. He had kept *his* voice discreetly low, but I had used my voice as part of my calculated weaponry. I had caught glimpses from the couple seated to my left. They had been picking up verbal tidbits as tasty as anything they were eating. I didn't care, Neil did. The change that came over him was unmistakable. Since he couldn't prevent me from using my armaments, he would fight back with his own.

"I'm sorry you're taking this tone," he said. "You're very

conscious of mistakes. Let me tell you that you're making one, a big one. I don't look for playmates. I happen to be in love with Jess."

"She tells me you're unhappily married," I said. "Why don't you get a divorce and marry Jess? I assume you've got lots of money. You can pay for all parties concerned. Perhaps you'd even be good enough to pay Jess's tuition."

Neil gave me a steady, granite look. Now he looked as indifferent to eavesdroppers as I had been. I thought he was going to suggest that we go outside and finish this discussion with our fists. That would have been all right. I think he would have broken me up rather efficiently, but that would have been all to the good. Naturally, he did nothing of the sort.

He did ask if I was through eating. I said yes, and he signaled for the check, which I immediately grabbed. After all, *I* had invited *him*. I went through the credit card routine, while the couple to my left fairly crepitated with silent, intense attention.

Outside, another beautiful day. We walked south on Third Avenue, while Neil Andrews explained to me how he felt about my daughter. He admitted he'd had affairs with other women because his was an unhappy marriage, but this was the first time he'd fallen in love with another woman. I retorted that I had only his word for all of the above, and that "love" was the most easily traded and quickly devalued commodity in the sex market. In just what way did he *love* Jess? He said he loved Jess eagerly and happily. He looked forward to seeing her, and he felt hollow when he left her. He had rearranged his life complicatedly but guiltlessly around this new, central thing.

"Then why don't you divorce your wife and marry Jess?" I asked again.

"Because my wife doesn't want a divorce," he said. "Because she would make a divorce as ruinous as possible, and the most ruinous thing for me would be to take the kids, make it just about impossible for me to have my career, have my kids, even part time, and have Jess. She could do it, too. She has the will and the means."

"Does she know about Jess?"

"She knows there's someone. Ironically, she has a lover."

"What's a nice Wasp like you doing in such a mess?"

"I ask myself the same thing."

"Suppose I were to say that I will do everything to ruin your political career if you go on with this," I said. "Suppose I were to say that I will wait for the right moment, and then I will go to every newspaper and magazine with this little 'love nest' story."

"Then that's what you would do, but I doubt that you will."

"Why wouldn't I?"

"Because you'd lose Jess, and I know that you care for her as much as I do."

"So what's going to be?" I asked him.

"I don't know," he said. "I hope that things will change. I will tell you this, and I hope you believe it: No matter how difficult for me, I will not make it difficult for Jess if and when she wants to end it."

"Are you going to tell Jess about this little session?" I asked him.

"No."

"Good. Neither will I."

I could imagine the Neil Andrews's face while it was taking lumps from his wife, from me, but I couldn't imagine that cool, dolichocephalic countenance in transitions of passion and tenderness.

That was Jess's secret.

22

Ted Samuels had stepped in at a pretty high level while I was still working for the network. Vice President. Program Development. I got the impression that he was even more important now that the pie was being cut into so many more slices.

We sat in the boardroom, just the three of us: Ted Samuels, Larry Graff, George Light. George Light spent the first few seconds trying to remember whether Ted Samuels was wearing a hairpiece or not. It seemed to me he was in a balding state those few times I saw him in the past. Now he had a nice, thick, black head of hair—a bit too nice and thick—the symmetrical perfection you find in ersatz teeth and hair. Anyway, what difference? There was nothing synthetic about his bright brown eyes or his open, friendly face. He wore old-fashioned horn-rimmed glasses, and he looked, all in all, like a man you'd want to strike up a conversation with at a party.

"I'm eager to read this treatment," he said, "but I wonder if you could generalize on its contents so we can talk."

I said, "Yes, I suppose I could, although I'm better on paper than I am extemporizing."

"You do pretty well in all forms," Larry said.

"I remember *The Search*," Ted said. "That was first-rate stuff."

"Thank you. Actually, what I've got here is more a statement of intent than a schedule of specific programs—although I have suggested several programs."

"That's fine," Ted said. "That's exactly what I'd like to talk about—intent. Larry knows—and I'm sure you do, too—how many talk shows have explored feminism, sexuality, et cetera. What I'm most curious about—"

"This is not feminism," I said.

"—what I'm most curious about is knowing in just what way this program will avoid what's been done in the past—or, for that matter, what's being done right now. What will give it immediate interest and a chance of continuity?"

Larry sat there in his best Buddhalike inscrutability, both hands folded before him on the polished table. The bulk of him reposed with a quiet, settled confidence. I wondered where Larry bought his suits. The ordinary Big Man's shop? Or was there a custom tailor somewhere in the city who bought yards and yards of the finest worsteds to cut up into a Graff outfit? Way back in my mind, a tiny reverberation, was an echo of the ridiculous ditty I had been singing all morning . . . *"I went shootin' with Rasputin, ate farina with Czarina, blintzes with the Princess and the Czar . . ."* It was something I had sung before, many times, but for the life of me I couldn't remember when and where I'd first heard it. Just a bit of lost detritus, the kind that occasionally comes loose and rolls around in my head until it settles down for another long sleep.

I told Ted Samuels that the principle, or philosophy, was taken from several sources. It was my belief that no matter how much one heard, personally witnessed, or read about, there would always persist the suspicion that some vital piece of the truth was being withheld. That went for other people's marriages, love affairs, life-styles. The most graphic manuals or intimate confessions will not erase the feeling that some arcane corner has been left unexplored. Put it another way: There is no amount of information that will pave over the mind completely. Cracks will appear and new weeds will thrust up. The reason is simple. Separate heads. The human condition. The instant you stop telling me something, you have become engaged with your own private thoughts. Ditto me to you.

All of which is especially true, aggravatingly true, between men and women. Love, sex, all kinds of sharing gives hope of a final dissolution between the thee and me, but those nice processes never seem to complete themselves. The ultimate mystery of selfhood remains—and there's your immediate interest and the source of continuity.

I watched Larry Graff watch Ted Samuels as Ted Samuels listened with ears, eyes, and a slim silver instrument he had taken out of the inner breast pocket of his jacket. As I spoke, Ted jotted down notes on the pad before him. Larry, I had observed, listened at first dubiously, apprehensively, not quite sure where I was going with my philosophy, but gaining his own confidence as I gained mine. The shining emblem of both our confidences was the appearance of that exquisite pencil or pen. There was something in my discourse that Ted Samuels wanted to pin down in my own words. That was a good sign. That was a sign that he intended to carry the whole idea one step further.

"I can agree with that principle," he said. "How will it apply to television?"

"By channeling and directing that curiosity," I said.

"Better than giving it free rein," Larry put in.

It sounded as though he were correcting some previous notion of mine. Had I said anything about giving it "free rein"? I couldn't remember having said that. This was just a Larry ploy to make it appear that he and I had been refining this idea, kicking it around for days, weeks, months.

"I want to hear about the channeling and directing," Ted said.

In truth, the whole thing had been worked up yesterday—well, the day before yesterday and yesterday. Not that I work better under pressure, but I knew damn well that my head wasn't going to stay with any project for more than a few hours at a time. I was too jumpy. I was not at all sure I wanted this project on TV, and even if it was inexorably bound for TV, I wasn't sure I wanted to be connected with it. I knew what would happen to it on TV. It would play more and more to the silly and salacious. But I'm a man who has always been employed, and fate had arranged for that employment to be mainly in TV, and I must take the necessary steps to continue my employment, because, knowing myself, I will be useless to myself and anyone else if I lose my self-respect. My self-respect depends on employment and income. I can't help it. That's the way I am.

I said, "This program will need the kind of sharpness that will know how to keep a good thing going and how to cut short the bad. A good thing is an area of inquiry that is gender-oriented and generally interesting. Do men like women's clothing? Do they really notice what a woman is wearing, or are they eternally fixed on the swish and contour beneath the clothes? Do women like men's clothing? Do they really notice what a man is wearing, and how much of that style enhances interest? Would a man resent a woman taking a hand in his haberdashery? Is a man's mind and personality more important than his face and physique? How about a woman's mind and personality? Do these things count? Yes, they do, but when? After a man knows he's not in the running for that sexy blonde? Do men and women throw switches in their minds, consult a swift-changing flow of possibilities, like one of those electronic stock exchange tapes? Do men tell women the truth about themselves before marriage? Do women tell men the truth about themselves before marriage? Is it largely a cover-up? Does it remain a cover-up after marriage? Does a man finally come to resent a woman who shows absolutely no interest in football, baseball, basketball? Does a woman finally come to resent a man who consumes so many hours of family time watching every bloody sport under the sun or dome, when they could be walking in the park, discussing home improvements, or making love? Are young interns turned off romance or sex because of their necessary scrutiny of the body? What kind of separation do doctors and nurses make in their minds between the facts of their profession and the fantasies of love? How do men regard older women? How do women regard older men? When is a man seen as 'old'? When is a woman seen as 'old'? Except for sex, do women actually prefer the company of other women? Women do seem awfully comfortable with each other—is that a recent phenomenon, or something that has been true for a long time?"

I had my own pad, which I had taken out of my own jacket pocket when I began my catalogue. I read the list of possible program subjects that I had compiled last night, and as I read I felt again the exfoliation of the whole idea. That was my cue. I glanced at Larry and thought I could actually see an increase in the man's specific gravity as assurance settled more deeply and made itself part of his bulk. His eyes went from Ted Samuels to me, from me to Ted Samuels, like a conductor making a unity of soloist and orchestra. I looked at Ted Samuels and saw his glance fall to his notepad as he listened and kept time by tapping the end of his silver writing instrument against the pad.

"Who do you think might be the right MC?" Ted asked without raising his head.

Larry named two names. Ted nodded. I could see that he had other names in mind. I could also see that a deliberate transfer had been made. It was no longer *my* idea, or even mine and Larry's; it was now Ted Samuels's idea, and through Ted Samuels's horn-rimmed obstetrics, it was being prepared for removal. I could see that it was now officially a "Program Idea."

"Would you object if we went to an outside producer with this?" Ted asked.

I looked at Larry. Larry was unhappy with that idea. So was I. We must have looked like a pair of surrogate mothers waiting for the adoptive parents to arrive.

"I only mention it," said Ted, "because it's an option more and more considered these days. That and outside development money. You're both familiar with the situation. We have to spread the costs of these new things . . . and, naturally, the profits. I'm not saying that's the way it will come out, but I thought you ought to . . . George, do you have anything more there . . . ?" He pointed to my pad.

I read off the men-women panel combinations that had occurred to me. Professionals and blue-collar workers. The active and the retired. Men athletes and women athletes. The married and the unmarried. The once-married and the re-married. Lady poets and men novelists. Men poets and women novelists. (Tie-in with recent publications?) The rich and the poor. Statesmen and studs . . .

"I don't think there'll be any trouble getting panels," I concluded. "No one says no to the tube."

Ted returned his sleek silver pen to his pocket and picked up his pad. Interview over. "I'd like to get back to you in about a week," he said. "Are you available?"

"Why, yes . . ."

"If you get a chance would you drop by my office later this afternoon?" he said to Larry.

"Sure thing," Larry said.

Warm handshake, friendly smile. I was surprised there was no caution about keeping mum. "Oh, by the way," Ted said, "have you thought about a possible title for the program?"

"*A Better Way,*" I said. "I think I mentioned it to Larry. I said there's got be a better way for men and women to be together."

Ted Samuels sampled the flavor of that title. I don't think it was to his taste. Should I care? Should I make a big hoo-hah over my creative rights, yell that it will be done my way, with my title, or fuck 'em all? No, I shouldn't do that, because I knew the business well enough to know that you don't out-tough the soft giants with their legal staffs and their mountain aeries lined with millions. Of course, you could take them to court, but only if you were a soft giant yourself. If you were a responsible man with the lifetime habit of being gainfully employed, you nod and take Ted Samuels's hand in a firm, friendly grasp.

"I would still get that treatment in final form, ASAP," Larry said. "Take it to your lawyer. Let him do whatever he thinks should be done. Get it on record. What did you think?"

"About what?"

"About Samuels."

"I think Samuels is a wise and noble man," I said.

"Come on. He's really not a bad guy."

"Where do you fit in?" I asked Larry.

"I want to produce some of the shows. Not all. Some."

"You have my blessing," I said.

"And you?" he asked.

"What do you think I should do?" I asked him.

"Scripts," he said. "Work with the director. Keep pumping ideas into the show."

"How about the MC?" I asked. "Don't you think I have the makings of a TV personality?"

"No," Larry said.

"I'm disappointed. Why not?"

"You have a worried look," he said.

I should have been elated. They were hungry for a new talk show. Talk shows were daytime communions where sins were confessed and grace conferred. Or evening talk shows. Did Ted have a daytime or an evening show in mind? Once a week or once a day? All things to be discussed. But later. The fact was, I wasn't elated. I was letting my man-woman thing get away from me. I couldn't have been serious about it if I was giving it to TV. Or perhaps that was as serious as you could get these days. Serious things get done on TV. Vietnam. Watergate. Irangate. But those were things that had happened, were happening, and TV had only to show them. Yes, well, wasn't my man-woman thing what was happening, and wouldn't a TV talk show simply show it?

If I had said nothing to Larry Graff, to Jess, to Ellen, kept the thing hermetically sealed, enriched the thing with research and meditation, would that have resulted in an important statement? I doubt it. And does that mean I'm giving up on a try to express my sense of the thing? No, I still hope to do that, but I see that the audience I'm addressing is shrinking, that I may be talking only to a handful, that I may be talking only to myself.

Right now, I have errands to do. I must spend the rest of the day seeking a birthday present, for Jess will be twenty-one in two days. I'd like to get her something so potently loaded with magic that when she hangs it from her neck or slips it on her finger she will drift to the phone, dial the right number, and tell Neil Andrews that given his world, hers, and the crackling new ideas she's had on her "news" thesis, she must, with regret, and with ever so much gratitude . . . of course, nothing like that is going to happen. I have seen Mr. Andrews, talked to him, taken in the strength of his rep tie and his character, and I have decisions to make. I would like to buy a small gift for Jessica. Something choice, expressive. Her ears are pierced. Perhaps a pair of stud earrings. Pearls set in gold. Diamonds set in gold.

"I think that's a good idea," Ellen said. "I'm not actually buying her anything on my own. She wants a new dress, and I told her to pick it out and charge it with my card."

"Have you been to her apartment?" I asked.

"Yes, it's quite nice."

"I haven't been there yet," I said. "Is the neighborhood safe?"

"Well, you know . . ."

"We must meet, Ellen," I said.

"Yes, we must."

"After Jess's birthday?"

"Yes . . . after . . . George, would you want me to have a birthday dinner for Jess here at the house? It could be just the three of us. Or if Jess wanted to have some special . . . perhaps Neil . . ."

"No, I don't think that would be . . . personally, that is . . . I don't think that would be such a good idea."

"Or a restaurant," Ellen suggested. "Just the three of us."

I was surprised at the distance from which my heart surveyed the prospect. It was not a tranquil distance. It was a rutted, hillocked distance, but it was there, established, measurable. Equally measurable was the compassion that had prompted Ellen to make the gesture. But I didn't want it. Not that I was that strong or proud, but that I suddenly found myself in *need* of distance.

"No, Ellen," I said. "I don't think so."

"All right, George."

"But I would like to set a date for our meeting," I said. We set a date.

The small gift will be easy, from the heart, but the big gift (which I deliberately chose not to tell Ellen about) will be difficult. It will be difficult because, frankly, I don't know whether to give it or not; or, if given, given with conditions. I find the latter more questionable than repugnant. If I thought there was the slightest chance of it working, I might try it, because the stakes (in my eyes, at least) were that high.

I have a ten-thousand-dollar certified check for Jess. I had planned to give this to her on the occasion most to be blessed with that practical blessing. I had hinted at this money in Denver, when she spoke of graduate school or going abroad. It had been meant for things like that. Or her marriage. But now the purity of motive and the joy of giving had been muddied by the politics of reality.

I could dangle that large bundle as an inducement: *"Get out of this Neil Andrews mess, my Jess, and it's yours. I know the method is crass but the motive is not. He is a most attractive man. I see what you see, I understand what you feel, but I can't see anything but heartache and loss."* Or I can alter that little speech slightly and *give* her the money. As far as getting results, neither will do the trick. I know that. The first approach would have the unmistakable smell of bribery (which it is), and I would have a saddened or infuriated or disgusted Jess to deal with. Or *not* to deal with. The second approach—now that I've had some time to think about it—could very well be worse received than the first. The second would shift the moral burden to Jess . . . *"Here, take this money, and then do as you please, knowing how much I disapprove."*

The third alternative is probably the one I'll use. Not say anything, not give anything, except the earrings. Oh, not *nothing.* She needs some money. I'm still sending the monthly check that is my contribution to family expenses, which of course includes Jess, but if she does decide to enroll this fall in the graduate program, she'll need a hefty outlay of bucks. And she surely needs money for this apartment. I'll give her a check for, say, three thousand . . .

I decided on the diamonds. I went to a jeweler I knew, one who had advised me on a gift for Ellen back in the primeval days of my own beginning. I was told that when it came to stud earrings, the gold setting was questionable. Most girls seemed to prefer the jewel itself on a post, the pearl or the diamond. Of course, a gold necklace with a single diamond or emerald was very popular. That would be a very delicate gold chain and probably something more than a karat for the stone.

"Do you find buying presents for your wife, mistress, girlfriend, or daughter more of an ordeal than a pleasure? Is that because for all the love and intimacy, you don't feel you really know that most mysterious and inmost of secrets—taste?"

"Do you find buying presents for your husband, lover, boyfriend, son, more of an ordeal than a pleasure? Or is present-giving a secret, ongoing campaign to bring a questionable product up to its true potential?"

"Just a minute, just a minute! I'd like to ask Mr. Smarty-pants why he framed those two questions differently!"

"Well, look, can the young lady come in and exchange it if she doesn't . . . you know . . . ?"

"Of course, of course."

But isn't that a cop-out? Isn't the whole meaning of a gift in the heartfelt commitment of the giver?

"Let me look at the necklace."

Why should I be surprised that Fredo's is still in place? We were all at Fredo's five Christmases ago, when Jess was a mere sixteen. Good God! What was Jess like at sixteen? Oh, come on, now! You're not going to do that bittersweet routine, are you? At sixteen, Jess's eyes were the same color they are now, and I suspect she was still a virgin. Wait a minute . . . I do remember something from sixteen. I remember she was discovering the lady poets. The Anne Sextons and Sylvia Plaths. And baroque music. Lord, you couldn't go back far enough. Gregorian chants. And from there, I recall, she leaped forward to the romantic ballads of Cole Porter, and the like.

"It's gorgeous! Oh, Dad, it's *exquisite!* Oh, thank you!"

I wasn't sure it was, but her saying so made it so. The gold chain with its single diamond lying on its bed of royal-blue velvet.

"Happy birthday, Jess. *Leben und lachen.*"

"What's that mean?"

"Live and laugh. Your grandmother used to say that."

She got up from her chair and gave me a public, ostentatious kiss. She kept the box open beside her, looked at the glitter of it, closed the box, opened it again, took out her necklace, had me help her put it on.

"Leave it on," I said. "I have something else for you."

I took the envelope out of my pocket and passed it over. She opened it and took out the certified check. Examined it. Her brow puckered and she shook her head.

"What's this?" she asked.

"Money," I said.

"I see that. Ten thousand dollars, it says. From where? Why?"

"It's yours," I said. "I've just been holding it until you were twenty-one."

"Why is it mine? Who gave it to me?"

"Your mother and I did. A long time ago. There's nothing either one of us can do about it now."

"I can't take this, Dad."

"Sure you can. It's easy. Just put it in your bank and draw checks against it."

"Why are you giving this to me?"

"Because I have confidence in your future."

"That's more than I have," she said. "I don't know what's going to be. Don't give it to me now."

"Yes, now. It's got to be now. If it isn't now, it'll be because we're hedging our bets, and we don't want to do that."

"But you and Mom—"

"That's something else," I said. "That can't be helped."

"And Neil?"

"Tell me about Neil."

I sat and listened as Jess told me about the unlooked-for shape her life had taken. She and Neil met two, possibly three, times a week. They would meet for lunch or dinner. If he went out of town, as he increasingly did, she would follow, stay at some hotel, wait for him. If Jess had told me that she had been through a series of medical tests and that the results condemned her irrevocably to some wasting disease—MS, something like that—my grief would have gone deeper and extended further, but what I was feeling now was in a comparable order of magnitude.

A kind of horror, a shuddering deprecation, which I was not as successful in hiding as I thought, for Jess reached across to me and said, her new necklace glittering in the yellow light. "I'm *happy!*" Maybe she was—she *was*—I could see she was—anticipation is pure oxygen to the soul—but *I* was not happy. She didn't carry around with her, as I did, an album of images, each absolute in promise. Asked if I thought Jess would ever arrive at the pitch of happiness I wished for her, I would say of course not. I knew life, and I didn't expect that my daughter had bought herself immunity simply because she was my daughter; but I did expect that even the mistakes and misadventures would be compatible with the promise.

What was happening was not compatible with the promise. Her real life brought to a halt while she scurried about picking up scraps, leavings. Oh, yes, that was no doubt an embittered way of looking at it, but the flat-out, sour truth was that I *was* embittered. Jess wasn't supposed to be at that end of the imbalance. She was supposed to be at the *other* end. The smoke-blue of her eyes had been a sign of ascendency, not this helpless vassalage.

"I wish you wouldn't look so glum," she said to me.

"I'm sorry," I said. "I don't mean to."

"This isn't the way I imagined it either," she said, as if again plugged into my thoughts, as she had so often been in the past, as Ellen had so often been in the past.

And having named "Ellen" to myself, the shadows that had crisscrossed my mind merged into solid memory. Jess's mother, too, had made a decision that might not have accorded with *her* father's dream. Ellen had decided not to be a concert pianist because the size and thrust of George Light's ego left no room for it. She might not have been a concert pianist in any case, but we were not dealing with finalities here, only expectations.

Violating my own strict injunction, I asked, "What do you think will happen?"

"I don't know," she said. "Neil's wife may tire of the sick game she's playing and make a divorce possible. If not, I'll stay with Neil for as long as we both . . ." She shrugged.

"Both what?"

"Both want to."

"How will you know when one or the other no longer wants to?" I asked.

"When one or the other says so." Jess looked at me and smiled. "It isn't as cold-blooded as it sounds," she said. "I'm sure I'm going to get those four credits, and I hope to get into the graduate program this fall. Neil wants me to. *I* want to. Dad, there isn't going to be a loss. There's nothing bad or deceptive between us. Neil and I are already connected in ways that go beyond being lovers. Do you understand?"

"I think so."

Yes, I understand, but how about the heart's cry for perfection? How about the cozy, rosy dream of you were meant for me and I was meant for you? Gone forever? Or never was? But my darling, my dear darling Jess, Jess of the housebroken tigers, why these quick and many compromises? Are you on the right track? Is this the way to be? Is your life going to be better because of it? It may be so, but I fear it. In some superstitious, narrow, deep way, I fear it.

23 I wonder why I didn't say
anything to Jess about the TV
thing. She would have found it interesting, and it wasn't as
though the possibility was so fragile that premature talk
might jinx it. My feeling is that it will happen. All the trib-
utaries seem to be flowing toward that confluence. The network needs a good new talk show. The other networks have
installed new formats, and the one this network has running
is beginning to try too hard. But it never occurred to me to
mention it at that birthday dinner. Nor did I mention it the
following day when Jess phoned to thank me once again for
the gorgeous gifts and the dinner and the terrific way I was
taking everything, helping her. . . . "Not the money, although God knows that's a help, but the way you're letting
me work this out in my own way."

"Do I have a choice?"

"You didn't have to give me that check now," she said. "That you did gave me a tremendous lift. What you said about not hedging your bets ... May I ask you something now?"

"You may ask," I said, "but I have no answer."

"I think you ought to be in touch with her."

"I was. Just before your birthday."

"Be in touch with her again."

"To say what?"

"Whatever has to be said."

"All right."

I didn't have any particular place in mind. The only thing I asked is that it not be in the house. Not because the house was too haunted with the past, but because it was too haunted with the present. I suggested a drive and Ellen said fine, that sounded like a good idea. So I drove to the house and Ellen greeted me at the door. She was dressed for the warmth of the day, a pocketbook in one hand. We went to the car and I began to drive.

"Where shall we go?" I asked.

"Anywhere. I don't care."

What we had both assumed was that we would go to places we had been to in the past, and this understanding took the form of a failed enterprise. It settled into the car like a large, immaterial third presence.

I drove to the Van Wyck Expressway onto the Southern Parkway, then headed east, then south, and before long I sensed the ocean. I parked the car on a sunny, sandy street, and we walked to the boardwalk. The sight of the ocean startled me. I must have experienced a sensation somewhat similar to Jess's when she was a little girl and she rediscovered the ocean each summer: a mixture of outrage and delight; a sense of immensities that carried on behind one's back, without one's blessing.

We had talked in the car, of course. We had talked about Jess. Jess had telephoned Ellen to tell her about the wonderful gifts she had received from her father—that is, her father and her mother—since I had insisted that Jess understand that the money came from both of us. Ellen knew about the separate account I had maintained with the money I had received out of the Henry settlement. *She* had insisted that that remain separate. I thought then that she had simply wanted it out of temptation's way, but now I wonder if there wasn't more prophecy than principle in her insistence. At any rate, she thought the check was generous, happily timed.

We talked about Jess and Neil Andrews, and I told Ellen that I had met and talked to Neil, and although I didn't succeed in my purpose of prying them apart, I came away feeling that I might have welcomed this same man were he unencumbered. That's scant comfort, but better than no comfort at all. The other feeling I came away with was one of powerlessness. Jess was in love with this man, he with her, and the story would have to play itself out within these circumstances.

"It's not the life I wanted for Jess," I said.

"Nor I," said Ellen.

The boardwalk we were walking on seemed sparsely populated, as did the beach that stretched away to our left. Perhaps that was because of the mistiness of the day. It was that mistiness that imparted a quality of light that made me think more of autumn than of summer. Perhaps it was because I wanted to be done with this sick season. I've always considered autumn a beginning, and despite everything that was happening, I felt an incipient something creep along the gray, cracked wall that separated Ellen and me. I'm not sure what. A different life, perhaps. Why "perhaps"? It would have to be a different life, wouldn't it? I turned toward Ellen and saw her squinting against the bright sun, saw the familiar lines of her face, filaments of her black and gray hair glinting into gold, and I felt that if the next few seconds didn't find for me a new medium in which to exist, I would spend an eternity howling in timelessness. For this woman walking next to me, this Ellen, was as unknown to me as the world's beginning or the world's end. I had explored her body, listened to the music she had made with her fingers, understood the nuances of her voice, but she was as much a stranger to me at this moment as the woman I might someday in the future meet and marry.

In this moment of my understanding, I remembered Ellen turning to me when I came into the hospital room just after Jess was born. There was no recognition in her eyes, and I thought it was due to the anesthetic she had been given. But I see now that it was not a drug at all, but an instant of unpreparedness in her life of careful preparations.

Since there was no question I could possibly ask, no statement I could possibly make, that would in any way approximate the tumult going on in heart and head, I reverted to the only personality available to me, and I said, "Last summer, when I visited, did you know then what you felt, about me, about Katie?"

"I knew only that I couldn't go back to the life I'd had before," she said. "I wasn't sure what life I was entering. Katie and I were friends then."

"How long have you known that you don't love me?" I asked.

"I don't know that, George," she said. "Even now I don't know that. Just as I don't know that I 'love' Katie. I know that I feel a freedom and therefore a closeness to her that I never felt with you. I will always want to know what's happening with you. That's a habit with me. I'm free to tell Katie that I feel this tie to you. She understands that. She would understand if I were to say that you and I were going to try to live together again. We would go on being as good friends as we are now. Do you understand that?"

"Since you're both women, I do," I said.

"You would not go on being interested in my life if we divorced, would you?"

"Would it matter?"

"Yes, it would. It would hurt me to know that you simply ceased being interested in my life."

"I couldn't very well be totally uninterested in your life, since you're Jess's mother. There will always be that connection."

"Then it would be for her sake, not for mine?"

"I don't know, Ellen. I'm afraid you're right. Just a moment ago, I felt actually dizzy in the realization of how much a stranger you are to me. For all the sex and talk and sheer *knowledge* of you, I know that you're a stranger to me. Am I to you?"

"No, you're no stranger."

"Why is that?"

"Because of the room I have made in myself for you. How much room have you made for me?"

There was an instant in which I wavered between understanding and not understanding. I could have made myself not understand, as I have done so often in the past, but something in Ellen's hazy, sidelong glance made me fear another such dereliction.

"Not much," I confessed. "Did you know it might be this way when we married?"

"I was afraid of it."

"Was that the reason for the long hesitation?"

"Yes."

"Not because—?"

"Because I wasn't sure of my sexual orientation?" Ellen filled in. "No, not because of that. I was sure of that. George, the sex we had was honest."

I could almost see the clean line of truth in her words, and it gave me some satisfaction. I wanted to go on trusting her honesty. I needed it to guide my own. I said, "It would be nice to say let's start again, I'll be a different man, but I know I won't."

"I know it, too," she said.

On the drive back, we began to speak of necessary arrangements. What we would tell Jess, what we would tell others. Questions grew like a tapeworm out of the reality of our marriage's end. We must tell a consistent story. What was that story? Let's say that we no longer love each other. But that would hurt Jess, particularly at this time. And besides, it wasn't completely true. Let's say that now that Jess is grown our separate careers have led us into separate ways. Or that the life-styles and value standards engendered by our separate careers have made our life together more and more . . .

Ah, what crap! Why not the truth? All right, what is the truth? The truth is that in this century of informed change, we have nothing to shield us from each other. We are too much exposed to the terrible sun of truth.

You have learned the truth about me—that I was incapable of admitting enough of you. I have learned the truth about you—that you were capable of turning to another, a woman, for love and understanding and comfort. You can forgive me for being what I am, even though you will no longer live with me, while I'm not sure that I can ever forgive you for what you have become.

But even as I ticked off these fatal truths, I continued to

look for a passage through the wall we had built. Five minutes from now, a day, a month, a year, would it be possible, given the ever-changing heart, for George and Ellen to live together?

I think I would have said yes up until that very moment. Now I feel a sad certainty infiltrating my blood. Ellen and I will never live together again. This is so not because of what has been revealed but because of what has been concealed. No matter how much either of us would be capable of forgiving, there would remain the alien place that Ellen had so frequently visited during all the years she had lived with me. Every silence, every half gesture, might signal a return to that other country.

I could never live with that.

But there is still the house to be settled. Shall we sell it, or will Ellen continue to live there? Shall we divide everything we have in half, or shall we give to each other what we cannot bear to possess?

"Ellen," I said, "I know this will seem like another of my cop-outs, but I'm going to leave these matters to you, to settle these matters in any way that seems fair to you, because you've been living with this much longer than I have, and, frankly, I can't . . . I just can't. . . ."

24 I think Mary Speros would have made a fine actress. The expression of bearable bereavement she put on at my leave-taking would have done credit to any great lady of the stage. Of course, the real trick is to manage it cold, before an audience or cameras, without the motivation that moved Mary. For I was only a transient, and the people who would be moving in promised a much longer stay, and Mary wanted very much to get it settled because she was planning a cross-country trip in her red Olds.

"It's better to have things settled," she said.

Yes. It is. Although I can't say that my new apartment in the West Eighties inspires a settled feeling in me. This, too, is temporary. I took it because it was available, and I didn't want to be driving over from Jersey every day when my job was in the city.

The tryout was successful. The problems were as anticipated. Not to let it descend too far into silliness and, conversely, to keep it from bloating with hot air. What hadn't been anticipated were the juicy flare-ups that happened at least once on every program. In fact, on the very first program, where a handsome, sharp-minded woman who was an administrator in a large corporation challenged a no less sharp-minded man who worked for a think tank to admit how he truly felt about women who achieved eminence in his field. His response was that he felt fine about them, but that he certainly wouldn't marry one. And why wouldn't he marry one? Because he was attracted to other qualities in women. It was as simple as that. No doubt, countered the woman, he was attracted to qualities that were less threatening. No, he didn't feel threatened, he just didn't feel enticed. Well, that might be what he told himself, but that lack of enticement might be due to a lack of courage. You may believe whatever you wish, the sharp-minded man retorted, but I know what I like . . . and what I *don't* like are women who don't know the first thing about me but think they understand me better than I understand myself. Yes, well, perhaps you dislike such women because they're not as deceived by you as you are by yourself. . . .

It was sheer good luck to get a pair like that, who would nick each other so expertly, drawing just enough blood to look good on TV. And on the first program! It was a terrific kick. The letters and phone calls were heavy, mostly positive. Some complained that there was enough conflict in the world and in the family, why encourage more?

Who listens to peacemakers?

Ted Samuels was the executive producer. Larry Graff was the field producer. I wrote the scripts and worked with the MC and director in preparing the program. The schedule for now is once a week, an evening show. The title settled on is *The Gender Trap.*

I have no idea how long it will run. All the ingredients for a long run are present, but the days are full of shifting winds that blow things in and out of favor. The political or economic climate may suddenly turn in a way that will make such games an irrelevance or an irritant.

Because it is a game. No one, neither the participants nor the viewers, will discover anything that will change or justify their lives. Certainly I don't expect to learn anything. The book I wanted to write has become this television program, and perhaps the only significance in the whole idea is in this ludicrous outcome. I know that something permanent and serious has happened, but there are no forms for permanence and seriousness. There's TV.

Jess has started graduate school and is engrossed in her classes. That boy she told me about, the one standing in the tawdry, depleted bazaar, remains where he was, but pushed somewhat to the background, while Jessica Light studies all the intricacies of communication. Naturally, she doesn't have as much time to be with Neil Andrews, but that was something they both had anticipated, and there was no resentment. As a matter of fact, Neil himself was having to spend more and more time out of town as the party geared up toward the next election.

You might say Jess has already absorbed the Neil Andrews experience. That tall, aristocratic gent with his wife and two children and political ambition has become part of her life without becoming an impediment in her life. So she says, and I believe it with my mind but not with my heart. Or maybe it's a matter of acceptance rather than belief. My mind accepts that Jess finds it possible to arrange her life this way, but my heart cries out against it. I guess I just don't like the idea of *absorbing* experience. If she goes on absorbing one experience after another, she will soon mithridate herself into a dangerous immunity. I don't want her to be immune. I want her to remain the eager, susceptible little girl strolling along the ocean's edge with a tiger on a leash.

But that's my vision, not hers.

The matter of divorce is not as automatic as I thought it would be. I didn't want lawyers, but I'm advised that a clean understanding protects everyone's interests best. Ellen said she'd be willing to let the thing ride for several years—go along, as it were—no divorce—but I was against it.

No, there wasn't another woman, nor the desire to be free in the event of another woman. It was as if the emotional momentum that had driven me into marriage to Ellen had reversed its course and was now with equal force driving me out.

"Do you hate me?" Ellen asked.

"I thought I might," I said, "but I think it's safe to say now that I don't hate you, never will."

And it's true. I would be willing to take an oath on the head of beloved Jess. I knew that I didn't hate Ellen; I just didn't understand her.

What I do understand is that it couldn't have been different. Even if the heavens had opened and the future was made visible in bleeding script, it couldn't have been different. It was wrong of me to have had that affair with Kim, but the deeper wrong I had been seeking in myself ever since my return from Denver was just not there. I see what it was that Ellen couldn't endure, but I also see that I had no way of knowing, no way in the world of knowing that who I was, the ambition and presumption and excessive demand of me, would cut off Ellen's life just as surely as it defined mine.

I couldn't be other than who I was. Knowing this, I could forgive myself. Forgiving myself, I could forgive Ellen.

But I wanted out of the marriage. Even the forgiven self remains the self.

As I've said, autumn for me is a time of beginning, and as if to celebrate the season I got a phone call from the reincarnation of the Empress Theodora. She had finally made it to Satan's capital. Could we meet?

"How did you find me?"

"I called Information."

So I took Terry to lunch in a restaurant high above the city, one with a view of Central Park, the rivers, the bridges. It was beautiful, beautiful! Terry looked wonderful. Everything about her seemed refurbished—her eyes, her nose, her freckles, her smart-looking outfit. She was traveling with her latest friend. They were going to head north from New York, through the autumn foliage of New England, and then go on up to Canada, where Dave had a six-month gig with a hotel orchestra in Montreal. Then they planned to drive across Canada, to Vancouver, where Dave had friends, where he was sure he could get another gig. Dave played the electric guitar. Terry was convinced he was the best guitarist in the world.

"How's the Empress Theodora these days?" I asked.

Terry nodded her head as if she had anticipated the question. "I know you don't believe in it," she said, "but the Empress Theodora is exactly where she wants to be. That's why I'm so happy."

"I'm delighted to hear it," I said. "I'm also very pleased that you looked me up, Terry. Why did you?"

"Because you were good to me," she said. "Because you were my friend."

Walking back to the studio, I decide that after the divorce, even before it, I will try to keep Ellen in my life. Jess plans to keep Neil Andrews in her life. Terry has faithfully kept the Empress Theodora in her life—and me, as well. I know that Jess has always been in mine and always will be. Why not Ellen? I can't be married to Ellen, but why go through an exorcism? She's *in* my life. Why not let her stay there?

Maybe that's where my man-woman project was intending to take me.

At least that's my sense of the thing, for the present.